THE GIRL FROM SICILY

SIOBHAN DAIKO

Boldwood

First published in Great Britain in 2025 by Boldwood Books Ltd.

Copyright © Siobhan Daiko, 2025

Cover Design by Head Design Ltd

Cover Images: Shutterstock and iStock

A CIP catalogue record for this book is available from the British Library.

Paperback ISBN 978-1-83633-093-6

Large Print ISBN 978-1-83633-092-9

Hardback ISBN 978-1-83633-091-2

Ebook ISBN 978-1-83633-094-3

Kindle ISBN 978-1-83633-095-0

Audio CD ISBN 978-1-83633-086-8

MP3 CD ISBN 978-1-83633-087-5

Digital audio download ISBN 978-1-83633-090-5

This book is printed on certified sustainable paper. Boldwood Books is dedicated to putting sustainability at the heart of our business. For more information please visit https://www.boldwoodbooks.com/about-us/sustainability/

Boldwood Books Ltd, 23 Bowerdean Street, London, SW6 3TN

www.boldwoodbooks.com

For Victor

1

JESSICA, APRIL–JUNE 2005

Rain splattered the paving stones in the garden outside Jess's ground-floor flat, and the melodious song of a blackbird echoed as she unfurled her umbrella. She opened her front door and stepped over the pile of mail on the mat: leaflets advertising pre-approved credit card applications, supermarket special offers, and 'fantastic' deals on replacement windows.

A white, formal-looking envelope caught her eye. Surely it wasn't another communication from Scott's solicitors. Jess sighed. Although they'd completed all the paperwork, their divorce had yet to be finalised.

With a frown, she picked up the envelope with 'McKirby Solicitors' stamped in the top left corner and a London address below. She and Scott were based in Bristol, as were their lawyers. Why on earth would a London law firm be writing to her?

Jess carried the envelope through to her kitchen, where she picked up a knife to slit it open. She pulled out a chair and began to read.

Dear Mrs Brown,

We regret to inform you that your grandmother has passed away in New York and we offer our sincere condolences. Probate has been granted, and you are the beneficiary of an inheritance. There are, however, certain stipulations. Therefore, we request that you schedule an appointment with us at your earliest convenience so that we can explain these stipulations to you in person.

Yours faithfully

Jonathan Burridge

Solicitor

Shock wheeled through Jess. She'd never met her grandmother. The one and only time she'd questioned her mother about her family background, she'd encountered a stony silence. The panic in her mother's eyes had stopped her from returning to the subject. All she knew was that Nonna Lucia used to live in Sicily, and that she'd moved to New York after the war.

A lump of sadness formed in Jess's throat. How she wished her parents were still alive. She missed them dreadfully – just thinking about them made her eyes prickle. The day they'd died, they were on their way down from Cheshire to console her after her latest round of IVF had failed. One of the many. She'd just turned thirty-five, advanced maternal age as the medical profession liked to call it. Scott had said they should stop trying. 'They' being the operative word. It hadn't taken him long to find a younger woman and impregnate her, hence the impending divorce. Scott was the proud father of a newborn baby boy now.

Jess gritted her teeth. She wouldn't succumb to self-pity; she was made of sterner stuff. Nevertheless, she couldn't help the lingering quiver of disappointment that Scott had refused to consider adopting. There was so much love in her heart for a child that Jess was even considering exploring the possibility of adoption on her own.

Tiredness seeped through her. What a day she'd had! Not only had she spent the entire morning target setting – a thankless task – but, in the afternoon, the computer system had gone down. Smoothing the ruffled feathers of impatient customers was part of her job description as a bank manager, but sometimes she wished that it wasn't.

And then, on top of everything, she'd learnt that her grandmother had passed away. Jess had intended to contact her after her mother's death, but now it was too late. Her heart grew heavy – the mystery of the rift between Nonna and Mum would never be resolved.

* * *

A week later, Jess found herself pulling out a chair in a dour, wood-panelled office on the first floor of a Victorian terraced building in the heart of London.

Jonathan Burridge pushed his glasses up his beaky nose and squinted at her from the other side of his wide rosewood desk.

'Your grandmother has left you a peasant farmhouse, a *baglio contadino*, on the outskirts of the village of Villaurora in central Sicily,' he said. 'Despite being empty, it has been well cared for. She has set up a trust fund for you to restore and maintain it, should you so wish. The money must be used solely for this purpose.'

Jess's mouth dropped open; she blinked rapidly and closed it again.

'I'm truly flabbergasted.' She could hear the disbelief in her tone.

'Your grandmother's great-niece, Giovanna Alessi, has the keys to the baglio and has been keeping an eye on it. If and when you decide to accept the inheritance, you'll need to contact a lawyer in Palermo, who will oversee everything.'

'How amazing!' It was all Jess could think of saying, she was so surprised.

'Indeed.' Jonathan Burridge steepled his bony fingers.

'Where is the village?' She'd forgotten the name. 'Central Sicily, did you say?'

The solicitor, obviously well prepared, picked up an atlas from a pile of books at his side, opened it at a bookmarked page, and spun the revealed map around.

'There.' He pointed with his finger at the island. 'The meeting point of Caltanissetta, Agrigento, and Palermo provinces forms a triangle apex.' Burridge inclined his head towards her. 'How should I respond to Signor Gentile?'

'Signor Gentile?'

'The *notaio* in Palermo.'

'Can I think about it? I mean, this is a shock, to say the least. How did he know where you could contact me?'

'Of course you must think about it. I imagine your grandmother left him your address.' A smile twisted the solicitor's thin lips. 'Let me know when you've reached a decision.'

Jess shook Burridge's hand and made her way out of his office. It was a short walk from Lincoln's Inn to Holborn, where she boarded the Tube to Paddington station and then the train back to Bristol.

As she stared out of the window of the bus taking her home to Julian Road, she barely registered the early-evening rush-hour traffic grinding up the hill past the university. She'd been mulling over her visit to Burridge the entire journey and myriad questions still flooded her mind. Should she go to Sicily and check out her inheritance?

She could kill two birds with one stone and find out why her mother, Carula, had cut herself off from her family. The thought snagged Jess like a hooked fish. She'd always felt as if part of her had been missing. Mum must have inherited her almost-black hair and olive skin from her parents, both of whom were Sicilian as far as Jess knew. That much she'd managed to winkle out of Dad before he'd told her to let the matter drop. Jess could see little of her blond, fair-skinned father in herself and, with her own dark hair, she looked nothing like her English cousins.

She couldn't wait to meet Giovanna Alessi. Wouldn't it be wonderful if she found more family in Sicily? Maybe that was why her nonna left her the baglio? Jess heaved a sigh. She was being fanciful and, besides, what would she do with a peasant farmhouse?

You're at a loose end, she told herself. *And you have used none of your holiday allocation this year. It wouldn't hurt to go to Sicily and look at the place. You don't need to decide until then.*

Two months later, Jess was driving a rented Fiat Punto along a *strada statale*, state road, heading deep into the heart of the island. She muttered under her breath as she swerved to avoid yet another pothole. Sunburnt peaks stretched across the far horizon, notching the hard blue sky like the points of a fever chart. The *strada* hugged the sharp ridges of dusty, ochre-coloured valleys, seemingly devoid of human habitation. She passed a series of grey-green prickly pear cacti, and it struck her that this was a harsh, uncompromising land.

Soon, her satnav was taking her through olive groves and then, finally, the verdant vineyards of the Tenuta Sacca di Melita estate, a winery where she had booked holiday accommodation. Imposing stone gateposts ushered her through to a white gravel driveway. She brought the Fiat to a halt in front of a long, beige-coloured two-storey building.

The perfume of roses invaded her senses and her eye was captured by a beautiful flower-filled garden sloping down to a massive vegetable plot. She stepped out of the air-conditioned Punto to be greeted by a whoosh of baking-hot air. Wiping sweat from her brow, she made her way to an enormous wooden door, painted Capri blue, set into a portal with a full lowered arch. A balcony presided above a wrought-iron half-circular rose window, the railings rendered the same blue as the wide door.

Taking a deep breath, Jess pressed the bell and waited. A dog barked from within. An attractive young woman with a mop of curly, short, bright red hair opened the door, a waggy-tailed black Labrador at her heels.

'Mrs Brown? I trust you had a pleasant journey. Please, come through. I'll help you with your luggage once you've checked in.'

Jess was swept into a huge quadrangle with a Judas tree at its centre. The shrill chirp of the crickets in its spreading branches meant she could hardly hear the beep of a message arriving on her phone.

It was her cousin, Mel, asking if she'd arrived safely. Jess promptly reassured her that everything was fine, then bent to pat the dog, who was sniffing at her shoes with interest.

'What's his name?' she asked.

'Cappero. It means caper. And I'm Stefania.'

'*Piacere.*' Pleased to meet you.

'You speak Italian?'

'I studied it at school, which is quite a while ago—'

'It will come back to you with practice, I'm sure.'

Jess gazed at her surroundings. It was as if she'd stepped into a small hamlet. Shuttered doors opened into the square inner courtyard, and wrought-iron balconies graced the upper floors. Terracotta pots of bright red geraniums filled the spaces between the steps leading up to the openings. Cappero went to lift his leg on one of them, making her smile. They walked into the cool of an office, and Stefania took Jess's passport.

'What a lovely place this is,' Jess said.

'I've been working here for a year now.' Stefania entered Jess's details into a computer database. 'Some might call it remote, but my boyfriend works in the vineyard and we love it.'

'It looks very old.'

'The winery dates back to the period of colonisation of the Sicilian countryside in the sixteenth century. Spain ruled the island and needed vast quantities of cereals for its people. The estate has belonged to the Sacca di Melita family since 1840.'

'How interesting! I need to research the history of Sicily. I'm ashamed to say I know little about it.'

'We are a mix of cultures and ethnicities because the Greeks, Romans, Byzantines, Arabs, Vikings, Normans, Spanish, and the Bourbon French conquered us.' Stefania ticked the list off on her fingers.

'I will definitely read more about it,' Jess said as Stefania handed back her passport.

'We have Wi-Fi in the cottages.' Stefania gave her a piece of paper with the log-in information. 'I'll take you to your accommodation now, Mrs Brown.'

'Please, call me Jess.' She wasn't sure if she was being too informal, but it seemed the right thing to say.

They went to the parked Fiat and retrieved Jess's suitcase, then Stefania led her to a separate building, set back slightly from the main house. Six blue-shuttered windows lined the upper floor. A terracotta-tiled roof jutted out below, shading a paved portico with three front doors.

'This is the place where the farm equipment was stored when the ground floor of the main building housed agricultural labourers. A couple of years ago, Piero took over managing the estate and turned it into holiday accommodation.'

'Piero?'

'He's the youngest son of Baron Gaetano Sacca di Melita.'

Stefania opened the door to the cottage, and Jess entered a cosy living space with a sofa and an armchair. A kitchenette held pride of place at the far end, next to an open-tread hard wood staircase.

'Let me take your suitcase up to the bedroom,' Stefania said. 'Then I'll leave you to get settled.'

Jess thanked her and shouldered her hand luggage. Upstairs, the sight of a king-sized bed, bedside tables, and an old-fashioned wooden wardrobe greeted her. Blue, yellow, and green glazed ceramic tiles covered the floor.

'There's an en suite bathroom.' Stefania showed a door to the left. 'I would keep the shutters closed during the heat of the day. Nights get cooler, but if you need air conditioning, here is the *telecomando*.' She handed Jess a remote control.

'It's perfect.' Jess smiled. 'I love it.'

'You're our only guest for now, as it's still early in the season. There's a welcome pack in the kitchen – fruit, cheese, cold meats, bread, butter, jam, etcetera. The nearest food store is in Villaurora. About half an hour's drive away.'

'I'll go there tomorrow,' Jess said.

'If you'd like a dip in the pool, just follow the pathway. Leaflets for day trips are available at reception. You can visit Agrigento, Syracuse, Enna and other places—'

'I might do that. But I'm also here to relax and enjoy Sicilian country living.'

'You've come to the right place, for sure.'

After Scott's bombshell and facing an impending divorce, Jess needed a place where she could isolate herself and heal in peace. Obviously, she'd have to make up her mind about her inheritance, but when she wasn't inspecting the farmhouse, she planned to indulge herself reading novels, going for solitary walks, and soaking up the sun. A new chapter was about to start in her life, and she wanted to be ready for it.

'Have a lovely evening,' Stefania said before taking her leave.

'*Grazie.*'

Jess unpacked, then went down to the kitchenette, where she made a cup of tea. Since it was still too early for supper, she set off for a short walk. Outside, the late-afternoon sun cast the garden in a golden glow. She took the path Stefania suggested and soon arrived at a rectangular-shaped infinity pool.

Sunshine sparkled on the water, inviting her to take a dip. Wishing she'd thought to change into her swimsuit, she perched on a lounger to enjoy the view. Rows of vines resembled a leafy army marching from the valley to the hill's crest. Beyond, a brooding dark wave of craggy mountains punctuated the skyline, and a bird of prey wheeled a taut arc above the peaks.

Jess breathed in the warm Sicilian air. She was here at last, the place where her grandmother had once lived, and she couldn't wait to visit Villaurora and find out more.

2

LUCIA, JUNE 1943

Lucia gazed up at the falcon circling over Villaurora. If only she could be free like that bird. Free to live her life. Free to soar. Instead, she was sitting on a chair on the step outside the family's one-storey house in the steep, narrow street, surrounded by flies in the hot June sunshine.

She wiped her brow. For the past eight years, since she'd travelled from Brooklyn, she'd been taking part in the annual pressing of the *pumadori*. Yesterday, the tomatoes had been cleaned, washed and left to dry overnight. This morning, she and her younger sister, Annita, had laid the *pumadori* out on bamboo frames in the sun before they'd added sea salt. Now she, Ma and Annita were working the extract with their hands prior to it being bottled. Hot, sticky work. *Women's work.*

'Face around, Lucia,' her mother admonished. 'Remember where you are.'

'Yes, Ma,' Lucia groaned.

How could she ever forget? As an unwed girl, she was required to turn her back to the street. Only after dusk could she turn her profile to passers-by so that strolling young men might assess her desirability. The marshal of the local cara-binieri, Giulianu Cardona, often looked at her like that, and even more blatantly during Sunday mass.

Lucia huffed to herself. She didn't want to attract the attention of a prospective husband. As soon as the war ended, she wanted to return to America, the country of her birth.

How she wished her father, Leonardo, an immigrant who'd worked as a garbage collector, hadn't needed to bring the family back to Sicily so he could look after his elderly widowed father. He'd been the only son and his married sisters had insisted the responsibility lay with him. Nannu passed away three years ago, but by then Mussolini had sided with Hitler against France and Britain. A year later, after Pearl Harbor, Germany and Italy declared war on the United States. It became impossible for civilians like Lucia and her family to travel across the Atlantic and, in addition, Ma and Pa would have been considered 'enemy aliens' and might even have been interned.

Ma nudged Lucia, breaking into her thoughts.

'You and Annita help me take the tomato paste indoors,' she said. 'Then I'll get on with finishing up making the supper.'

After washing her hands, Lucia went outside again. The church bells were ringing the Angelus, which meant that Pa and her twin brother, Dinu, would be home soon from working the small patch of land Pa had inherited from his father.

The smallholding, known as a *campagna*, cultivated most of the fruit and vegetables they needed, with some extra produce to sell for the cash to buy wheat. The only meat they ate was rabbit, and Lucia's stomach rumbled as the aroma of a delicious stew came through the open door. She smiled to herself, remembering how she and Dinu had gone out hunting late yesterday afternoon.

It was something they would often do. She dressed in his clothes – he was quite short and she was almost as tall as him – and she would tuck her mane of dark brown hair into a cap. It made her existence more bearable.

They'd hiked up to the corridor of jagged peaks forming a rocky ridge behind the village. Clusters of small, pale grey snails had fallen from the sisal plants with a faint dry rattle as their feet brushed past them. Long black snakes slithered among the stones, and there were insects everywhere – big, bright butterflies and dragonflies and hornets, legions of twittering grasshoppers, and great armies of ants.

Lucia had known, from experience, that the rabbits would be feeding on clover at the foot of the crags. Hearing her and her brother approach, the animals hid as usual. But she and Dinu raced, zigzagging towards them, shooting and flushing them out of hiding. They'd learnt to be quick on the trigger and it hadn't taken long to bag a couple for the cooking pot.

Dinu had hugged her and kissed her on the cheek.

'You did well, *soru*.' Sister. 'You're becoming an even better shot than me.'

She'd put him in his place, slapping him playfully on the arm.

'I've always been a better shot than you, *frati*.' Brother.

Lucia loved her brother Dinu to the depths of her soul, but she also worried about him. He was intelligent yet ambitious, resilient yet hot-headed, and there was a dark side to him that could lead him into terrible trouble one day.

She could hear her twin's voice before she risked turning her head to see him leading their mule down the street towards her. There was another man, a rucksack slung over his shoulder, walking between him and Pa.

As they drew nearer, she realised that the man, dressed in

the usual peasant clothes – baggy trousers and an open-necked shirt – appeared familiar. Thick, dark brown hair, cut short at the back and sides. Chocolate-brown eyes. A chiselled chin. But it was his confident, white-toothed smile that made her gasp with surprise.

It was Gero Bonanno from the Bronx, the eldest son of fellow emigrants from Villaurora. He'd become as handsome as a Greek Apollo, and he'd grown taller and broader than most Sicilians. What the hell was he doing walking down the street with her father and brother? As far as she knew, his family was still in New York.

She crossed her arms. She'd got to know Gero, a little, on outings with the Bonannos to Coney Island. He was a couple of years older than her and Dinu, and she'd always thought him arrogant despite having a little girl's crush on him.

'Look who we found asleep beneath the bridge over the dry riverbed,' Pa said as if it was an everyday occurrence. 'Let's get him indoors.'

They trooped through the front door, and Lucia felt a quiver of shame. Their only room served as a stable on one side. On the other side, a rectangular wooden table and eight chairs stood on the earth floor. Acrid smoke, from the straw fire under the cooking pot, billowed towards them. Lined up along the wall were the *quartare*, terracotta jugs used for keeping fresh water. There were also the family's bunk beds. They all lived together in this miserable hovel. It was like something out of the Dark Ages.

Lucia and Dinu's younger sister, Annita, shyly held back.

'*Bedda Matri!*' Ma exclaimed, stepping forward. 'I can't believe my eyes.'

'*Bona sira.*' Gero from the Bronx wished her a good evening.

'What are you doing in Villaurora and how did you get

here?' Ma asked bluntly. She was never one for measuring her words.

'I was flown over from our base in Africa and parachuted down in the valley below Villaurora late last night. Walked up here and then fell asleep while I waited for nightfall.'

'You're with the US army, I presume?' Pa said, pouring water from a jug into the basin and scrubbing at his hands. 'Are the *americani* on their way?'

'I can't say.' Gero put a finger to his lips, then accepted a glass of rough red wine from Dinu. 'It was lucky I met you, though. Dad said you'd come back to Villaurora. I'm here with a message for don Nofriu Vaccaru. They chose me to deliver it because my father is a *paisano*.' A compatriot.

Lucia had seen don Nofriu around the village, wearing his trademark short-sleeved shirt, a cigar in his mouth and a cap pulled down almost to his tortoiseshell spectacles. He was Villaurora's godfather, a so-called man of honour. Not someone to be crossed, for sure.

What on earth could the American army want with him?

'Come, Lucia, give me and Annita a hand serving dinner.' Ma grabbed Lucia's arm. 'It's a good thing you and Dinu bagged those rabbits yesterday.'

Lucia caught Gero looking at her curiously.

She turned away and went to help her mother and sister.

Gero was just as arrogant as he'd always been, bragging about his mission. She hoped that, once he'd delivered his message, he'd get the hell out of Villaurora. It would be better for the family if they didn't draw don Nofriu's attention.

* * *

'That was the best rabbit stew I've ever eaten,' Gero said to Ma later, after accepting a second helping.

Thankfully, there'd been more than enough to go around. They didn't have a refrigerator – none of their neighbours had one – so it made sense for them to finish off what was in the pot.

While eating, the conversation had focused on how well Gero's father was doing. Lucia remembered hearing that Alfonso Bonanno had travelled to the USA with his pregnant wife, Filomena, about twenty years ago when Mussolini had become prime minister. Gero had been born soon after they'd arrived in New York. They'd had four more children – all of them girls. Gero informed Lucia and her family that his dad had started a film distribution company, importing and leasing Italian films to US theatres.

He's bragging again, Lucia thought.

She whispered to Annita that they needed to help Ma with the dishes, so they cleared the table and went to the kitchen area.

'Gero can stay here tonight as it's too late for him to visit don Nofriu,' Ma said, passing Lucia a plate.

'But where will he sleep?'

'There's a spare mattress. He can have that.'

Feeling that quiver of shame again, Lucia told herself that it was Gero who was imposing on them, that he should take them as they were. It wasn't their fault that they'd become so poor. It was merely because of circumstances. By the time she rose in the morning, hopefully Gero would be gone.

3

DINU, JUNE 1943

Dinu had woken early, and when he returned from the outside toilet, everyone was still asleep. Ma and Pa were snoring loud enough to wake the dead. God, it was dank in here, he thought. He left the door open to let in some light and fresh air.

Pa had asked him last night to take Gero to don Nofriu, and Dinu had agreed. Not because he liked Gero – far from it. The guy was a stuck-up punk. But the opportunity for an intro to the village boss was too good to pass up.

Dinu's muscles tightened at the thought. He didn't want to stay in Villaurora all his life; he didn't want to live like a nobody and die like a beggar. Dinu had made a pact with his cousin, Francu Bagghieri – the son of Ma's sister, Giuseppina – that as soon as the war was over they'd go into business and make piles of money. If they cosied up to don Nofriu, did him some favours, he might help them. Dinu and Francu had no qualms about what that would involve. They'd heard don Nofriu was always on the lookout for new *picciotti*, soldiers for his 'family'. But they hadn't secured an introduction to him yet.

Dinu sensed Lucia coming up behind him before he saw her; they were always in tune.

'*Bon jornu, frati.*' Lucia wished him good morning. 'Are you taking Gero to don Nofriu? *Accura.*' Be careful.

'Don't worry about me, *soru.*' Dinu patted her hand.

'I wish I could go with you. I'm fed up with being treated like a second-class citizen in this country.'

For once, he was glad of the status quo. Lucia plainly thought of herself as his guardian angel and made it her business to keep him on the straight and narrow. It had always been so. Even in New York, when they were kids, she'd stop him from shoplifting and getting involved in playground fights. All it took was one piercing look from her grey-blue eyes and he'd crumple.

'I'll be fine,' he said. 'Gonna ask Francu to come with us—'

'Do you think that's a good idea?' She creased her forehead.

Francu's family was even poorer than theirs. They had no land, and Francu worked as a day labourer. He spent his time waiting until a *campiere* – a steward who worked for a big landowner – would be hiring and 'did him the courtesy' of letting him bend over his hoe for twelve hours at a time.

Of course it would be a good idea for Francu to meet don Nofriu.

'*Bon jornu!*' Gero's voice came from behind. 'Can I invite you both to breakfast in a diner?'

Lucia laughed out loud, and Dinu joined in with her.

'This isn't New York,' he said.

'I know. I was just kiddin'.' Gero chuckled. 'Dad told me there's a bar in Villaurora, though.'

'Lucia has to stay home to do her chores,' Dinu said, putting the *americano* straight. He caught his sister's scowl as she huffed and went to stoke the fire.

'Now I'm here in Sicily,' Gero said, 'I'm beginning to get why so many Sicilians have emigrated. The poverty is unbelievable.'

'Who are you calling poor?' Dinu bunched his fists.

'Sorry, I didn't mean to offend—' Gero held up his hands.

Like hell you didn't, punk. Dinu kept his thoughts to himself.

'We can grab a coffee in the piazza,' he said. 'I always meet my cousin, Francu, there before Pa joins us and we head for the *campagna*. This morning, Pa will go to work on his own.'

'I'm sorry to put you guys out. Maybe I can find don Nofriu's house by myself?'

'No. It's okay. I'll take you.'

'Thanks. Let's go, then!' Gero shouldered his kit bag.

Dinu led Gero down the hill to Piazza Vittorio Emmanuele. As they walked, they left behind the poorest one-storey dwellings and approached a street flanked by houses with two floors and balconies festooned with washing. Long and narrow, the village square had been terraced into a flat platform. The parish church of San Pietro, constructed of pale beige tuff blocks like most of the buildings in the area, occupied one end of the piazza, and the Bar Centrale stood opposite.

Francu was already propping up the counter, a cup of barley coffee in front of him. A smile spread across his tanned face.

'Who's that with you, *kuxinu?*' Cousin. He wiped his dark, pencil-thin moustache with the back of his hand.

Dinu introduced Gero, giving his fake name 'Ino' and recounting that he was a distant relative from Canicatti. He ordered more coffees and suggested they sat at a table in the corner where they wouldn't be overheard. Then he explained the real reason for Gero's visit.

'*Sciatiri e matri!*' Francu exclaimed. Wow.

'Can you tell me something about don Nofriu before I meet him so I know who I'll be dealing with?' Gero turned his gaze from Dinu to Francu and back to Dinu again.

'Many years ago, bandits infested the roads between Villaurora and the coast, where farmers sent their grain to be milled.' Dinu glanced around, making sure no one would hear him. 'Don Nofriu started his business by arranging protection with a man of honour named Varsallona, whose hideout was in the Cammarata mountains.'

'Protection meant he was getting paid to keep the grain safe?' Gero shuffled his chair forwards.

'Then, during World War One, the Italian army began requisitioning horses and mules in Sicily for their cavalry and artillery.' Francu took up the tale. He might have been a peasant farmhand, but he was as sharp as a pin. 'Don Nofriu came to an agreement with the Army Commission to delegate the responsibilities to him. He collected a tax on the animals whose owners wanted to avoid requisition. He was also a broker for other animals that were being rustled, buying at a cheap price from the rustlers and selling at market prices to the army.'

'Sounds real ingenious to me.' Gero laughed, delving into his kit bag for a packet of Camel cigarettes, which he offered to Dinu and Francu.

'He got his comeuppance.' Francu took a box of matches from his pocket and lit everyone's smokes. 'Many horses and mules died of diseases or old age before they even reached the battlefield. The army ordered an inquiry. After the war, don

Nofriu received a twenty-year sentence for fraud, corruption and murder, but he was absolved thanks to powerful friends who exonerated him.'

'By powerful friends, you mean men of honour?' Gero asked.

'Of course.' Dinu took a deep draw of his Camel. 'In the early twenties, after a group of disgruntled peasants tried to grab land from aristocratic absentee landlords, don Nofriu bought three estates in the Villaurora region. He divided them up and handed them over – allegedly without making a penny, according to some – to a cooperative he'd founded.' It was a well-known story.

'Not every peasant got a plot,' Francu said, tapping ash from his cigarette. 'And don Nofriu kept over twelve thousand acres for himself.'

'What happened to the godfathers when the fascists rose to power?' Gero asked, changing the subject. 'In the US we've been led to believe that Mussolini got rid of them, but that doesn't appear to be so—'

'Like many men of honour, don Nofriu was exiled to the south of mainland Italy,' Francu said. 'But he returned to Villaurora six years ago and no one dares to persecute him any more.'

'Mussolini didn't get rid of Cosa Nostra like he claimed.' Dinu exhaled smoke. 'It's still very alive in Sicily.'

'It thrives here because the population respects *"omertà"*, the law of silence, of personal revenge. We feel contempt for the state and its institutions, which have done nothing for us,' Francu added.

'No one can disrespect a man of honour and get away with it,' Dinu said, taking a last draw of his cigarette, then stubbing it out in an ashtray.

'Thanks for the intel.' Gero smiled. 'Now I'd be grateful if you'd take me to meet the man himself.'

Gero paid for the coffees and soon Dinu was leading him and Francu out of the square, around a corner to a side street running parallel with the piazza.

'This is don Nofriu's place,' Dinu said, stopping on the pavement outside an iron gate in front of the wooden door to the ground floor of a three-storey house.

His chest squeezed with anticipation as he rang the doorbell. A man with dark stubble opened the door and peered through the entrance.

'What do you want?' he asked in a gravelly voice.

Gero stepped forward and explained.

'Wait here,' the man said, slamming the door.

Gero handed around his packet of cigarettes and they all lit up to smoke in silence while they waited.

Before too long, the man returned.

'Don Nofriu will see the American.'

'We're with him,' Dinu said.

'The American and no one else.'

'We'll wait for you in the piazza,' Francu told Gero.

Don Nofriu's man opened the gate to Gero, then slammed it and the door shut. Dinu was speechless with disappointment. There was nothing to be done but to make their way back to the square.

'You thought we'd get an intro, didn't you?' Francu said as he and Dinu lowered themselves onto the middle row of steps leading up to the church.

'I was counting on it, *kuxinu.*'

'We'll just have to ask the American to put in a good word for us.'

'If he sticks around.'

'Hmmm. My guess is that he'll be here until this godforsaken war is over.' He smirked. 'There'll be rich pickings when the Allies arrive, you'll see. Don Nofriu will need extra men for his business. We're in with a chance.'

'I hope you are right,' Dinu said as he gazed up at the falcon circling in the thermals above.

4

JESSICA, JUNE 2005

By the time Jess got up from the lounger, the falcon she was watching had disappeared. She remembered reading that the raptor's aerial agility and speed symbolised freedom, and the ability to navigate life's challenges with grace and precision. What an amazing bird!

She left the pool area as Cappero, the dog, bounded up to greet her. A tall, bronzed man glanced up from where he was pruning leaves from the vines as she strolled past. Could he be Stefania's boyfriend? Jess recalled she'd told her he worked in the vineyard.

An image of her soon-to-be ex-husband flashed into her mind. She'd met Scott at uni, where they'd both been accounting and finance undergraduates. Fair-haired and blue-eyed, he'd attracted her from the start with his cheeky northern humour, his confidence and his intelligence. The two of them were more than a bit nerdy; they'd bonded over their love of *Star Trek*, as well as their shared core values of working hard and respecting others.

Sadness scratched in Jess's throat. She'd always thought

they had integrity in common too, but that was not the case. Jess had been devastated when she'd found out Scott had gone behind her back and was seeing a colleague at the accounting firm where he'd recently been made a partner. The fact that Kimberly was already pregnant had put paid to any hopes she might have had of salvaging her marriage. She gave herself a shake, refusing to let the hurt and betrayal fester.

'Good boy,' she said to Cappero and continued walking, the Labrador snuffling along in front.

Reaching the door to her accommodation, she turned to gaze at the view. The beauty of her surroundings was like a balm to her soul. Scott wouldn't have liked it here – he'd have considered it too remote. His idea of a pleasant holiday was a fortnight at an all-inclusive resort, which they'd barely leave for the duration. In the early days of their marriage, she used to enjoy the rest and relaxation, especially when they were trying for a baby. But latterly, she'd yearned to go somewhere more interesting.

Well, she'd certainly come to the right place for that. Stefania's potted history of the conquerors of Sicily had made Jess realise how ignorant she was about the island, and she was looking forward to learning more about it.

She stepped into the cool of the cottage and went to open the fridge. A platter of cold meats and cheeses graced the middle shelf, along with a bottle of *Tenuta Sacca Chardonnay, Bianco Sicilia DOC*. She retrieved the food and drink, then found a bottle opener in the top drawer.

The flavour of apples and lemons tingled on her tongue. The wine was delicious, but she restricted herself to just the one glass. She'd need her wits about her tomorrow when she drove up to Villaurora. Jess thought about the woman she'd be meeting, the woman who had the keys to the farmhouse. Giovanna Alessi was her second cousin.

What's she like? Jess wondered.

* * *

The next morning, when Jess awoke, it was already very warm, with high temperatures forecast. After a cooling shower, she picked out a pale green t-shirt and khaki shorts. Armed with her first coffee of the day, she booted up her laptop. It was a slow connection, but eventually she found the email Giovanna had sent her with details of the time and place where they would meet.

After munching on a couple of slices of bread with butter and strawberry jam, Jess set off. The narrow winding road took her through miles and miles of olive groves and vineyards, and she marvelled at the rose bushes planted at the ends of the rows of vines, their bright colours contrasting with the verdant plants. Before too long, she'd reached the bottom of the vale and the signpost for Villaurora.

Grateful for the air-conditioned car, she motored past small farms – one-storey houses with tracts of cultivated land. The stubble of newly harvested wheat fields painted the countryside a pale-yellow colour. The *strada* climbed steadily, looping through the ever-present bamboo thickets, vineyards and olive groves. The wide valley spread out below, and she could see the rolling hills behind the Sacca estate.

Wild. Primitive. Beautiful.

The *strada* switched back on itself in looping bends, lined with the ubiquitous grey-green prickly pear cacti and yet more farms. Soon Jess spotted another road sign. *Villaurora C.*

Presuming it pointed to the centre of the village, she took the indicated turn.

A couple of low-rise modern apartment blocks, with washing hanging from balconies, faced the *strada* to her left. On her right, a house displayed a shrine built into the wall, where a crucifix hung above a vase of flowers in front of an image of the Virgin Mary.

Jess's chest tightened in anticipation as she drove up a road with pink oleanders on either side and a clock tower at the far end. The piazza would be just beyond, where Giovanna had said she'd be waiting in the Bar Centrale.

After finding a parking space for her car, Jess stepped into the heat and headed for the square. She found that it was built on a type of platform, with stairs leading up to it and the small church. A steep street rose from the middle, pavemented with a series of broad steps. Jess crossed the piazza. A woman was sitting at a table outside the bar, and she approached her.

'Giovanna?' she asked.

'*Sono io.*' It's me. '*Ciao,* Jessica.'

Giovanna looked just like she'd described herself in her email. Her hair was mid-length, curly and dark brown, and she was of slim build. She'd told Jess that she was in her early forties, but Jess thought she appeared younger.

'Would you like a coffee?' Giovanna asked in Italian.

Jess replied that she'd prefer a glass of water. The warmth of the morning had made her thirsty.

'We can get you one inside,' Giovanna said. 'Then we'll go straight to the baglio.'

* * *

Surrounded by olive trees that hid it from the road, the farmhouse perched at the top of a short dirt track below the pointed fever-chart crags towering above the village, appearing to have been dropped from space onto the hillside. The small, low white building with a terracotta-tiled roof featured a big rustic wooden door in the centre. She parked out front and, while Giovanna produced a key to unlock the door, a feeling of excitement stirred in the pit of Jess's stomach.

They went inside. Bare beige stone walls lined the square structure, which was built around a central atrium like the Sacca's main building. But the property her grandmother had left her was much smaller, of course. Jess remembered the solicitor had referred to it as a *baglio contadino*, meaning peasant farmers had once lived there. Eight doors opened onto the paved courtyard, two on each of the four sides.

'Are they locked?' Jess asked her cousin as she went to try a handle.

'No. We keep the farm equipment inside.'

'Is this a working farm, then?' Jess took a step backwards in surprise.

'Your grandmother asked us if we could work the land, in return for keeping an eye on the place,' Giovanna said. 'So that's what my husband, Angelo, and I do. Besides the olive trees, we grow lentils, tomatoes, chickpeas and beans.'

'Wow! How big is the farm?'

'Twenty-five hectares.'

It suddenly occurred to Jess that Giovanna would probably inherit the baglio, if she herself decided not to accept it. Nonna had put her in a difficult position, for sure. Why had she left it to her, the granddaughter she'd never met? Jess felt an overwhelming need to find out.

'I'm grateful you and Angelo have been taking care of

things.' She glanced at Giovanna. 'It's good that you're farming the land. I hope you'll want to carry on doing so in the future? I mean, I know nothing about farming—'

'So you've decided you want to keep the place?' Giovanna's tone came across as curt.

Jess shook her head, slightly put out by the directness of the question.

'I haven't made up my mind yet. After I've spent some time here mooching about on my own and weighing up the pros and cons during the three weeks of my holiday, I hope to come to a decision.'

'Angelo is away today, but he'll be back tomorrow.' Giovanna folded her arms across her chest. 'You can have supper with us at our house in the village and meet our two boys after you've come here, if you like.'

'I was hoping to find more family in Sicily.' Jess smiled. 'How old are your sons?'

'Bernardo – we call him Binnu – is seventeen. And Salvatore – Turiddu – is fourteen.'

'I love their Sicilian names.'

'Our language is in decline, unfortunately. The youngest generation prefers to speak Italian.'

'Oh, that's a shame.' Her grandmother had undoubtedly spoken nothing but Sicilian, back in the day. How she wished she could have met her.

Jess turned a door handle and peered inside. A small tractor and trailer were surrounded by various agricultural attachments. They must have cost a pretty penny. The next door opened into an empty room. Jess couldn't wait to explore the rest of the baglio at leisure. She asked for a key, and Giovanna handed her a spare set.

'Angelo will be here all day tomorrow,' Giovanna said. 'But

he'll be out on the land and won't disturb you.'

'I'm looking forward to meeting him.'

'I usually pick him up at around six o'clock.' A smile crinkled Giovanna's mouth. 'See you then!'

Feeling like she'd just been dismissed, Jess asked for directions to the nearest grocery store.

'Follow me back into the village. I'll stop outside the shop and point it out to you.' Giovanna checked her watch. 'I'm sorry to be in such a rush, but I need to get home and make lunch for my boys.'

That's put paid to me having a wander about the baglio on my own today, Jess sighed to herself.

* * *

Later, following a quick meal of juicy ripe tomatoes and mozzarella cheese back in her cottage, Jess decided to go for a swim. After changing into her tankini, she put a towel from the bathroom cupboard into a bag along with a bottle of factor 30 and a book. She slipped her feet into a pair of flip flops, found her sunglasses and headed outside.

Tiled in blue, the pool had been built into the hill on one side, with high stilts below the other. As soon as Jess got down there, she deposited her things on a lounger and dived in. As she swam a leisurely breaststroke towards the far end, she truly had the feeling that she was on the way to infinity.

This is such bliss, she thought. *I could stay here forever.* She remained in the pool until the tips of her fingers turned as wrinkled as prunes.

The decking scorching her feet, she ran back to the lounger. The sun had burnt her while she was ploughing up and down in the water, so she unfurled a big umbrella and positioned herself under it.

She settled her sunglasses onto her nose and opened her book. But it was impossible to concentrate. Her thoughts filled with her first impressions of Villaurora, the baglio and her cousin.

The village itself, apart from the oleander-lined street leading into the centre, seemed rather nondescript. Certainly not a location to entice tourists. Inside the bar, the few tables looked as if they'd seen better days, and the grocery store appeared to only sell the bare essentials.

The baglio, however, was another matter. She'd felt immediately at home there, and could imagine that lovely paved courtyard adorned with potted geraniums. The rooms opening onto it could be restored and would make a perfect place to invite family and friends to spend their holidays.

But she was getting carried away, she told herself. She needed to go back there several times at least, maybe even get quotes for restoration work, before she made up her mind. Hopefully, her grandmother's trust fund would cover the cost of that.

As for Giovanna Alessi, there was something 'off' about her. The directness of her questions, the curt tone of her voice. She could have prepared lunch for her boys prior to meeting Jess. After all, it wasn't every day one met a long-lost cousin. But then, said cousin had inherited the property which provided her with an income. Giovanna and her husband had probably been expecting it to come to them. Jess exhaled a slow breath. She couldn't fathom why her grandmother had left it to her and not them.

Cappero came into the periphery of her vision. He flopped

down on the grass at the edge of the decking, panting, and wagged his tail apologetically that he hadn't ventured across the hot wooden slats to greet her.

But it was the appearance of someone else approaching that made Jess startle. She caught sight of the tall, bronzed man she'd seen working on the vines the day before. Lean and toned, dressed in swim shorts, he walked towards her. Stefania's boyfriend appeared older than Jess had thought he'd be – possibly in his early forties, given the slightly receding light brown hair and the crinkles at the corners of his hazel eyes. He stopped in front of her sunbed and held out his hand.

'I'm Piero Sacca,' he said. 'I hope you're enjoying your stay with us, Mrs Brown.'

Jess extended her hand to shake his. But that didn't happen. Instead, he placed his hand under hers and brushed a whisper-soft kiss to her knuckles.

'Please, call me Jess,' she said, abruptly withdrawing her hand. 'And yes, I'm enjoying my visit here very much.'

Men in Italy only kissed married women's hands. It was a gesture of respect, but the practice had almost died out, and so Piero's gesture had taken her completely by surprise, and she could feel her cheeks flaming.

'I hope I'm not disturbing you, Jess.' He placed his towel on the sunbed next to hers.

'Of course not.' She smiled. 'This is your pool, after all.'

'Indeed.' He smiled back at her, turned and executed a perfect dive into the deep end.

She watched him swim a fast crawl, his muscular arms breaking the surface in a steady rhythm. Conscious that she was staring, she picked up her book and attempted to read. Except, the words on the page weren't half as interesting as Piero Sacca.

Her phone bleeped. A text from her cousin, Mel, asking how she'd got on today.

The baglio seems to have potential. I'll let you know more tomorrow after my second visit.

5

JESSICA, JUNE 2005

The next day, after spending the morning at the pool and making herself a late lunch, Jess prepared to go out. She packed the digital camera she'd treated herself to before leaving Bristol and the bottle of red wine she'd bought yesterday, then headed to where she'd parked her rented Fiat. She glanced up as Stefania came through the wide door.

'I'm glad I've caught you,' Stefania said. 'Would you be free tomorrow evening? You'd be a bit of a guinea pig, I'm afraid. Piero is planning to open a restaurant for our guests and we're trialling a tasting menu.'

'*Grazie*. That would be lovely.' Jess didn't need to think twice.

'Good. Piero's brother, Fabrizio, and his brother's wife, Cristina, are visiting from Monreale and will join you.'

'What about Piero's wife?' Jess risked the question that had been at the back of her mind since she'd met him.

'His ex-wife, you mean?' Stefania shook her head. 'Eleonora lives in Palermo with their two children. She never visits, but

Teresina and Gigi love it here. They'll be coming to stay for a few days during the summer vacation.'

'How old are they?'

'Gigi is ten and Teresina seven. They're fantastic kids.'

Stefania stared pointedly at the ring on Jess's finger. She should remove it, she supposed, but hadn't got round to doing so yet.

'I'm getting divorced,' she said, and left it at that.

Stefania blushed and apologised for staring.

'It's okay,' Jess said, and it was. She'd stopped fretting months ago. 'Well, I'd better get going.' She took her car keys from her bag. 'Thanks again for the invitation. It's very kind of you to think of me.'

'Piero insisted. And he stressed I ask you to give your honest opinion on the food.'

Stefania waved her off and soon Jess was following the same route she'd taken yesterday to Villaurora. Instead of cutting through the centre of the village, however, she carried on driving and presently she arrived at the dirt track leading up to the baglio.

She parked in front of the building, grabbed her bag, and went to open the big wooden door. But before doing so, she stopped to gaze at the view. The village hugged the slope further down, its narrow streets forming a grid-like pattern. She counted twelve parallel roads descending, criss-crossed by six vertical ones. The valley below appeared practically devoid of human habitation. Only a few farmhouses were dotted here and there.

Would she enjoy living in such a desolate place?

It's certainly peaceful...

A fresh breeze had sprung up and cooled the skin on Jess's

bare arms as she turned the key in the lock. Her chest squeezed with anticipation and she stepped inside.

* * *

After a couple of hours wandering around, taking photos and imagining the various outcomes of a restoration project, Jess was still no closer to arriving at a decision about her inheritance. She leant against a doorframe, and her chest hitched as she felt a little overwhelmed and in need of advice.

But who could she ask?

The walls between the eight rooms were so thick, it would be hard to knock through to make them bigger. But why would she want any larger rooms? She would only come in the summer and the courtyard itself would provide a gorgeous outdoor area. A Judas tree planted in the centre and some parasols for shade, perhaps? Tables and chairs for alfresco meals. One room had an old-fashioned kitchen that would require updating. And the bedrooms needed en suite bathrooms. The list was daunting, to say the least.

All the while, she carried on wondering why her grandmother had left her the baglio. There had to be a valid reason. Something momentous must have occurred for her mum, Carula, to cut herself off from her family and not even speak about them to her own daughter. Maybe Nonna was hoping to mend bridges?

Jess returned her camera to her bag. She'd see if she could spot Angelo, and Giovanna should be here soon. After locking up, Jess made her way around to the back of the building, where a man was hoeing the earth between rows of crops.

He waved and came towards her. Of medium height, with a

broad face and a full head of thick, dark hair, he introduced himself.

'*Bona sira. Sono* Angelo.'

'*Piacere.*' Jess held out her hand.

But he didn't shake it.

'I need to wash,' he said with a bow. 'Sorry.'

'No problem.' She smiled.

There was a standpipe at the edge of the field, and he went to rinse his fingers under a stream of water.

'Giovanna should be here any minute now,' he said.

As if on cue, the rumble of a motor echoed from down the road. Giovanna's car juddered to a halt and she wound down the window.

'*Ciao*, Jess.' Giovanna greeted her as Angelo got into the front seat. 'We should park near the village church as our street is too narrow. Follow me!'

Jess did as instructed and, about ten minutes later, she squeezed her Punto into a tight spot a couple of cars behind Giovanna's. Grabbing the bottle of wine, she stepped onto the pavement.

'For you,' she said, handing her gift over to her cousin.

Giovanna thanked her, then led her across the square to the steep road she'd seen yesterday. The pavements on either side were wide and stepped, and it would be impossible for two vehicles to pass each other in between, let alone park. They entered a two-storey house, the top floor fronted by a bulging balcony of swan-neck railings.

Binnu and Turiddu were lounging on the sofa inside the front room, playing some kind of video game. After getting to their feet, they introduced themselves before going back to what they were doing.

'Let's go through to the kitchen,' Giovanna suggested. 'I can put the pasta on while we have a drink.'

Looking as if it dated from the 1970s, the room – filled with the aromas of fresh basil, rosemary and sage – appeared spacious with avocado-green cabinets, harvest-gold-coloured plastic chairs around a beige laminate-topped table, and a brown ceramic-tiled floor.

'Take a seat,' Angelo said, pulling out a chair for Jess. 'Can I offer you a glass of white wine?'

'I'd better not, as I'm driving.'

'Oh, we don't bother about such things in Villaurora,' Giovanna said from where she was standing by the stove.

'I'd love some cold water.' Jess gave her a smile.

Angelo fetched a bottle from the fridge and poured her a glass. An awkward silence ensued, and Jess searched her mind for a neutral topic of conversation. But Angelo obviously had no qualms about addressing the elephant in the room.

'Have you decided to accept your inheritance?' he asked without preamble.

'Not yet.' Jess collected her thoughts. 'I know you have a vested interest and I can assure you that I'm happy with the way things are. I mean, that you continue to farm the land.'

'We'd appreciate something in writing,' he said. 'Perhaps you could lease the terrain to us for a nominal rent?'

'I'm sure I can arrange that, if and when the time comes.'

'Good.' He nodded, and a smile creased his broad face.

* * *

After an amazing meal of *pasta alla norma* (maccheroni with a tomato, aubergine, salted ricotta and basil sauce) followed by *arancini* (deep-fried rice balls stuffed with minced meat) and a fresh green salad dressed with olive oil, Jess declared she couldn't manage another mouthful.

'That was truly delicious,' she said. 'You're an excellent cook, Giovanna.'

'She's not bad.' Binnu, the eldest of the boys, wiped his mouth with a serviette.

'Can you get Sicilian food in England?' Turiddu made direct eye contact with Jess.

'Not as good as your mum's,' she said.

Throughout the meal, her youngest cousins quizzed her about life in the UK, declaring their ambition was to leave Villaurora as soon as they'd finished school and maybe try to get jobs in London.

'All our young people are leaving the village.' Angelo poured Jess another glass of water. 'There's no work for them here.'

'I was wondering why the streets are so empty.'

'In the old days, Sicilians would emigrate to America for employment. Now they go to places like Milan and Torino. Or further afield to England.'

'There're plenty of opportunities in the UK if you're prepared to work hard.' Jess chose her words with care. She didn't want to give the boys false hope. 'Especially in the big cities.'

'We would do that,' Binnu affirmed. 'Work hard, I mean.'

Giovanna rose from the table to do the dishes, and Jess went to help her while Angelo and his sons headed for the front room to watch TV.

'Your boys are a credit to you,' Jess said as Giovanna handed her a tea-towel. 'You must be so proud of them.'

'They keep out of trouble, unlike some.' Giovanna flipped her hair back from her face.

'I was interested in what Angelo said about Sicilians emigrating to America.' Jess took a plate from Giovanna and wiped it dry. 'I'm completely in the dark about my grandmother's family. All I know was that she came from Sicily. It was only when a lawyer contacted me that I found out the name of this village.'

'I too find it strange that we knew nothing about you until a couple of months ago.' Giovanna handed Jess another plate. 'I never met Lucia in person. She went to America before I was born.'

'Was her husband Sicilian?'

'I don't know, Jess. All I know is that he passed away some time ago. My parents looked after the baglio for her and, when they got too old, Lucia wrote to me and asked if Angelo and I could take care of it. We also have a smallholding on the other side of the village, so it made sense to farm your grandmother's land as well. She was happy we could do so, even bought us some new machinery.'

'Does she have any other family in Villaurora besides you?'

'My grandmother was her youngest sister. There was a brother too.' Giovanna stared down at her hands. 'He's no longer with us.'

'What was his name?'

'I don't know.' Giovanna shook her head. 'Sorry I can't be more helpful.' It was as if the shutters had come down.

Jess carried on helping until all the plates were washed and dried. She told Giovanna about her English family. While her father was a Bristolian, born and bred, Jess grew up in Cheshire, where her parents both worked in the animal pharmaceuticals industry. Her father was one of four children and Jess's uncles, aunts and nine cousins all lived in Bristol. She hadn't been back to Cheshire since her parents' funeral.

'My condolences,' Giovanna said. 'I'm sorry for your loss.'

'A lorry driver was on his phone, apparently. He ploughed into Mum and Dad's car. They didn't stand a chance.'

'How terrible!' Giovanna's eyes widened.

'I still miss them so much,' Jess said, her voice trembling.

'What about your husband?' Giovanna touched her hand to Jess's arm.

'I don't want to dwell on it,' Jess said, after unburdening herself and recounting the whole sorry Scott saga. 'The baglio is like a new chapter in my life. I feel as if it's helping me, somehow.'

'So, you think you'll keep it?' Giovanna glanced at her. 'Isn't it too remote for you here?'

'It is in the middle of nowhere, I agree, but that has its attractions. I can forget all about my busy life in England and truly relax.'

Giovanna seemed about to say something, but shrugged instead.

'I'd better make tracks for the tenuta,' Jess said, knowing when she'd overstayed her welcome. 'It'll be a tricky drive in the dark.'

Giovanna took her through to the front room, where Angelo and the boys got to their feet to say goodnight. Everyone kissed each other on both cheeks, Italian style, and Angelo saw her to the door.

'Would you like me to walk you back to your car?' he offered.

'I'll be fine, thanks. I'm hardly likely to get mugged in Villaurora.'

Angelo chuckled at her joke, and she laughed along with him.

'*Buona notte*,' she wished him goodnight.

'*Bona notti*,' he responded in Sicilian.

She walked down the road and crossed the square, taking a moment before getting into the car. Above her, with the lack of light pollution, the sky billowed with billions of stars. *Peaceful* was the first word that came to her. This might be the middle of nowhere, but she couldn't help being captivated by its beauty, just like her grandmother must have been all those years ago.

6

LUCIA, JUNE 1943

Lucia gazed up at the stars, embedded in the velvet blackness of the summer night. It was hot inside, and she'd come outdoors to sit in the cool. Many of their neighbours were doing likewise, and the street murmured with the sound of whispered conversations.

Dinu pulled up a chair next to her and sat himself down.

'*Ciao*,' she said, turning to smile at him. She'd barely seen him since Gero Bonanno had arrived, and she wasn't happy about that.

The other day, after he and Francu had shown the American how to get to don Nofriu's, Dinu had come home in a rage. Gero had accepted the boss's offer of a room in his house, and Dinu said it was an insult to the family that he'd preferred to live in comfort rather than bunk down with them.

Lucia had been relieved, not offended. Getting Gero out of the house meant he'd have less chance of being a bad influence on her brother. She worried about Gero's connections with the village godfather.

But Ma had taken Dinu's side.

'It's like a slap in the face,' she'd said.

It wasn't too long before she changed her mind. Gero came the next morning with half a kilo of ground beef for her to make a ragù to stuff *arancini* with. He'd become Ma's number one favourite person since then.

Lucia huffed to herself. Don Nofriu traded in meat on the black market, she knew for a fact. Gero would have arrived with money to fund his activities on the island, and he'd have used some of it to purchase the beef. He must have further use for her family, she'd thought.

And he soon proved she wasn't wrong. She'd found out yesterday from her twin that Gero had hidden his radio down in the valley after he'd parachuted from the plane. Dinu and Francu had set off with him after nightfall to bring it back to Lucia's family home.

'Why can't he keep it at don Nofriu's?' she'd asked her brother.

'He doesn't want him getting wind of his business.'

'And what business might that be?'

'He wants to snoop on troop movements for a start,' Dinu had said. 'I know I can trust you not to breathe a word.'

Time to change the subject, Lucia thought.

'So, *frati*.' She glanced at her twin. 'How about we go hunting tomorrow?'

'I can't, *soru*. Gero would like me to show him where the nearest division of the Italian Sixth Army is camped. Remember, we spotted them last month while we went looking for rabbits further afield?'

'Please, take me with you,' she begged. 'I'm going crazy cooped up here all the time.'

'Not sure that's a good idea, sis.' Dinu rubbed at the back of his neck. 'I don't want Gero getting the wrong idea about you.'

'That I'm a tomboy? I don't care a jot if he does and neither should you.'

'Life here isn't like in America.' Dinu cleared his throat. 'You're not supposed to be out and about with a guy unless you're married.'

'Oh, for heaven's sake,' she said, folding her arms over her stomach. 'That'd only apply if I was alone with him. Which I wouldn't be as you'd be with us, stupid.'

'Who are you calling stupid?' He shot her a look.

'Just kiddin'.' She laughed to dispel her disquiet at Dinu's sudden dark tone. 'But seriously, what could be the harm?'

'Let me run it by him tomorrow, okay? He's meeting Pa and me for a coffee in the Bar Centrale before we go to work.'

'Thanks, *frati*.' She leaned across the space between them and gave him a hug. 'I won't embarrass you, I promise.'

'You'd better not,' he said.

Again, there was a dark edge to his tone, a darkness that made her shiver.

* * *

The next evening, Lucia dressed in her brother's clothes and headed off with her brother and Gero at nightfall by the light of a full moon. Her parents thought she was going to hunt rabbits with Dinu, and she hadn't put them straight. The danger was minimal. They were only going to verify the exact position of the encampment and wouldn't go anywhere near the troops. As they walked, they chatted about their childhoods in New York.

'Remember when we used to meet up on Coney Island?' Gero reminisced.

They didn't go to Coney Island to swim, Lucia reflected.

Neither she nor Dinu had ever learnt because there was never enough room in the water. There were also those twenty-thousand leaks under the sea, which turned it into the biggest urinal in the city. She gave a shudder of revulsion.

'The beach was sardine-packed with oiled bodies, most of them funny-looking,' she said.

'They were all in varying shades of sun-toasted red.' Gero flung his head back in laughter.

'I remember our sandcastles would always end up being trodden on,' Lucia said, thinking back to how everyone staked out their territory, leaving just enough space for folks to walk past. Many crotches would approach at the level of her nose, and her view of misshapen rumps would make her feel like throwing up. Not to mention all those beer bellies spilling out over waistbands.

'My parents wouldn't let us use the bath houses to get changed in,' Gero said. 'They reckoned they weren't as clean as our bathroom at home.'

Lucia smiled ruefully at the memory. Ma had been of the same opinion, even though they shared theirs with the apartment next door. Furthermore, the bath houses cost fifty cents to rent and Pa only earned about fifteen dollars a week.

'Ma and Pa made us ride back to Brooklyn on the trolley car in wet bathing suits full of scratchy sand,' she said.

'Didn't you just love the boardwalk, the penny arcades and the frozen custard?' Dinu's voice vibrated with pleasure.

'Oh, yeah. The frozen custard.' Gero appeared to bounce on his toes. 'Twelve thousand per cent butterfat. How could I ever forget?'

Lucia was glad he hadn't mentioned Luna Park. She and her family didn't have twenty-five cents to waste at a shooting gallery, nor the fifteen required for the rollercoasters. She used to gaze longingly at the Mile Sky Chaser, which surrounded the park on three sides and featured drops of nearly eighty feet.

'Have you been to any of the beaches here in Sicily?' Gero asked.

What a crass question, she thought. Did he really believe people like them indulged in breaks at the seaside? She'd been warming to him while they chatted, hoping against hope he wouldn't involve her brother in anything to do with don Nofriu.

'Only time I ever saw the coast was when we approached Palermo on the cargo ship bringing us here from New York.' Dinu shook his head. 'Sometimes I forget we're living on an island.'

They lapsed into silence as they trudged on through the night, Lucia's legs feeling as heavy as lead. She prayed they'd get to their destination soon. Finally, to her relief, they arrived at a bamboo thicket.

Dinu put his finger to his lips and motioned that they should crouch down. The camp appeared lightly defended; Lucia could only spot two sentries. There were about twenty tank-sized shapes, covered with camouflage nets.

'I've got what I came for,' Gero whispered. 'We can leave now.'

Not a word of thanks, Lucia huffed. She wished he would leave for good.

* * *

The next day was Sunday. In the morning, before heading off to mass, the entire family took it in turns to have a bath and wash their hair. It was quite a rigmarole. Ma supervised the proceedings, heating water in an enormous cauldron over the fire, then pouring it into a huge iron tub. The least dirty of them went in first – always Annita – followed by Lucia, Ma, Dinu and Pa. A sheet was strung up across the room for privacy, and by the time the show was over, the bathwater was filthy and stone cold. Dinu and Pa didn't seem to mind, thankfully.

Lucia relished the feeling of cleanliness. The rest of the week, she and the other members of her family made do with a sponge down at bedtime. She put on a fresh clean dress and braided her hair before helping Annita with hers.

'You look lovely, *tisoru*' – darling – she said to her sister. 'Come, link your arm with mine and we'll walk down to the church together.'

Ma and Pa herded them out of the house, and soon they joined their neighbours on the street as the entire village went to mass.

Lucia spotted Dinu and Francu and gave them a wave. Her brother had set off earlier to meet their cousin.

The air inside the church was redolent with the scent of incense and the stench of bodies that hadn't partaken of a weekly bath. Gero was in don Nofriu's pew on the opposite side of the aisle to where Lucia, Annita, Pa and Ma were sitting. Lucia gritted her teeth. It looked as if Gero had been accepted as a member of the godfather's 'family', or Cosa Nostra clan.

Dinu and Francu had wormed their way into the bench behind the American. Lucia hated the way they were constantly cosying up to him. She knew her brother well and feared his intentions.

Without warning, she felt hot eyes burning into her. She chanced a quick glance and caught sight of the marshal of the local carabinieri, Giulianu Cardona, an unattractive man with oiled black hair, protruding ears, a pencil-thin moustache and fleshy red lips. He was always looking at her and she disliked him for it.

To distract herself, she gazed around the congregation. The pew in front was occupied by the village schoolteacher, Alberto Spina, his wife, Donata, and their little boys, Lele and Pinuzzo. Rumour had it that Spina was anti-fascist, but it was probably only gossip.

A gruff voice came from the back of the church. Carlo Russo, the village's fat mayor. Lucia turned around to look at him. As fascist as the black shirt he was wearing, he was sandwiched between his chubby wife, Nilla, and their adolescent sons, Fonziu and Mariano.

Lucia curled her lip. The mayor had done nothing to help the people of Villaurora, and she despised him. Thank God she had the love she felt for her family, or she'd go sour with so much hate. And she loved the blessed Virgin Mary and Jesus, of course. Her faith was strong, she'd been brought up a good Catholic, and she knew that if the life she was living now was lacking in material things, it wasn't the be all and end all of her existence. She would live in a perfect union of love with God when she went to heaven.

The congregation rose to its feet as Father Michele walked slowly to the altar with his servers. He was don Nofriu's brother; the two men were like day and night. The priest's open, smiling face was a complete contrast to the man of respect's cunning, foxy appearance.

Lucia closed her eyes, and a vision of the velvet sky lit by shining stars came into her mind. She longed to be out in the countryside, hunting rabbits with Dinu without a care in the world. A feeling of dread came over her, and she wished Gero Bonanno had never come to Villaurora.

7

JESSICA, JUNE 2005

Jess woke with a feeling of tranquillity, her dream of Villaurora, of the night sky emblazoned with stars, fading into sunlight. The incredible clarity of the vision was still with her as she swung her legs from the bed and made her way to the bathroom. Crickets, twittering in the umbrella pine tree outside the window, heralded what promised to be another hot day.

After a quick shower, Jess dressed in a pair of shorts and a t-shirt. She brewed a coffee, then grabbed a brioche from the packet she'd bought in the village, before heading to the portico where a small wrought-iron table and two chairs held pride of place.

The buttery taste of the pastry coated her tongue as she thought about last night with her Sicilian cousins, and the mystery of Giovanna not being able – or not wanting – to tell her more about Nonna's brother. World War Two ended sixty years ago. Perhaps the brother – Jess's great-uncle – was killed in the conflict? But if so, surely his name would be remembered?

She sipped her coffee, her mind flitting between one idea

and the next. Was the baglio Nonna's family home? That being the case, though, Giovanna – Nonna's sister's granddaughter – couldn't have been disinherited, could she? No, Nonna must have obtained it by another means.

Jess rubbed a hand through her mane of hair, untangling the wayward tresses. She'd make an unannounced trip to the property, she decided. Yesterday, she'd told Giovanna she didn't know when she'd go back, but the day stretched before her. Tonight, she was expected at the wine and food tasting. She could spend the day reading, or she could visit the baglio.

Decision made, about half an hour later, she found herself in the paved courtyard of the farmhouse, searching for something, anything that might provide an answer to her questions. If there were any stones she'd turn them over, but the place was as empty as a bird's nest in December.

Jess swept her gaze around the place, and her eye was drawn to a strange turquoise ceramic figurine, cemented onto the wall to the left of the entrance door. How could she have missed it yesterday? She approached and sucked in a sharp breath. Truly one of the weirdest things she'd ever seen. At the centre presided a clay head surrounded with entwined serpents for its hair. A medusa. Ears, twisted to look like corn, were disproportionately large at the sides. Three legs, bent at the knee, emerged from the head. The toes on the feet curled upwards. If the head was a clock, the legs would be at the twelve, four and eight o'clock positions.

The sudden whirr of a motorbike engine echoed through the building. Wondering who it could be, Jess pushed open the rough wooden entrance door and stepped outside. Nothing out front, so she walked around to the back of the house, where she saw a mountain motorbike cresting the hill above the property, leaving a cloud of dust behind it. She hadn't even realised there was a path going up there. Some hundred metres away, she spotted Giovanna, hoeing the earth between a row of crops.

'Did you see that mountain bike?' she asked after hurrying over to her.

'What bike?' Giovanna stared at her blankly. 'You must be mistaken. I didn't see anything.'

She might not have seen it but must have surely heard it, Jess thought.

'Is there some kind of track leading in that direction?' She pointed towards the hilltop.

'Oh,' Giovanna said, not meeting Jess's eye. 'The path is very dangerous. Full of potholes and extremely steep. The sides fall away sharply, so no one ventures up there in case they have an accident.'

Jess chewed at her lip, certain she hadn't been mistaken. Either she accused her cousin of telling a blatant lie, or she backed down. She opted for the latter. Maybe it wasn't such a big deal.

*   *   *

Jess spent the afternoon relaxing on the portico, finishing her book and thinking about the morning she'd spent at the baglio. She wondered who had cemented the strange ceramic figurine to the wall and why Giovanna had lied to her about the motorbike. Instead of denying she'd heard it, she could have concocted a story to explain why someone had driven through the property. With hindsight, Jess wished she'd pressed her more on the matter. She'd been too reticent; she shouldn't have backed down. A hiker might have found the path dangerous, but surely a mountain bike would have handled it easily.

The sun dipped lower in the sky and, with a sigh, she went

to get ready for the wine and food tasting – the last thing she felt like doing, but she couldn't get out of it now. She showered and changed into a sleeveless pale green linen dress. She felt too hot to leave her hair down, so she tied it back in a ponytail. Just mascara and lip-gloss for make-up and she was done.

Piero, handsome in an open-neck fitted white shirt and dark blue jeans, was waiting with Cappero to greet her at the giant blue wooden door.

'Thank you for joining us,' he said, taking her hand and bowing over it.

'Thanks for inviting me.' Smiling, she bent to pat the dog.

'My brother and his wife are looking forward to meeting you.' Piero spoke in English, his voice deep and melodic, his accent barely discernible. 'Let's go inside. It's too warm to stand around out here.'

As he ushered her through one of the sets of double wooden doors facing the courtyard, her breath caught in awe. She gazed at a series of pristine bare stone arches linking the separate areas. The same terracotta-tiled floor formed a cohesive whole, interspersed with flat-weave pale carpets, and white matte plastered walls made the most of the available light. The whole effect was cosy and inviting. Casual with a touch of sophistication.

'This is so beautiful,' she said. 'I love what you've done with it.'

'*Grazie*. In times gone by, my ancestors hired extra labour when needed, and they were housed here during the wheat planting and harvest seasons.'

'Do you still grow grain?'

'Only a few hectares of durum wheat. We have some cows and sheep, but the rest of the land has been taken over by vines and olive trees. The estate spans nearly 600 hectares of which 400 are devoted to the production of wine.'

'I saw you working in the vineyard.'

'I keep my eye on things, but I also have a team. Not just Stefania and her boyfriend, who's my manager. We also have a wine specialist and an agriculturalist as well as three generations from two families, who've worked for us since my grandfather decided to expand our wine business.'

'Oh, when was that?'

'Not long after the second war. It was an experiment at first. He planted native vines of the Perricone and Nero d'Avola variety, then blended the product to create the first original wine from a single vineyard in Sicily. He named it *Rosso del Barone*, and I'm proud to say it holds its own with the best European and New World vintages.'

'How amazing!'

'Indeed. My father took over after Nonno passed away, and cultivated the first international vines to be grown in Sicily. He also modernised our winemaking systems.'

'Does your father still live on the estate?'

'No. He's retired now, lives in Mondello, a beach resort near Palermo.' Piero paused, as if to collect his thoughts. 'My focus is on sustainability these days.'

'Sustainability?' Jess tilted her head.

'Our aim is to prevent damage to the ecosystem. We no longer use any chemical or technical methods that could be harmful and instead rely on manual labour and environmentally friendly technology.'

'That's wonderful,' Jess said. 'You should be proud of yourself.'

'Kind of you to say so. My brother, Fabrizio, runs our sister winery, Tenuta Milangeri, in Monreale near Palermo, along the same lines. He and his wife, Cristina, are waiting for us in the dining area.' Piero made direct eye contact with Jess. 'Shall we go through?'

A good-looking couple were sitting on stools in front of a bar. They got to their feet as Jess and Piero approached, Cappero padding at their heels. Piero introduced Jess to Fabrizio – a slightly younger version of himself – who aimed a kiss at her hand, and Cristina – tall and elegant with expertly styled, short blonde-highlighted hair – who air-kissed both her cheeks.

Piero and his family certainly are kissy.

'It's lovely to meet you,' Jess said, taking the flute of sparkling wine Piero had poured for her.

'Cheers,' he said, and they all clinked glasses. Jess took a sip, tasting dryness and a slight hint of sweetness.

'Is this champagne?' she asked, eyeing the label on the bottle, *Melita Brut*, the bubbles still bursting on her tongue.

'We aren't allowed to call it that, but it is – for all intents and purposes,' Fabrizio responded. 'To clarify, all champagne is sparkling wine, but not all sparkling wine is champagne. We make it using the traditional method, just like the French.'

'What method is that?'

'We pick the grapes by hand, and press them carefully to keep the juice clear white. Then we put it into a tank and start the first fermentation.' Piero sipped his drink. 'About five months after the harvest, we blend it with wine held in reserve. Afterwards, it goes through the second fermentation process.'

'That's so interesting,' Jess said, intrigued.

'A mixture of yeast and sugar is added to the wine.' Fabrizio held his champagne flute up to the light. 'Then it's put into thick glass bottles sealed with a bottle cap before being placed in a cool cellar to ferment slowly, and to produce alcohol and carbon dioxide.'

'That's the most important part of the process,' Piero said. 'The carbon dioxide can't escape from the bottle and as it dissolves, it creates the bubbles.'

'Fermentation takes months, but the wine continues to age in the coolness of our cellars for several more years,' Fabrizio carried on explaining.

'I hadn't realised it took so long,' Jess said, surprised.

'I love the final stage,' Cristina added. 'We keep the bottles upside down, their necks frozen in an ice-salt bath. A plug of frozen wine forms, containing dead yeast cells. We remove the bottle cap, and the pressure of the carbon dioxide gas in the bottle forces the plug of frozen wine out, leaving behind only clear liquid.'

'We add a mixture of white wine, brandy and sugar – it's a secret recipe – to adjust the sweetness level and to top up the bottle.' Piero's eyes lit up with a smile. 'The bottles are corked and the corks wired down to secure the high internal density of the carbon dioxide in the wine.'

'And now we are drinking it,' Jess said, raising her glass. 'It's really delicious.'

'These are our appetisers and a perfect pairing with the *Melita*.' Piero pointed to a tray on the counter.

'My favourite Palermo street food,' Fabrizio said. '*Panelle*, which are made with deep-fried chickpea batter, and *panzerotti*, which are like mini pizza *calzoni*.'

'So delicious,' Jess said after tasting one of the *panelle*. 'I really like the taste.'

Crispy, with a nutty, salty flavour. A bit like French fries, only thicker.

'Good.' Piero took a *panella* for himself.

Jess tried one of the *panzerotti*. The mini pizza pocket held an enticing filling of melty cheese and tomatoes. She declared it to be scrumptious before discerning Stefania coming into the room.

'Dinner is ready,' Stefania announced. 'Please take your seats.'

The table was big enough for twelve, but their places were at the far end – Piero and Jess opposite Fabrizio and Cristina. Cappero flopped down on the floor by their feet.

Stefania and her helper – the daughter of one of the estate workers, whose mother worked as the cook – served ravioli stuffed with ricotta and mint. White wine appeared in a magnum – *Nozze d'Oro 2000*.

'This is a fifty-fifty blend of sauvignon blanc and inzolia,' Piero said as he poured Jess half a glass. '*Nozze d'Oro* means golden nuptials, and we created it on the occasion of my parents' fiftieth wedding anniversary.'

'Everything is perfect.' Jess relished the balance between the acidity and peachiness of the blend.

During the main course – beef involtini, the meat rolled around a delicious filling – Cristina asked Jess about herself. More wine had been served, this time the estate's trademark *Rosso del Barone*. Jess swirled the ruby-red drink in her glass and inhaled the enticing cherry-vanilla aroma before taking a sip. She went on to tell Cristina and the others about her job at the bank.

'Sounds stressful,' Piero said.

'It is, but I cope. I'm loving the chance to recharge my batteries here, though. It's so peaceful.'

'What about your husband? Does he work in banking as well?' Cristina stared blatantly at the ring on Jess's finger.

'He's a partner in a firm of accountants.' Jess felt her cheeks burn. 'But we're getting divorced—'

'I'm sorry. I didn't mean to pry,' Cristina said before changing the subject. 'Is this your first time in Sicily?'

'Yes.' Jess pondered if she should mention her inheritance. Maybe they could give her some advice? 'My grandmother was Sicilian,' she said. 'In fact, she's left me a property. A *baglio contadino* near Villaurora.'

'Wow!' Cristina's eyes widened. 'What's it like?'

Jess went on to tell them about the farmhouse. She mentioned her cousins, but kept the mystery of her grand-mother's background to herself.

'I need to decide whether to accept the bequest or not,' she added. 'The baglio needs renovating, and I was wondering if you knew a good, reliable builder I could ask for a quote.'

'Of course.' Piero lifted the bottle to refill Jess's glass, but she placed her hand over it. She'd taken care not to overindulge, sticking to just half a glass per course.

Stefania and her helper cleared the dishes, then brought dessert, the Sicilian staple, *cannoli*. Tube-shaped shells of fried pastry dough, pumped with creamy, sweetened ricotta, paired with a *passito* sweet wine made from white malvasia grapes. Jess could only manage one forkful and a small sip from her glass.

'I've eaten too much,' she said. 'I'm in danger of bursting.'

'I hope you don't!' Piero laughed.

Jess giggled, feeling a little tipsy despite the care she'd taken.

'What is your verdict on our tasting menu?' Piero asked.

'Everything is almost spot-on, as far as I can judge.' She thought for a few seconds. 'Just one thing. Ricotta's in both the ravioli and the dessert. Maybe you could have something different?'

'Excellent idea,' he said. 'Other than that, do think our guests will enjoy it?'

'How can they not?' She gave him a smile. 'Thank you so much for trialling it on me. I've enjoyed every mouthful.'

'I have a meeting with a group of wine producers in Agrigento tomorrow. It's where you can view some magnificent Greek temple ruins.' Piero crinkled his eyes. 'You could be a tourist while I'm busy. Afterwards, we can have lunch in my favourite fish restaurant, if you like.'

Taken aback, Jess swallowed the lump of surprise in her throat. But a visit to the temples was on her to-do list, so how could she refuse?

'That would be lovely,' she said. '*Grazie.*'

'We're heading home now,' Cristina said as she and Fabrizio got to their feet. She bent to give Cappero a pat. 'Do come and see us in Monreale before you return to England. We're only a short drive from the magnificent Norman cathedral.'

Jess thanked her and went to stand next to Piero in the courtyard while they waved Cristina and Fabrizio goodbye.

'I need to take Cappero out, Jess,' Piero said. 'So I'll walk you back to your cottage.'

The dog raced ahead, and she fell into step beside him. She felt comfortable with Piero, as if she'd known him for years. Should she tell him about her quest to discover her family history? But by the time she'd decided to do so, they'd stopped at the door to her accommodation and he was bending to kiss her hand.

'Good night, Jess. We'll leave at eight in the morning, if that's all right with you?'

'I'll be ready, and thanks again.'

She unlocked her door and went inside. Thoughts of Piero, Fabrizio and Cristina filled her mind after she stretched out on her bed. She'd enjoyed the evening. Fabrizio and Cristina were super-friendly and Piero such a gentleman. It was kind of him to offer to take her to Agrigento. She wondered what she might wear for the journey, imagined herself in sunglasses, laughing with Piero, her hair blowing in the breeze as they drove along...

Take care, Jess. You're only here for a short time and a holiday fling is the last thing you need, she told herself.

Instead, she thought about the baglio and a vision of the strange clay figurine came into her head, its serpent hair and corn-like ears. But sleep soon chased it away, and she knew nothing until the dawn chorus of sparrows outside her bedroom window was welcoming the start of a new day.

8

LUCIA, JULY 1943

A flurry of small, brown-feathered sparrows swooped down, chattering away in high-pitched chirps while they pecked at the grit by Lucia's feet. She was sitting on the front doorstep, sipping her barley coffee. The morning sun cast long shadows across the narrow street as it appeared over the top of the houses opposite. There was no one about – Dinu and Pa had already gone to work – and Lucia was relishing the chance to show her face without being reprimanded for shamelessness.

She thought about the progress of the war. It was July now, and Gero had been supplying Lucia and her family with information about what was occurring. In the Pacific, the conflict had finally turned against Japan. She gave a deep sigh. If only that would happen in Europe, where heavy fighting had been going on for nearly four years.

A couple of days ago, while eating with the family – Ma had made involtini with the beef Gero had brought – he'd said Nazi Germany was bogged down in a costly defensive war in the Soviet Union, fighting to protect their ever-shrinking occupied territory. That meant an Allied initiative on the Western Front of Europe might take place any day now, whilst the enemy's resources remained diverted.

Yesterday, Gero had gone with Dinu and Francu to observe a German camp near Enna in the centre of the island. On their return, Dinu told Lucia it was most likely only a temporary base, given the lack of permanent structures. By all accounts, the Nazis had reduced the strength of their presence in Sicily. Another reason for the Allies almost certainly picking the island as their first objective in liberating Europe from Hitler.

Lucia's chest tensed. Although she and her family would be safe from direct contact with any fighting – Villaurora was too remote – she couldn't help worrying. Allied aircraft flew over the village ever more frequently on their way to bomb Palermo. What if one of them crashed? She gave herself a shake; she was being silly. The chances of a plane coming down on her home were practically zero.

Footfalls sounded. Someone was approaching. It was Gero, and Lucia groaned inwardly. What was he doing here so early? Usually, he only came to use his radio in the evenings. She wished he'd found a different location for the purpose. Not because he'd be discovered; Gero had explained he wasn't putting Lucia and her family in any danger. The nearest military camps, where the enemy might have detection devices, were far enough away.

She pressed her lips together, feeling conflicted. If he weren't such a show-off, she might have swooned. His almost-black hair was swept back from his face and his Greek god good looks wouldn't have looked out of place in Hollywood. It was the fact he was living with don Nofriu that worried her.

'*Ciao*, Lucia,' Gero said, a smile twinkling in his dark brown eyes.

She wished him good morning and rose to her feet. If

anyone saw her talking to him without a chaperone, they would brand her a *pulla* and she'd bring disgrace to her family.

He followed her inside and went to the suitcase housing his transceiver, where he began sending a coded message.

Curious, she pulled up a chair and sat next to him, breathing in his smell of fresh soap and cigarettes.

Ma brought him a coffee, for which he thanked her.

'I suppose you're not gonna tell me what you're communicating,' Lucia said.

'Sorry.' He shook his head. 'Top secret.'

'Are the Americans coming soon?' Lucia fixed him in her gaze.

She knew for a fact that, almost a month ago, the Italian island of Pantelleria, located just over one hundred kilometres southwest of Sicily, had surrendered to the Allies unconditionally after nineteen days of aerial bombardment. Would Pantelleria be a suitable base for launching the invasion of Italy?

'Can't say.' Gero leant away from her.

'Can't or won't?' She could hear the annoyance in her tone.

'I'm just trying to do my best in a difficult situation, Lucia.' He exhaled a deep breath. 'You're a smart girl. You don't need me to spell things out to you.'

'You think I'm smart?' She huffed. 'How come?'

'I've seen the way you look at me, like you can see right through me.'

'And what can I see, then?'

'That I'm *un sceccu*.' An idiot. He laughed. 'Every time I open my mouth, I put my foot in it.'

'You're always bragging, Gero.'

Another laugh. This one embarrassed.

'It's your fault,' he said.

'Mine? I don't get it—'

'You're so beautiful.' He stared down at the ground, then shrugged ruefully. 'I wanna impress you, but my words always come out wrong.'

'I'm not beautiful.' A flush warmed her cheeks. 'I think you need glasses.' She shoved her hands into the pockets of her apron.

'Have you looked in a mirror lately? You have the most incredible eyes, the glossiest hair, and the most perfect oval-shaped face.'

'You're making me uncomfortable.' Lucia suddenly felt impossibly hot, but resisted the urge to fan herself.

'Sorry 'bout that,' Gero said. 'I was only telling the truth.'

'When did you enlist in the army?' she asked, wanting to change the subject.

'They drafted me just over a year ago. I was supposed to be an infantryman but, on the first day, they did a roll call and deployed those of us who had Italian last names to the Office of Strategic Services.'

'The Office of Strategic Services? What's that?'

'I probably shouldn't tell you, but it's an intelligence agency set up to get information and to sabotage the military efforts of enemy nations. They enlist bilingual personnel like me for missions behind adversary lines.'

'Were you happy about being sent over here?'

'I've always wanted to visit Sicily. But not under these circumstances. I guess it's better than fighting somewhere else, though.'

'Was the training difficult?'

'Jeez, you ask a lotta questions, Lucia.' His smile belied the criticism of his words. 'Our camp was in the Blue Ridge Mountains. A typical day began with a five-mile run. We then had to do two hours of gymnastics. After lunch we attended lectures on various topics, such as personal disguise, observation, communications, and field craft.'

'*Bedda Matri*,' she exclaimed. 'That must have been amazing.'

'Sure was. In the afternoons we trained with explosives in an open field, practised with small arms at a basement firing range, parachute jumped from a ninety-foot jump tower, and crawled under barbed wire while machine guns fired live rounds overhead.'

'*Mizzica!*' Woah. 'Was it very tiring?'

'Yep. In the evenings, we either had to study assignments, go out on night manoeuvres, or undergo simulated interrogations by instructors or by one of the German officers from an enemy officer internment camp nearby. The course ended with us having to find our way back to the camp after parachuting into a forest thirty miles away.'

'So that's how you managed to work out how to get to Villaurora—'

'It helped that my dad could draw me a map. I didn't tell anyone he'd done that, or he could've been in trouble.'

Lucia caught his sudden melancholic expression and asked, 'Do you miss your folks?'

'A lot. But there's a war on and I need to prove my allegiance to Uncle Sam.'

'I heard Italians are considered enemy aliens in America.'

'Only those not born in the States. The government could have interned my parents, but they're keeping them under surveillance instead.'

'I miss New York.' She sighed. 'Can't wait for the war to end so I can go back there.'

She didn't say how she hoped to achieve her dream. It would take a lot of money. Money she didn't have.

Gero gave her a searching look. He appeared about to say something, but Annita chose that moment to come bounding up to them.

'Ma needs you to help sweep the floor,' she said, then turned to Gero. 'And she'd like you to go now, so we can get on with our day. She also said she'd love you to come for *cena* if you can manage to bring some beef.'

Trust her mother to send Annita as her messenger, Lucia thought as she glanced at Gero.

He was smiling widely.

'Tell your mother her wish is my command.'

Lucia kept her gaze firmly fixed on him as he made his way out the door.

Gero came for supper and, as promised, he arrived with a packet of ground beef. Ma cooked *purpittuni* meatballs, which she served with macaroni and some of their tomato paste made into a sauce. After they'd eaten, they all sat outside in the cool night air.

Without warning, a terrific noise echoed from above, and Lucia looked up at the sky. Bombers were flying in a V-shaped formation, shining silver in the moonlight. A chill squeezed at her stomach. The Allies were on their way to rain death and destruction on Palermo and on her fellow countrymen.

It was the first time she'd considered herself to be Sicilian, she realised. Up until that moment, she'd always thought of herself as American.

Gero went inside to listen to his radio. Not long afterwards, he returned and whispered something to Dinu.

'We're going for a drink at the Bar Centrale.' Dinu turned to Lucia.

'Can I come too?' she asked.

'Sorry, sis.' He shook his head. 'You know that can't happen.'

'I know.' Her shoulders sagged.

'Keep your chin up. We'll go huntin' rabbits soon, I promise.'

'With Gero?' she asked. 'I wanna challenge him to shoot better than me.'

'If that's what you want.'

Lucia gazed at Gero, and her heart skittered a beat as she caught him staring at her with a mixture of amazement and admiration.

'I want that a lot,' she said.

9

DINU, JULY 1943

Early the next day, after Pa had given him a day off work, Dinu set off with Francu and Gero for the Sacca de Melita estate. It wasn't somewhere he'd ever imagined himself going. Since arriving in Sicily eight years ago, he'd kept well away from the 1,200 hectares of the *latifondo*.

Having spent more than half of his life in 'the land of the free', he hated the fact that four-fifths of Sicily was divided into noble fiefs. The immense fortunes of a small, privileged group of aristocrats contrasted horribly with the extreme poverty of the rest of the people.

But, when Gero had told him last night that his commander, Colonel Charles Rinelli, had been staying with Baron Aurelio Sacca di Melita, posing as his butler, and that he'd ordered Gero to report to him, Dinu hadn't hesitated in offering to help.

'I'll be too conspicuous walking there on my own,' Gero had said.

So Dinu and Francu had proposed going with him and, if they were stopped, the three of them would pretend to be agricultural labourers in search of work. Dinu was curious about the American colonel and mindful that he might be able to take advantage, somehow, of the situation. Don Nofriu's men protected the estate, and Dinu had yet to secure an introduction to the boss. Maybe, if he made himself useful to the colonel, the American would recommend him?

It was a vain hope, but he kept it alive in his heart as he made his way down the long winding road to the valley.

'Tell me about Rinelli, Gero,' he said.

'He's the son of Italian immigrants from Varese, near Milan. Born in Vermont. He went to Harvard Law School and became an attorney about twenty years ago.'

'He sure did well,' Dinu said.

'Yep. He became active in politics and served as lieutenant governor of New York from '39 to '42.'

'What's he doing here in Sicily?' Francu chipped in.

'He's a Civil Affairs Officer with the US army.' Gero brushed a lock of hair back from his forehead. 'That means he'll be responsible for rebuilding and restoring democracy in Italy after the Allies defeat Hitler and Mussolini.'

'And you work for him?' Dinu asked.

'You won't breathe a word?' Gero turned his gaze from Dinu to Francu and back to Dinu again.

Both Dinu and Francu nodded.

'Don Nofriu considers Rinelli "one of his good friends", if you know what I mean. That's why I was sent to Villaurora.'

'Thanks for sharing that with us, Gero,' Dinu said. 'Can't wait to meet him.'

They carried on walking, and Dinu's step lightened at the thought of the possibilities ahead. An intro to the 'man of honour' would surely happen soon, wouldn't it?

A couple of hours later, he and his companions entered the

Sacca estate. The undulating land was covered with yellow wheat stalks and bales of straw that would be used for cattle winter bedding. The morning had turned hot and sweat ran down Dinu's face. Flies swarmed, and he waved them away with the back of his hand. Eventually, the gated part of the property, guarded by armed men, came into view.

'Let me do the talking,' Gero said. 'I have a password to give them.' He stepped forward and spoke to a burly man with a handlebar moustache.

The man nodded, and Gero signalled that Dinu and Francu should follow him.

They walked up the drive to the front of the baron's *baglio padronale*, or *bagghiu* in Sicilian. Dinu eyed the outside walls of the nobleman's residence, which were much bigger than the more humble bagli occupied by peasant farmers near Villaurora.

Gero pressed the bell and, before too long, a heavy-set man, with dark wavy hair receding from his broad forehead, swung open the hefty wooden door. Dressed in a black suit, which must have been stifling in the summer heat, it could only be the colonel who was pretending to be the baron's butler. Gero saluted the man, confirming Dinu's impression.

'Let me introduce my compatriots,' Gero said as they went into a large square courtyard. 'They helped me find don Nofriu. And they escorted me here, providing me with the cover story that I'm an agricultural labourer looking for work.'

'Good call.' The colonel swept his gaze over Dinu and Francu. 'Come into the kitchen and I'll rustle up some refreshments.'

Dinu noticed Francu eyeing the upper storey of the edifice, where presumably the master and his family lived. The ground floor accommodated itinerant farm workers like him, and was used for storing supplies and fodder. There were also the stables and other areas for keeping the farm tools and for garaging the baron's vehicles.

Dinu and the others crossed the courtyard, passing under a shady Judas tree, and went through the central door opposite. The kitchen had an enormous iron cooking range, where a middle-aged woman was stirring a pot.

She turned to greet the colonel deferentially. Clearly, he was only the 'butler' to the outside world.

'Brigida, fetch the young men a glass of water,' he said before pulling out a chair at the rectangular wooden table.

Rinelli stared thoughtfully at Dinu and Francu, then said to Gero, 'I need to talk to you in private.'

'These guys are on our side, sir.' Gero glanced at the colonel. 'Whatever you wanna tell me, you can say it in front of them.'

'You sure we can trust them?'

'We are like family.' Dinu squared his shoulders. 'I swear on my ma's life we're trustworthy.' When a Sicilian man invokes his mother, you know he's telling the truth.

'Okay.' Rinelli gave a curt nod. He waited as Brigida served glasses of fresh water and they had all taken a drink. 'The Allies have planned to start their assault in the early hours of tomorrow.'

'Where?' Francu leant forwards.

'I know Gero said I can trust you, but that's info I can't give. Sorry.'

'I hope they defeat the Germans and Italian fascists quickly,' Dinu said.

'That's partly why Gero and I are here.' A smile curled the colonel's lips. 'As soon as our boys break through from the coast, there's a plan we need to put into action.'

'What plan?' Francu asked.

'Have you heard of Lucky Luciano?' Rinelli cocked his head.

'I remember hearing the name when I was a kid.' Dinu grinned at his own ability to recall. 'Ain't he the boss of the Genovese crime family in New York?'

'Yep. He's been imprisoned in upstate New York since '36, but he still has his hand firmly on the controls of his business empire. He's notorious, and carries on wielding a lot of influence.'

'The Office of Naval Intelligence contacted him in '42 to ask for his help in protecting New York harbour from enemy sabotage,' Gero added, taking up the tale.

'It was helpful that Luciano was both able and willing to provide assistance through his contacts,' the colonel said.

'So what's he got to do with you and Gero being here?' Francu asked.

'Luciano is Sicilian by birth. He still has plenty of links with the Old Country, and, more to the point, with members of the *Onorata Società*.' The colonel lowered his voice. 'Don Nofriu is the most esteemed of the men of honour. Getting him on our side is a big part of our strategy. The message Gero took to him was vital. Thanks for your help with that, by the way.'

'So, what happens next?' Gero asked.

'I want you to go back to the village and wait. As soon as our guys have broken through, you'll be contacted. All you'll need to do then is to follow the plan.'

'What plan?' Dinu risked the question.

'That remains confidential, young man. But you'll find out soon enough, I hope.' The colonel snorted out a laugh. 'In the meantime, Brigida will give us all some lunch. It will be too hot for you to walk back to the village this afternoon, so you should rest here and wait for the cool of the evening.'

And that was what they did. They filled their bellies with *pasta alla norma*, washed down with good-quality red wine, took a nap on hay bales in one of the storage areas, saluted the colonel, and then made their way through the heavy wooden doors.

Sparrows had roosted in the tall bamboo thickets beside the road and were bickering noisily over the best places to perch as Dinu and his friends walked past them. Dinu remembered the saying that sparrows never die of hunger, because they're cheeky and fearless.

He smirked to himself – he could be cheeky and fearless, too. One day he would die – everyone died in the end – but it wouldn't be of hunger, for sure.

10

JESSICA, JUNE 2005

Enjoying the dawn chorus of sparrows chirping outside, Jess pondered staying in bed a little longer, stretching out lazily. But she was meeting Piero at eight and didn't want to rush.

After a leisurely shower and a quick breakfast, she connected her laptop to the internet and read about the Agrigento temples. The site dated from the fifth century BC and was one of the most outstanding examples of ancient Greek art and architecture in Italy. The images looked amazing, and she couldn't wait to visit.

She checked her appearance in the mirror. The pink floral cotton slip dress was a little 1990s, but it was almost as cool as wearing shorts, which she'd decided might be too informal, given that Piero had said they'd be having lunch in a restaurant. She fetched her wide-brim straw sunhat and canvas tote bag, into which she placed a bottle of water, her digital camera, her wallet and a tube of sunscreen. Then, settling her sunglasses on her nose, she went to meet Piero.

She found him standing beside a red Alfa Romeo coupé,

dressed in his trademark outfit of dark blue jeans and an openneck fitted white shirt.

He wished her good morning, and she offered him her hand. But instead of taking it, he bent to kiss her on both cheeks.

Flustered, she breathed in the spicy scent of his aftershave. Clearly, their friendship had progressed. *Don't read too much into it, Jess!* She settled herself into the front passenger seat.

'I connected to the Agrigento website earlier,' she said as Piero drove them out through the vineyards. 'The temples look amazing. I can't believe they've remained standing for over two and a half thousand years.'

'The Concordia is the best preserved. You'll love it.' A smile tugged at the corner of his lips. 'I'll drop you at the eastern entrance and pick you up at the western one. It will take you about three hours to walk from one end of the site to the other.' He glanced at the hat, which she'd placed on her lap. 'You've come well prepared. Just make sure you keep hydrated.'

'I'll do that,' she said, grateful for his concern.

'My meeting will be over by twelve thirty. That'll give us ample time to get to Licata.'

'Licata? I thought the restaurant was in Agrigento.'

'Sorry. I should have clarified. Licata is further down the coast.'

'I'm looking forward to seeing the Med. Here in the middle of Sicily, it's hard to believe we're on an island.'

'The sea is never far away, Jess. We'll be in Agrigento within an hour.'

'It's really kind of you to take me. Oh, and thanks again for including me in your wine and food tasting yesterday.' She fidgeted with the rim of her hat. 'I hope you didn't think I was being critical of the ricotta.'

'Not at all. It was a fair observation. We use ricotta a lot in Sicilian cooking. But Stefania is already thinking of substituting the cannoli with a lighter dessert.'

'I feel bad about it now.'

'I assure you there's no need.'

She looked down at her side, and his competent hand on the gear stick captured her attention. Well-shaped with smooth skin. Manicured fingernails. Her gaze fell on his long, lean thighs. Feeling the heat flushing through her, she tore her eyes away.

What the hell was she doing? She was still married to Scott. True, she was getting divorced, but she shouldn't be looking at another man already.

Wanting to distract herself, Jess stared out of the window. They'd reached the *strada statale*, noticeably in better condition than the road she'd taken to get to the winery from Palermo the other day. Piero had inserted a CD into the car's sound system, and the sultry tones of Mina singing '*Il Cielo in Una Stanza*', 'The Sky in One Room', filled the air.

'Beautiful,' Piero said.

She turned to look at him, her cheeks warming up.

'The scenery,' he said, nodding towards her window.

'Of course, yes, it is,' she said, making herself focus on the fields whipping by.

* * *

Later, after snapping countless photos during a gruelling walk, nudging her way through groups of tourists along the ridge between the temples, Jess arrived at the pickup point she'd arranged with Piero. Thankfully, there were water fountains at intervals, where she could refill her bottle to prevent her dying of thirst. And she was glad she'd remembered her sunscreen, or she'd have been burnt to a crisp. But the temples were as magnificent as they'd promised to be. Well worth a visit.

'How was it?' Piero asked as Jess settled herself into the front passenger seat.

'Wonderful! The Concordia is so well preserved.'

'Local people converted it into a Christian place of worship in the sixth century, which meant they maintained it better than the other temples.'

'It reminds me so much of the Parthenon in Athens.' She'd gone there with her parents when she was a teen.

'Both are Doric temples built on platforms,' Piero said, starting the car.

'How was your wine producers' meeting?' she asked.

'Very successful, thanks. My father and two acquaintances started the association seven years ago to present Sicilian wine to the world. Last year, we organised an exhibition in Palermo, "Sicilia en Primeur", to showcase the quality of the latest harvest and the excellence of the wines about to be marketed. This year, the event will be held in Agrigento. Our plan is to hold the exhibition in the different provincial capitals on a rotating basis.'

'I know so little about Sicilian wine. But what I tasted last night, I really liked.' She inclined her head towards him. 'When will the Agrigento event take place?'

'At the end of August. Not long now.'

'Are there vineyards all over the island?'

'There are. Sicily is the number one Italian wine region in terms of vineyard acreage and the tenth in the world.'

'Gosh! I had no idea.' The conversation starter, used for politeness, had turned into something that had truly grabbed her interest.

'We're in a privileged position at the centre of the Mediterranean Sea.' Piero steered the car down a straight road below the temple ridge. 'And our ideal climate – sufficiently varied – makes Sicily the perfect region to grow high-quality grapes.'

'It's good that you practise sustainability,' Jess said, remembering what he'd told her last night.

'We have over two and a half thousand hours of sunshine a year. That means the plants remain healthy and producers can avoid the use of chemicals in the vineyards.'

'Does it ever get cold in the winter?' She was thinking of the baglio. Would she need central heating if she were to accept it?

'Oh, yes. We've even had snow at the tenuta.'

'That's incredible,' she said, surprised.

'Sicily only enjoys a mild Mediterranean climate along its coasts.'

Jess gazed out of the window. The landscape was much drier and rockier than inland. She indicated towards what looked like enormous plastic tunnels.

'What do they grow in those?'

'Vegetables of all types, cherry tomatoes on the vine and cantaloupe melons, exported all over the world. The economy of this area is based on agriculture and fishing.' He glanced at her. 'Is Sicily like you expected?'

'To be honest, I didn't know what to expect. My grandmother came from here, but a family rift meant I knew very little about it.'

'What kind of rift, if you don't mind me asking?'

'I'm completely in the dark. All I know is, something made my mother cut herself off from her family. Probably happened before I was born, or when I was too young to remember.'

'How mysterious. I recall you said your nonna left you a

baglio near Villaurora. It must have been a surprise, given what you've just told me.'

'It was. The crazy thing is, I'm already falling for the place. But I'd be mad to hang on to it. My life is in Bristol. My second cousin and her husband have been farming the land and were probably expecting to inherit it. Depriving them of it would be selfish of me.'

'Perhaps you can come to some form of arrangement?' he asked, signalling right at the sign for Licata.

'Perhaps,' she said.

Should she give voice to her concerns about Giovanna and Angelo? No, she decided. She didn't know Piero well enough.

* * *

The restaurant overlooked the marina, and Jess exclaimed with delight at the myriad pleasure craft lining the waterfront and piers.

She and Piero had been seated on a shaded terrace with a stunning view through the palm trees of boat masts bobbing on the deep blue sea.

'This place is beautiful.' Jess swept her gaze around. 'Thank you for introducing me to it.'

'Glad you like it. Just wait until you taste the food. I hope you'll like it even more.'

A waiter arrived to take their drinks order, and they both opted for sparkling water while they perused the menu. Before they could choose, the chef, a bespectacled young man who went by the name of Salvo, came up to their table to explain the dishes of the day. He spoke rapidly in Italian with a heavy Sicilian accent, and Jess asked Piero to translate for her.

'I'll have the tuna tartare followed by roasted sea bass,' she said.

'Excellent choice.' Piero's smile crinkled the edges of his eyes. 'I'll have the same.'

He requested the wine menu, then said, 'We can go for a walk after lunch so I can metabolise the alcohol before I drive.'

'Sounds like a good plan.'

Their server returned, and Piero ordered a bottle of Grillo.

'It's a Sicilian white wine,' he said. 'My brother produces this variety in his tenuta.'

'I enjoyed meeting Fabrizio and Cristina.' Jess smiled. 'Do they have any children?'

'Only the one. Five-year-old Damiano. He's a bit of a handful, runs rings around every nanny they get for him.'

'I'm an only child too,' Jess said. 'Like my mother.' She'd been told that much, at least.

'Do your parents live in Bristol as well?'

Jess shared the tragic story of the accident with Piero, and he said how sorry he was.

'I have a lot of English cousins,' she continued brightly. 'And now I've met my Sicilian ones.'

'Won't they be able to recommend a builder to you for a quote on restoring the baglio?'

She shook her head.

'I'd rather the referral comes from someone without a vested interest, if you know what I mean—'

'I understand.' He cleared his throat. 'Would you like me to take a look at the baglio before I contact someone on your behalf? Just so I can explain what's involved.'

'That would be wonderful, Piero. Thank you.'

Their waiter arrived with the wine, which he uncorked and decanted for Piero to taste.

'*Perfetto.*' He nodded to the server, who then poured a glass for Jess before leaving the bottle in an ice bucket on their table.

'Lovely,' she said as the acidity exploded on her tongue.

Their first course was served, and they both picked up their forks.

'*Buon appetito,*' Piero said. 'Enjoy your meal!'

The flavour of the tuna was fresh, and rich with buttery undertones. Jess was relaxed enough in Piero's company by now not to feel the need for polite conversation, so she relished the dish in silence. While they waited for the roasted sea bass, she caught Piero eyeing the ring on her finger.

'I suppose I should take this off,' she said, blushing.

'I only removed mine after my divorce was finalised.' He held up his own ring finger.

'Oh, when was that?'

'Last year. But Eleonora and I had been living apart for a long time.' He took a sip of his wine. 'She's a city girl at heart. When the kids started attending a private school in Palermo, she stayed in our apartment there during the week. They would all come to the tenuta for the weekends and holidays. Eventually, she met someone else.'

'I'm so sorry,' Jess said. 'I know how that feels. My ex met someone else as well.'

Their waiter approached to clear their plates and bring the main course. Piero waited until he'd gone, then asked, 'Do you want to talk about what happened? Tell me to butt out if you'd rather not.'

'I don't mind telling you,' she said. And so she did. She told him about the endless rounds of IVF and all about Scott's betrayal. 'I'm fine with it now,' she added. 'A new chapter is starting in my life and coming to Sicily has been like an epiphany. I'm no longer in love with Scott.'

'It's good you've moved on, Jess. That's something I, myself, can't do.' Piero stared down at his hands. 'Truth is, I'm still in love with Eleonora. I'll be in love with her until the end of my days.'

He lifted his gaze to Jess's and her heart went out to him.

* * *

Later, after lunch and a friendly argument over who would settle the bill – which Piero won – they went for a walk along the waterfront.

'I like this place,' Jess said, enjoying the change of scenery. The fresh sea breeze cooled the skin on her arms and she licked the taste of salt from her lips.

'Licata was the first city liberated by the Allies in July 1943,' Piero said. 'The Americans came ashore here and at Gela, just down the coast.'

'How interesting.' Jess glanced around, imagining the port devoid of pleasure craft and teeming with warships and troops, and the shore a morass of exploding shells. She'd seen enough World War II movies to know what it must have been like.

'How did your family cope during the conflict?' she asked as they made their way down a quay extending into the sea.

'My grandfather helped the Allies. When they set up AMGOT, he became the mayor of Palermo.'

'What does AMGOT stand for?'

'Allied Military Government of Occupied Territories.'

'Poor Sicily. Conquered once again.'

'*Appunto*.' Precisely. 'We've had so many rulers, it's easy to lose count. We were joined to Italy in 1860. Six years later, there was a revolt and the Italian navy bombarded Palermo. It caused a lot of resentment.'

'I can well believe that.'

'We have our own regional government now. But we still answer to Rome.'

The erstwhile breeze had stiffened, taking Jess's breath and making conversation difficult. She and Piero carried on walking in silence until he suggested they returned to the car. Back in the front passenger seat, as she listened to Piero's choice of music – an eclectic mix of Mariah Carey, The Killers, and Coldplay – she mulled over his revelation of still being in love with his ex-wife.

How terribly sad for him.

She sighed to herself. Any temptation she might have had of starting a holiday fling with him had been put to bed. She smiled at the saying. There'd be no 'going to bed' with Piero Sacca. Instead, she'd focus on deciding about the baglio with no silly nonsense – as she now considered it – to distract her.

Her eyes felt heavy as they began to close and, before Jess knew it, she'd fallen asleep. She only woke up when Piero brought the Alfa to a halt in front of the tenuta's main building.

'Sorry for dropping off,' she said. 'I hope I didn't snore.'

'I didn't hear a thing.' He chuckled and got out to open her door.

Ever the gentleman, she thought as Cappero rushed up to lick her hand and she gave him a pat on the head.

'Thank you for a lovely day, Piero,' she said.

'It was my pleasure. Let me know when you'd like me to look at your baglio.'

'I'll do that.'

He kissed her on both cheeks and, steeling herself not to react to him, she kissed him demurely in return.

At the cottage's portico, she gave a gasp. A trail of ants was leading up the front step and under the door. She must have left some food out in the kitchen. Quickly unlocking the door, she took a deep breath and rushed inside. Sure enough, there was an open jar of strawberry jam on the counter. And it was completely covered in ants.

Ants must be a feature of life in Sicily. Something she'd have to get used to if she decided to accept Lucia's bequest and live in Villaurora.

11

LUCIA, JULY 1943

Lucia was staring at the ants marching along the sidewalk like a miniature army as they made their way towards a dead cockroach. There were always ants in Villaurora, like there were always flies. She couldn't remember ever seeing so many of the varmints in New York.

She'd come outside early, hoping despite herself that Gero would turn up like he'd done the other morning. Yesterday, he'd taken Dinu and Francu off with him somewhere. Curiosity burned within. Her brother had returned late last night and had gone off to work with Pa before he could tell her anything.

Lucia thought about Gero while she waited. She got a funny feeling in her stomach whenever she remembered his words to her. He'd said she was beautiful, and the way he'd looked at her with puppy dog eyes had given her such an unexpected thrill.

The sound of footfalls alerted her to the fact that someone was approaching. Was it Gero? Lucia's heart pounded in anticipation. But it was the marshal of the carabinieri, Giulianu

Cardona, who was striding up the road, and her breath hitched with disappointment.

'*Bon jornu*, Lucia. What are you doing out here on your own?'

'Only getting some fresh air.'

Cardona's eyes roved down her body, and embarrassment made her cheeks grow hot.

'Is your brother around?'

'He's gone to work.'

'Tell him to report to me when he returns.'

'Why? What's he done?' Lucia crossed her arms.

'Nothing for you to worry about, *zuccareddu*.'

'I'm not your "little sugar".' Her flesh crawled.

Cardona laughed and raked his eyes over her again. Hungry eyes that made her feel sick to the stomach.

'One day,' he said. 'When this war is over—'

Ma's voice calling her from within the house interrupted whatever the marshal was about to say. She spun on her heel with relief and went indoors, glad to remove herself from Cardona's predatory gaze.

* * *

That evening, Gero arrived with more ground beef – which Ma gratefully took off him to make a ragù for pasta. After greeting the rest of the family, he went to his radio transceiver.

In the periphery of Lucia's vision, he sent a coded message, and a reply came through almost straight away. She knew his code book was in the same suitcase that housed the radio; she watched him quickly transcribe the communication, then heard him let out a whoop.

'The Allies have arrived in Sicily,' he said. 'They got here in the early hours of this morning. The Americans have taken Licata and are fighting their way into Agrigento.'

'*Bedda Matri!*' Wow, Ma exclaimed. 'Is it really true?'

'No doubt whatsoever.' Gero got up from where he was sitting and Dinu and Pa enveloped him in bear hugs.

Lucia hung back, suddenly shy. She caught Gero looking at her over Dinu's shoulder and her heart gave a flutter.

'I'll go open a bottle of wine,' her twin brother said, extricating himself from Gero and Pa. 'We should celebrate.'

'What happens now?' Pa asked, pulling out chairs for himself and Gero at the table.

'The US army will push west to Palermo and north to Messina, where they'll meet up with the British. That's confidential intel, by the way. But you've become like family, and I trust you.'

Was Gero bragging again? Lucia frowned. Or was he merely a trusting person by nature? If she'd been given similar information, she wouldn't have breathed a word to anyone. She went to join the men at the table and accepted a glass of wine.

'How long do you think it will take the Allies to break through?' she asked.

'Your guess is as good as mine.' Gero winked at her.

Lucia glanced away, hoping her father hadn't seen. She was definitely starting to develop feelings for Gero, and Pa mustn't find out. If he had any inkling, he'd be fearful about her reputation and keep her even more under lock and key.

'Well, I hope it's sooner rather than later,' Lucia said. 'Then we won't have you beneath our feet any more, Gero.'

Her heart sank as she caught the look of devastation on his face. Somehow, she had to get him on his own and explain what was at stake.

'How about we go huntin' rabbits tomorrow night, Dinu?' she suggested to her brother.

'Sounds like a great idea,' her twin said before turning to Gero. 'You up for it too, *paisano*?'

Gero shot Lucia a look, and she nodded as imperceptibly as she could.

'Count me in,' he said.

* * *

At sunset the next day, with a hunting rifle slung over her shoulder and dressed like a boy in Dinu's clothes, Lucia was hiking up towards the corridor of jagged peaks behind the village. She brushed past the sisal plants, hearing the rattle of the snails falling to the ground. A grey viper with black stripes slithered across her path. It was more intent on hunting lizards than worrying about any humans, but she took care to avoid stepping on it – the venom in its bite would hurt like hell.

Dinu was forging the way in front, but Gero had fallen into step beside her. She asked him about the progress of the Allied advance; he'd been on the radio prior to them setting off.

'The Italian army is putting up some resistance, forcing the Americans to battle their way into Agrigento. I don't have any info about how the British are getting on—'

'I feel a little sad that the Americans are fighting our countrymen,' she said. 'Even though, basically, I'm a US citizen as I was born there.'

'Yeah, I get it. I kinda feel the same way.'

'Sorry about what I said last night about your getting out from under our feet.' She tugged at her shirtsleeve, thinking about what to say next. 'It's just that Pa is very protective of me, like all Sicilian dads with their daughters. If he thought there was anything between us, he wouldn't let me anywhere near you.'

'Are you saying there's something between us?' Gero's face broke into a smile.

'I dunno. Is there?' A blush warmed her cheeks.

'I'd like there to be. How about you?' His smile widened.

She took a step back, sudden doubt quivering in her stomach. Was this what she wanted? Getting close to Gero and his connections might not be such a good idea.

'Hmmm.' She pursed her lips. 'There's a war on. Maybe we should wait for it to end?'

'What are you two talking about?' Dinu's voice came from up ahead. 'We need to be quiet or we'll scare the rabbits.'

'They always hide when they hear us coming,' Lucia said. But she and Gero lapsed into silence until Dinu gave the order to run and shoot.

Lucia was quick on her feet and took the lead. She felt energised in the cool of the night with the stars and moon above to light her way. Besides, she knew the terrain so well she could navigate it blindfolded. She ran like the wind, crisscrossing through the clover, shooting at the confused bunnies. For a moment, she felt sorry for them. But she'd been missing Ma's delicious rabbit stew – and she also wanted Gero to see this side of her.

I can be a show-off too.

After she'd shot two rabbits and the men one each, Lucia suggested they take a rest in a cave she and Dinu had come across years ago in the cliff face.

Gero took a packet of Camels from his pants pocket and handed one to Dinu.

'What about me?' Lucia asked.

'Didn't know you smoked,' Gero said.

Lucia didn't smoke. But she took a cigarette anyway and leant in to Gero's lighter. After attempting one drag, tears streamed down her face and she coughed and coughed and coughed, causing Dinu to crease up with laughter.

'That'll teach you, *soru*! You can play like a boy, but you'll never be like a man.'

'I don't wanna be like a man. And, for your information, women smoke all the time. It's simply that I'm not used to it.'

'I don't think it's very feminine.' Dinu smirked.

'You're just like Pa. And all the other men in this country. You think you're so much better than us women.'

'Hey, you two.' Gero held up his hands. 'Quit bickering!' He glanced at his wristwatch. 'I think we should head back down to the village. Don Nofriu's guys will lock up soon, and I don't want to wake them.'

Lucia gave a huff. Gero could sling his hook as far as she was concerned. If he liked her as he'd said he did, he should have stood up for her. His mention of don Nofriu also made her wary. It would be best that she kept well away from him.

* * *

The following day, news of the Americans coming ashore in Licata reached Villaurora. The church bells rang, but the village became like a ghost town. People stayed indoors, the few shops kept their blinds drawn – as if a funeral was passing – and Lucia could taste a mixture of expectancy and anxiety in the air. Gleaming aeroplanes rumbled in the sky, but no soldiers came, and she thought she'd forever be anxious and waiting.

Every evening Gero came to listen to his radio. Four days after Licata had surrendered, he reported Agrigento was in

American hands. Almost a week later, they'd taken Enna, in the centre of the island, and now were heading for Palermo.

As for Dinu, he'd yet to report to Giulianu Cardona. Whatever the marshal of the carabinieri wanted him for could wait, Dinu said.

Lucia was out on the front step with Ma and Annita when she heard loud, confused shouting. It was as if someone had switched the radio on in the middle of a soccer game, just as a player was about to score a goal.

Surprise at the clamour paralysed Lucia for a moment, but she guessed the reason for the noise straight away. She grabbed Annita's hand and, against all caution, ran with her down the narrow street.

Ma yelled, 'Come back, girls! You might get shot.'

But it was too late. They were being swept along with their neighbours to the piazza, where villagers were clapping and shouting, 'Long live the United States!' People were swigging wine, which was passed from hand to hand over the crowd.

Lucia pulled Annita towards two Jeeps loaded with five Americans, who were wearing dark glasses and shouldering rifles. Father Michele, the parish priest, dressed in his trousers, collarless, pale and sweating, was talking to the men, repeating, 'Please, please.' Was that the only English word he knew?

But the Americans didn't appear to be listening. They held their rifles at an angle and looked about them, drawing cockily on their cigarettes. The villagers filled glasses with red wine, and offered them with gentle insistence to the soldiers, urging them to join in the celebrations. The Americans refused the drink and exchanged a few words between themselves, ignoring the priest – who was still trying to communicate with them.

Without warning, Giulianu Cardona appeared on the scene

with four carabinieri. The Americans raised their rifles and, when the men were close, one of them jumped off the Jeep and adroitly unhooked the police officers' pistols.

Another round of cheers broke out. *'Viva la libertà!'* Long live freedom!

Unexpectedly, an American flag blossomed above the crowd, gripped by the village schoolteacher, Alberto Spina. But the Americans took no notice of the procession forming behind the Stars and Stripes. They were finally speaking to Father Michele, and Lucia overheard the priest saying to the marshal, 'They want you to fetch don Nofriu.'

Cardona hurried out of the piazza, leaving his four disarmed carabinieri staring sheepishly at the ground.

Before Lucia knew it, the marshal had returned with don Nofriu and – Lucia's eyes almost popped out of her head – Gero, dressed in a US army uniform.

Don Nofriu, wearing his ubiquitous short-sleeved shirt, braces holding his trousers up over his paunch, a cigar in his mouth and a cap pulled down to his tortoiseshell spectacles, went up to the lead Jeep. He unfurled a large yellow kerchief with a big black 'L' embroidered on it.

The soldier in charge of the Americans saluted Gero, who helped don Nofriu clamber into the back of the Jeep before sitting himself next to him. It was only then that Gero appeared to realise Lucia was in the crowd. His gaze met hers and he mouthed the words *'A dopo.'* See you later.

She couldn't help raising a hand and smiling back at him.

The crowd opened up, cheering as the Jeeps left the piazza; the soldiers threw them cigarettes, and one took snapshots with his camera.

Lucia didn't know why, but she felt a wave of tears welling up inside her. Perhaps it was for the carabinieri, or for the flag raised above the crowd, or for Gero disappearing with don Nofriu – God knew where – or for Pa and Dinu working in the *campagna* and missing the entire show.

Grabbing Annita's hand, she raced back up the road and, as she closed the front door behind her, she began to feel as if she were in a dream. But it was as if someone else were dreaming and she was in that dream, stumbling across the room, emotionally exhausted, with a tight lump of tears choking in her throat.

'There you are, girls,' Ma said, looking so dejected she reminded Lucia of a bag of sawdust dropped on the floor. 'Put your aprons on and help me sweep these godforsaken ants from the room.'

12

DINU, JULY 1943

A week after Gero had disappeared with don Nofriu in the back of an American Jeep, Dinu was outside on the front step, smoking. He was still annoyed that he'd missed the boss's dramatic unfurling of the yellow kerchief with a big black 'L' on it. Plainly, it stood for 'Lucky Luciano', and it must have been with the message Gero had taken to don Nofriu soon after he'd parachuted down.

Dinu set his jaw; the time had come to lay his cards on the table with Gero. Dinu had done him a lot of favours and, as soon as the American came back to the village, Dinu would ask for the favours to be returned.

He spotted Francu coming down the street, swinging his arms by his sides.

'I found out that don Nofriu and Gero have arrived back in Villaurora.' Francu sat down and took the cigarette Dinu offered him. 'Gero drove him in a Fiat car.'

'Remember Rinelli told us that, as soon as the Allies had broken through, a plan would be put into action?' Dinu exhaled smoke. 'My guess is they've been networking in the

Onorata Società.'

'I believe you could be right.' Francu took a deep draw of his cigarette.

'Gero should stop by, now he's back in the village,' Dinu said. 'He still might need to use his radio.'

Francu smirked, then said, 'Speak of the devil—'

Gero looked different in his khaki uniform. Older, somehow. He wore the golden oak leaf major's insignia on his shoulder loops and there was an air of authority about him.

'*Ciao, paisani, comu state?*' He asked how they were, lighting himself a Camel.

Dinu and Francu replied they were well.

'Where have you been?' Francu asked.

'Here and there. Mostly in Palermo.'

Dinu fixed Gero with a firm gaze, eager to get the truth out of him.

'What was don Nofriu up to?'

Gero tapped the ash from his cigarette, then shrugged.

'He met with his friends in Cosa Nostra and they've been sending emissaries to encourage Sicilian troops to lay down their arms to the Americans.'

'*Mizzica!*' Dinu could hear the surprise in his voice. 'Did they succeed?'

'Two divisions of Americans closed in on Palermo the other day. Both were massed on the hills overlooking the capital, ready for a fight. The opposition was minimal – only occasional pot-shots, sabotaged bridges and mines. The Sicilian coastal divisions put down their arms and either surrendered in droves or disappeared.'

'So Palermo is now in American hands?' Francu whistled.

'Not sure how big a part don Nofriu's machinations with his fellow godfathers played in that.' Gero shook his head. 'But the battle for Sicily isn't over yet. German and Italian forces are fiercely defending the area around Mount Etna.'

'Where the *Onorata Società* has a much smaller presence,' Francu said with another smirk.

'Yep.' Gero got to his feet. 'I'll pay my respects to your parents, Dinu. Then I'll head back to don Nofriu.'

'I was gonna ask you if you'd introduce us to him.' Dinu lowered his voice. 'To return the favours you owe us for helping you out.'

Gero stared at Dinu long and hard. He appeared thoughtful, then he barked out a sardonic laugh.

'Be careful what you ask for, *paisano*. Don Nofriu plays the role of the kindly village godfather but, in reality, he's an extremely dangerous man.'

'I can handle him,' Dinu said with confidence. 'Remember, I grew up in New York.'

* * *

The next day, Dinu and his father were working in the *campagna*. After spending the morning harvesting figs, they took a break from the scorching July sun to eat the packed lunch of cheese and bread that Ma had wrapped for them in waxed cloth parcels. The two-hectare smallholding, on a terraced slope leading up from the village, boasted a hut made of bamboo. A bamboo plantation was part of almost every *campagna*, and theirs was no exception.

Sitting on the beaten earth floor of the shack, Pa muttered about Gero's revelation to the family last night that he'd been appointed the civil affairs officer for Villaurora.

'He's not much older than you, son. What's the world coming to?'

'At least that fat fascist mayor has been sent packing.'

'To be replaced by don Nofriu.'

'Better a man of honour than a socialist, I say.' Dinu grinned.

Pa grimaced and took a bite of bread and cheese. He heaved a sigh.

'Or a communist like the schoolteacher, Alberto Spina.'

'I thought he was simply anti-fascist,' Dinu said.

'They're all as bad as each other.' Pa passed him the water bottle and shot him a glance.

'What are we gonna do about our rifles?' Dinu asked.

Gero had also announced last night that he'd instructed the marshal of the carabinieri to collect all weapons in possession of the villagers.

'Giulianu Cardona will give them back to us.' Pa frowned, creasing his forehead. 'Gero promised.'

The American had justified the employment of Cardona, saying the carabinieri had sworn an oath of allegiance to the king, not to Mussolini. The marshal had also kept his job because the Allies needed to employ the carabinieri to enforce the laws they would enact.

'I'll make sure Cardona obeys Gero's orders,' Dinu said, growling deep in his throat.

* * *

That evening, Gero was conspicuous by his absence at the dinner table.

'I hope now everyone knows who he really is, he won't forget us,' Ma lamented, clearly missing the parcel of meat he always brought her.

'Wouldn't surprise me if he has,' Lucia said, twirling pasta around her fork. 'I heard there was a ceremony in the carabinieri barracks and that he officially made don Nofriu our mayor. Francu's ma was there. She came by this afternoon and said there was a vast crowd outside the building, clapping and cheering as the boss appeared. Gero must be a very good friend of his—'

'I don't think he's joined don Nofriu's clan.' Dinu met his sister's eye. 'Gero's just using him.'

'More like don Nofriu is using Gero,' Pa said, picking up a piece of bread and scooping tomato sugo from his plate.

'Shush.' Ma shook her head. 'We mustn't talk about don Nofriu.'

Dinu sat back and contemplated his family. He would get rich one day and, when that day came, he'd look after them. Even if the village capo didn't offer him a job, Dinu would find a way to make money on his own.

His sisters cleared the table before going to do the washing up and getting ready for bed. The fact that the entire family slept together in the only room of the house had been riling Dinu more and more of late. The first thing he'd do, when he had the funds, would be to buy a bigger place for them all.

He pushed his shoulders back; he'd have a family of his own in the future. Attractive village girls with good dowries would catch his eye at Sunday mass, and he'd be tempted and feel a stirring in his loins. But now was not the time to think of such things. He always distracted himself by thinking of something else. Francu was the same; they'd discussed the matter. Dinu's cousin was as hungry for wealth as he was. Women could wait for now – they'd only be a distraction.

Later, in his bunk bed, Dinu woke with a start. Outside, the silence of the summer night had been broken by someone shouting, 'Citizens, wake up, they've arrested Mussolini. I heard it on the radio.'

Dinu rushed into the street, swiftly followed by Pa. Lights shone from windows. Front doors burst open. Men were out on the sidewalks, embracing each other, telling each other the news.

Their neighbour informed everyone that the king had nominated the marshal of Italy, Sir Pietro Badoglio, as Head of Government, Prime Minister and Secretary of State. He'd also said that the war would go on and Italians would be true to their word.

Whatever that meant.

When Dinu and his father went back indoors to tell Ma, Lucia and Annita what had happened, the girls cheered, but Ma was more concerned about the army of ants she'd discovered marching across the floor. She grabbed a broom and began sweeping frantically.

'Come to bed, Paola,' Pa said, taking the broom off her. 'You can deal with them in the morning.'

Dinu lay back in his bunk, his mind buzzing with thoughts of the future. Change was coming fast and he wouldn't fall victim to it. He would be a catalyst of that change.

By fair means or foul.

13

JESSICA, JUNE 2005

It took Jess an age to scoop the ants and jam into a rubbish bag and dump everything in the bin outside. She rinsed the jar and put it away. After a cheese salad for her supper, she took a shower and headed for bed.

She lay stretched out on the mattress, but sleep eluded her. What an amazing day she'd had. Villaurora wasn't as remote as she'd first thought. The road to Agrigento was better than expected, and the town itself appeared to have all the necessary facilities, including supermarkets where she could head for a weekly shop – if she kept the baglio. But how would she solve the mystery of why her grandmother had left it to her? All her enquiries had hit a dead end.

Her thoughts turned to Piero. His revelation about still loving his ex-wife made Jess's heart ache with sympathy. She couldn't imagine feeling that way about Scott. Although she'd loved him for years, through thick and thin, his unfaithfulness had been like a bucket of water thrown on a fire; it hadn't taken long to extinguish all the love she'd once had for him.

It was far too soon to be thinking about embarking on

another relationship. Now she knew there was no hope of a holiday fling with Piero, she would focus on the reason for coming to Sicily. Tomorrow she'd make her way to Villaurora and try to find some clues.

In the morning, Jess put dirty laundry in the washing machine, made some coffee and toast, and read her novel while she waited for the cycle to end. It would be too much of a rush to go to the baglio and then do food shopping in the village – she'd found out that the grocery store shut from half past twelve to four – so she decided to chill and stay in the winery until late afternoon.

She hung out her washing on the portico, then got ready to head for the pool. After swimming leisurely lengths for about thirty minutes, she moved a sunbed into the shade and retrieved her book, sunscreen and a bottle of water from her tote bag. Sunglasses settled onto her nose, and factor 30 rubbed wherever she could reach, she lost herself in her book until the sound of Cappero's panting filled the air.

'Hello, you,' she said, reaching down to stroke the over-heated dog. 'What have you been up to this morning?'

'He's been with me in the vineyard.' Piero's voice came from behind.

'*Ciao.*' Jess gave him a smile. 'Hope you both had fun.'

'We've been checking the roses at the ends of the rows of vines.' Piero dragged a lounger into the space next to hers and sat himself down.

'I've been wondering why there are rose bushes in the middle of your vineyard.' Jess always marvelled at the iconic plants with their beautiful blooms each time she drove past them.

'They're delicate shrubs, and act as a thermometer to tell us if the vines have caught a "fever".' He made quote marks with his fingers.

'I don't understand,' she said.

'If there's a fungal disease in the vicinity, the rose will catch it before the vine does. It gives us time to intervene to prevent the problem from spreading.'

'So, the roses are like spies, then?'

'*Appunto.*' Precisely.

'How fascinating. I'll never look at a rose in the same way.'

Piero's smile lit golden sparks in his hazel eyes.

'Just going for a dip,' he said, peeling his shirt off over his head before getting to his feet.

As he sauntered across the decking towards the pool, Jess fixed her gaze on the swimming shorts that melded his rounded backside. And when he dived into the deep end, she had the silly urge to go sprinting over and dive in alongside him. She pushed the idea aside and returned to her book. But she couldn't focus – she was too distracted by the sight of his powerful arms and shoulders ploughing through the water.

Don't look, Jess told herself.

When he got out of the pool, she risked a quick glance. He was shaking the water from his hair and the droplets were running down his beautifully tanned, toned body. She felt her face flame and lowered her eyes to her book again.

'What are you reading?' he asked, coming up and receiving a joyful welcome from Cappero, who'd stayed in the shade.

Jess showed Piero the cover of *The Time Traveller's Wife*, explaining that it was an unconventional love story about a man who is unavoidably whisked through time, and that he meets his future wife when she's still a child.

'Problem is that while his age darts back and forth according to his location in time, hers moves forward in the normal manner, so the pair are often out of sync.'

'Sounds like a crazy read,' Piero said, drying himself with the towel he left on his sunbed.

'It's so different from anything I've read before.'

'What do you usually read?'

'All sorts.' Jess took a sip of water. 'I like historical, contemporary, even science fiction.'

'What about movies?'

'I'll watch a range – from *Star Trek* to *The Notebook*.'

'I've never heard of *The Notebook*,' Piero said. 'But I've seen the entire television series of *Star Trek* as well as all the films.'

'The entire series? All of them?'

'Yes, all of them. *Voyager* is perhaps my favourite.' He looked straight at Jess. 'I think it's Captain Janeway that keeps me transfixed. I love a strong female character.'

A knot formed in Jess's stomach. She and Scott had bonded over their love of science fiction and she couldn't to go down that route with Piero – much as she might have liked to. She'd develop romantic feelings for him, and that would only lead to tears.

'I enjoyed it yesterday when you told me about the American landing in Licata,' she said, rapidly changing the subject. 'You mentioned that your grandfather helped the Allies. Did they pass through this area?'

The story Piero then told her, about the godfather of Villaurora's involvement with the Americans, made Jess's chest tingle.

'It sounds even more fantastical than the book I'm reading,' she said, taking another drink from her bottle of water.

'The tale could have been embellished by don Nofriu. It's impossible to gauge just how much he and his friends in Cosa Nostra encouraged Sicilian soldiers to lay down their arms. More likely, bad morale, poor leadership, outdated equipment and the sight of vast numbers of superior troops hurtling towards them in mechanised columns had more to do with it. Not to mention aircraft leading the way in the skies above.'

'It must have been terrible—'

'The British invading force on the other side of the island met with huge casualties. They could only advance slowly, from what I've read. The American army accomplished its mission far ahead of schedule and with very little loss of life.' Piero held Jess in his gaze. 'It makes me believe that Cosa Nostra must have had something to do with the US success.'

'I'm interested in what you said about the American crime boss.' Jess had never heard of the man before.

'That part of the story is a bit of a myth. But the Office of Naval Intelligence did contact Lucky Luciano in 1942 to ask for his help in protecting the New York harbour from enemy sabotage. The authorities denied asking him to assist with the Allied occupation of Sicily, though. As well they might, given that he was a notorious criminal.'

'All I know about the Sicilian Mafia,' Jess said, 'is that they murdered magistrates and carried out terror attacks in the 1990s. It was on the TV news, I remember.' A memory came into her mind of her parents' reaction to the bombings, how horrified they'd been and how her mother's face had turned ashen.

'There's a new leadership now, apparently, and murders of state officials have been halted,' Piero said. 'Italian law enforcement is far more successful at acting against Cosa Nostra these days.'

Jess pushed her sunglasses up her nose and asked him to tell her when the Sicilian Mafia had been created. He responded that it was a tough question to answer, but most people believed it started in the nineteenth century.

'There were many small private armies, or *mafie*, hired by absentee landlords to protect their *latifundi* from bandits,' Piero said. 'The ruffians in those private armies organised themselves and grew so powerful that they turned against the *padroni* and became the sole law on several estates, extorting money from the landowners in return for protecting their crops.'

She listened with rapt attention while Piero told her that the different *mafie* would meet with each other to settle disputes. In the twentieth century, they evolved from enforcers of feudal law into the administrators of an alternative legal system for much of Sicily's economy. And just as in any legal system, the most important law was that a person could never seek justice outside the system – a code of silence developed known as *omertà*.

When Jess expressed surprise that the government hadn't tried to do anything about it, Piero explained that, in the mid-1920s, Mussolini appointed Cesare Mori, a retired member of the police force, as the new prefect of Palermo. For four years, Mori's forces terrorised the towns in which Cosa Nostra held sway. By the end of the decade, the fascists had arrested over eleven thousand people, and many mafiosi had fled to the United States.

'How did the Mafia become so powerful again if Mussolini had got rid of it?' she asked, intrigued.

'His battle against the godfathers wasn't as successful as he'd claimed. The fascist-controlled press was ordered to follow the party line and avoid mentioning Cosa Nostra.' Piero exhaled a slow breath. 'Continued incidents of crime, violence, and lawlessness went unreported. Many of the gangsters jailed in Mussolini's four-year campaign were released, and the Mafia problem became worse.'

'You're a walking history book, Piero.' Jess leant forward. 'I'm truly fascinated.'

'I could also give you the rundown on Klingon law and their various battles with the Federation.' He grinned ruefully. 'All wars are basically the same, no matter the species.'

'Good point.' Jess laughed. 'What happened after the Allies occupied Sicily?' Her grandmother would have experienced the occupation, and she felt a burning need to know.

'The Allies released several mafiosi from prison, categorising them as victims of the fascist regime. The military government replaced fascist mayors with various community leaders, and many of these were also godfathers or their associates.'

'Like don— don—' She couldn't remember his name and wondered if Lucia had ever met him.

'Don Nofriu. I could tell you some stories about that man.' Piero checked his watch. 'But they'll have to wait for another day. Now I must get back to work. It was nice chatting with you, Jess.'

'It was nice chatting with you too, Piero.' She glanced at him. 'I'm heading up to Villaurora later this afternoon, by the way. I'll visit the property, then go to the grocery store.'

'I haven't forgotten about taking a look at your baglio. My kids are arriving tomorrow for a brief visit, so maybe we can arrange a day next week after they've gone back to Palermo?'

'That would be lovely, thank you,' she said.

'I'll look forward to it.' He rose, picked up his shirt and towel. 'Come, Cappero.'

Jess gazed at his retreating backside until he was out of sight.

The drive to Villaurora had become familiar to Jess, and she tuned in to easy listening music on the radio as she made her way up to the village.

At the baglio, she unlocked the heavy rustic door leading into the square courtyard. She went indoors and gazed around, imagining how the place would look with a little TLC. Arches left bare between the rooms. Walls matte plastered white. The red-brick floors polished until they shone like stars. Window shutters painted sage green.

She would fill the property with her English family and friends. They'd love a swimming pool, and so would she. Perhaps she could add an upper floor on one side of the quadrangle for extra space? It would have a fabulous view.

Jess couldn't wait to show everything to Piero and get his advice. Her chest fluttered as she thought about him. Why did he have to be so incredibly good-looking and charming, yet so unavailable? She heaved a deep sigh.

Her gaze fell on the strange turquoise ceramic medusa cemented onto the wall to the left of the entrance door. Curious, she went up to it and touched her finger to the corn ears and three legs. What might it represent?

Perhaps Piero will know.

She locked up and made her way around to the back of the building, hoping she'd find Giovanna there so she could ask her some questions. But there was no one about, so Jess set off for a short walk. Bells echoed from the village below, calling the faithful to evening mass as she headed up through the olive groves towards the track where she had seen the motorbike disappear in a cloud of dust two days ago.

The pointed fever-chart crags forming a rocky ridge above the village towered in the distance. She brushed past agave cactus plants and something fell from them with a faint, dry rattle. Hopefully not a snake. She hurried on, the path not nearly as dangerous as Giovanna had made it out to be. Some kind of shepherd's hut had been built in the middle of a sloping field ahead, but Jess couldn't see any sheep.

Stones scattered beneath her feet as she approached the hut. The door and windows had been boarded up and the place had an abandoned look to it which made her think it was unoccupied. Why should someone come up here on a motorbike?

Stopping to catch her breath, Jess glanced at her watch; she'd better make tracks to the village shop or it would be closed before she got there. There was something about the hut that called to her, but she'd put off exploring further until she had more time to do so.

14

LUCIA, AUGUST 1943

On the first Sunday after the Allies had captured Messina, Lucia was strolling down the road to church. Booming bells called the faithful to mass, and they seemed to be ringing louder than usual, she thought. She'd linked her arm with Annita's and they both had a spring in their step. The Sicilian campaign was over. After only thirty-eight days of fighting, the British and Americans had successfully driven German and Italian troops from the island and were now preparing to assault the Italian mainland. Surely the war in Europe would soon end.

In the church, Lucia sat in a middle pew, sandwiched between Ma and her sister, with Dinu and Pa on her other side. Feeling eyes burning a hole in the back of her neck, Lucia twisted around to find Giulianu Cardona staring at her, looking like a cat who'd got the cream.

She gave a shudder and turned back to face the altar. That man had been strutting through the village, puffed up with his own importance, ever since don Nofriu had reconfirmed his position as marshal. Rumour had it Cardona's house over-flowed with tinned food and cigarettes, thanks to the godfather.

Lucia's stomach rolled with disgust. Don Nofriu controlled the black market in Villaurora and his illegal trade in scarce commodities was thriving. She drew in a slow, steady breath, angry that prices of goods had rocketed to figures only the Allied occupiers – flush with cash – or those who profited from the black market could afford.

The weapons of four armies – Italian, German, British and American – were now a commodity hoarded and sold to those who would pay the highest price. Lucia bristled, remembering Dinu and Francu had gone to the coast a couple of weeks ago, and had collected as many discarded munitions as they could find. Horrified, she'd come across a stash of guns hidden behind their mule's hay bale at the back of the house. When she'd asked her brother about them, he'd told her to mind her own business.

She clasped her hands together with worry, suspicious Dinu and Francu were up to something. Lately, her brother had been shirking his duties in the *campagna* to go off with their cousin for long hours. Lucia vowed she would wheedle the truth out of Dinu. By hook or by crook, she'd get to the bottom of whatever he was up to. Fervently, she hoped it was nothing to do with don Nofriu.

As expected, Gero came into the periphery of her vision. Recently, he'd taken over two rooms in the town hall, next to where the godfather was actively wheeling and dealing. Fulfilling his duties as the representative of AMGOT, Gero had given don Nofriu two trucks and a tractor to help clear rubble in the area. But Lucia had found out that the *capo* had been using them to carry food supplies stolen from various Allied and Italian military warehouses instead. No one said anything because of the *omertà* code of silence.

'*Assabbinidica*, Signura Paola,' Gero greeted Lucia's mother as he sat beside her. '*Comu sta?*' How are you?

Ma said she was fine, and would he come for dinner tomorrow and please bring some meat.

Lucia leant forward to pray. She snuck a quick peek at Gero, then looked away quickly when she realised he was also gazing at her. Her stomach tensed with uncertainty, her feelings for him so confusing. One minute she liked him a lot. The next, she found herself lamenting the fact that he appeared so naïve and trusting. How could he have been taken in by don Nofriu? Or, God forbid, had he joined the godfather's clan?

No, he wouldn't do that. Gero had been nothing but kind towards her and her family. There wasn't an evil bone in his body, she hoped. Lucia tried to concentrate on the service, but it was impossible. Giulianu Cardona's eyes were burning a hole into the back of her head again.

Finally mass was over, and she linked arms with Annita to make her way out onto the village square, where people were milling around, passing the time of day before heading home for their Sunday lunches. Lucia spotted Pa, deep in conversation with Cardona. They must be discussing getting her father's hunting rifles back, she concluded.

'Come, Annita, let's catch up with Ma,' she said, pulling her sister along with her up the road.

* * *

After helping her mother serve *pasta alla carrettiera*, spaghetti seasoned with oil, garlic, chilli pepper, the last of their pecorino cheese and parsley, Lucia took her seat at the table.

The entire family tucked in, and chat was sparse while they filled their bellies. She gazed at her mother, noticing a tightness in her expression. Wondering what was bothering her, Lucia was about to ask when Ma suddenly put down her fork.

'Prices are too high for us to buy any more grain. How will I make flour?' Ma's voice had gone up an octave. 'Without our daily bread and pasta, we'll starve.'

'Don't worry. I have a plan to take care of things.' Dinu leant across the space between them and patted Ma's hand.

'What plan?' Lucia stared at him, her heart sinking. No good would come of it, she was sure.

'You'll find out soon, *soru*.'

'Enough, son!' Pa banged his glass down, his nostrils flaring. 'Cardona told me his men have seen you and Francu acting suspiciously. He's still waiting for you to report to him.'

'I'll do so when I can.' Dinu laughed, cocking his head to the side. 'I've been a bit busy of late—'

Pa shook his head in obvious despair, and then he turned his attention to Lucia. He gave her an encouraging smile.

'I have some news, daughter. The marshal also asked me for your hand in marriage. He doesn't want a dowry, and he promised he'll look after us, your family, in return.'

Lucia's mouth dropped open. Nausea squeezed in her stomach and she felt sick. How could her father even entertain such an idea? The marshal was odious and corrupt, to boot.

'I can't marry that man. I don't love him.' She could hear the despair in her tone.

'Love comes later,' Ma said, smiling at Pa. 'Your father and I barely knew each other when our families arranged for us to marry. We grew to love each other as time went by.'

'How can you think of selling my sister to that mercenary

pig?' Dinu pushed back his chair. He narrowed his eyes and clenched his fists. 'I told you I'll take care of things, and I will.'

'By breaking the law?' Pa shook his head again.

'There is no law, Pa. Sicily has fallen into complete chaos. It's every man for himself nowadays.'

Lucia had had enough of being discussed like some kind of product. She got to her feet and held out her hand to Annita.

'I'm going out for a walk.' She grasped Annita's wrist. 'Come with me, sis. We can chaperone each other. When we get back, I don't want to hear any more talk about me marrying that pig, Cardona. I would rather kill myself first.'

The next morning, after a sleepless night of intense worry, Lucia rose before everyone else and went out to sit on the front step. Ma and Pa had argued long and hard with her when she'd returned from her walk. They'd accused her of being selfish, of not putting the family first. It was her duty as a loving daughter to marry whomever they chose for her. The marshal of the carabinieri was a good catch – he would provide for her and for them. She would grow to love him when they had children, they'd said. It was how things were always done.

Tears filled Lucia's eyes. Of course, she knew that one day someone would come along who wanted to marry her. But she'd always thought she'd be able to get out of it. But now the war had changed everything. The current situation meant that her family depended on her. Her parents had made that clear last night. The money they earned from selling the fruit and vegetables grown on the *campagna* wasn't nearly enough to pay for the wheat they needed. It was up to her to save them and she'd cause their starvation if she refused to do so. Lucia hiccupped on a sob and wrapped her arms around herself. She would have to marry Cardona. There was nothing else she could do.

Sudden footfalls sounded, and she glanced up. She smoothed the tears from her cheeks with the back of her hands as she caught sight of Gero approaching.

'What's wrong?' he asked.

Clearly, she hadn't wiped away the tears fast enough. She took a deep breath, then told him the whole depressing story.

'If I don't agree, my family will starve,' she said, making direct eye contact with him.

'Can I?' he asked, raising his hand to her cheek.

She nodded and let him trail his finger down the tracks of her tears.

'I'm going to have to marry Cardona,' she said. 'I have no choice.'

'You're wrong, Lucia. I believe you do have a choice. Why not marry me?'

She almost fell off the step, she was so surprised.

'What? But why?' Lucia couldn't keep the shock from her voice. 'We aren't even courting.'

'I feel something for you,' he said. 'And I think you feel something for me.'

'Feelings are not the same as true love—'

He reached for her hand, and she let him take it. Her fingers seemed tiny compared with his.

'Do you feel anything for Cardona?' he asked, his gaze on hers.

'I hate him.' She spat out the words.

'They say that love and hate are similar emotions—'

'I swear to you that Cardona disgusts me.'

'Do I disgust you?' Gero took a quick breath.

'Not at all. I quite like you,' she said. 'But how can we be married, you and me? Where would we live? And what if you're sent somewhere else with the army?'

'I came by to tell you I've just bought a house from don Nofriu. It's a *baglio contadino* above Villaurora. We could start our wedded life there, if you agree. Then, when the war is over, I'll take you back to New York. You once told me you wanted to return to the US. Well, what better way than as my wife?'

'I don't know, Gero.' She struggled to find the right words. 'This is so sudden—'

'If you're worried about intimacy, I swear I won't touch you until you're ready,' he said before lifting her hand to his lips and kissing it.

The thought of going to bed with him, of doing what married people did, made her nerves jangle. At least Gero didn't disgust her. But her worries about his connections with don Nofriu had intensified of late because of Dinu. If she were to leave Sicily and move to America after the war, who would keep an eye on her twin brother?

'It's a big decision, Gero,' she said.

'Take the time to think about it, sweetheart.'

Lucia looked him deep in the eye, and what she saw there made her heart give a stutter. His gaze was burning with love, but how could that be? Okay, they'd met years ago, except they were children then. Now they were adults, they were different people. No, it was far too soon for love; she must have misunderstood what she'd seen.

15

DINU, SEPTEMBER 1943

The pistol Dinu had tucked into his trousers and hidden under his shirt chafed at his side as he shifted the heavy sack of grain he was carrying on his back while he hiked across country. The trek from Caltanissetta had been long and difficult – almost nine hours. He and Francu had set out at nightfall, so as not to attract the attention of any carabinieri. Now it was nearly daylight, they'd have to be careful. Villaurora was in Palermo province and transporting wheat over the provincial boundaries was against the law.

To distract himself from the pain the load was causing to his shoulders, Dinu thought about his sister's upcoming marriage to Gero Bonanno. No one had been more surprised than he when the American had asked Pa for her hand. Pa had thought he was joking at first. But Gero had been adamant. He wanted to marry Lucia, to love and cherish her for the rest of his life. In return, he'd promised to help her family, to make sure they had enough food, and to fund their passage back to the USA when the war was over.

Dinu muttered under his breath; Gero's actions had taken

the wind out of his sails. If only he and Francu had managed to get their grain-smuggling business up and running in time to make it unnecessary for Lucia to marry the American. But Gero had delayed setting up a meeting with don Nofriu so they could sell him their stash of weapons and get paid enough money to buy their first lot of wheat. They would distribute it among friends and relations and not charge black-market prices. It would take them at least a couple of months before they'd save the sum to buy their own mule. The beast of burden would carry as many as five sacks at a time, and it would only be at that stage that they'd make a profit.

The weight of the wheat bore down on Dinu as he trekked along the path. Don Nofriu hadn't asked him what he planned to do with the money. The godfather had barely acknowledged him during their exchange. Dinu had gone to the town hall on the pretext of a meeting with Gero, who'd taken him through to the boss's office. Don Nofriu was sitting at a wide oak desk, smoking his habitual cigar. He'd pushed his tortoiseshell glasses up his nose, glanced at the bag of munitions Dinu opened before him, and haggled over a price. It was considerably lower than what Dinu had asked for. But the don had said, 'A poor man like you isn't in a position to call the shots,' and he had a point.

Dinu remembered Lucia telling him she wasn't in love with Gero, that it would be a marriage of convenience. Under normal circumstances, an American serviceman like Gero wouldn't be able to marry a local girl until the war was over. Except Gero's commander, Charles Rinelli, had pulled the right strings. And so, as soon as the necessary paperwork had been completed, Pa would walk her down the aisle.

Smirking to himself, Dinu thought about Giulianu Cardona. The marshal's nose had been well and truly put out of joint. There was nothing the *bastaddu* Cardona could do about it – Gero had the backing of don Nofriu, who counted Charles Rinelli among his friends.

Maybe Lucia marrying Gero wasn't such a bad idea? He'd be part of their family and on account of Gero's favours, the village boss would surely show greater consideration towards Dinu than he'd done before.

Dinu's thoughts turned to his parents. His father worked all the hours God sent on their *campagna*, and his mother had known a much easier life in America. There'd been running water in their Brooklyn apartment. In Villaurora, Ma and the girls had to carry water in pails from the village pump to their house, where it was stored in Ali Baba terracotta jars. Dinu resolved to change his family's fortunes by becoming as rich as don Nofriu one day. Their poverty would be a thing of the past and maybe they wouldn't even need to move back to the USA.

Day was breaking and Dinu and Francu would soon be home. But the path they were following was well known to smugglers, so he and his cousin would have to watch out for carabinieri. He put a finger to his lips and motioned to Francu to stop walking. All was quiet, except for the twitter of the cicadas, already chirping in the early-morning heat.

Stealthily, Dinu and Francu moved forwards until they came to a dry riverbed with a rough floor of tiny stones, lined by a bamboo thicket and an olive grove. From there, the track would drop in a long, winding spiral to Villaurora.

Suddenly, a flash of light like the striking of a match caught Dinu's eye. He held up his hand to Francu. About thirty metres away, three men had stepped out from behind the bushes and they were dressed in the black uniforms with white piping of the carabinieri.

'*Medda.*' Shit.

The police officers fanned out, sunshine glinting off the metal on their rifles and handgun-style submachineguns. An older carabiniere with sergeant's stripes on his sleeves took centre position, flanked by two younger guys. Smiling with clear self-importance, the sergeant came forward and pointed his rifle unwaveringly at Dinu's chest. The other two carabinieri closed in from both sides, waving with their guns that Dinu and Francu should put their sacks down.

'Give us a thousand lire as a gift, and we'll allow you to go,' the sergeant said, glancing from Dinu to Francu, and back to Dinu again.

'Never,' Dinu spat.

'Show me your documents. If they're not in order, I'll make you shit and wipe your asses with them.' The sergeant's face turned red with anger, and he narrowed his eyes.

Dinu thrust his chest out, icy fury pounding in his veins. He wouldn't let himself be arrested, wouldn't let these godforsaken men rob him of his family's food. Planning to get beneath the arc of the pointed rifle, he took out his identity card and walked towards the sergeant.

'Throw it on the ground,' the sergeant growled, motioning with his rifle.

Dinu did as ordered, keeping his gaze on Francu, five paces to his left. His cousin knew he had a pistol under his shirt, and was trying to distract the sergeant's attention by waving his arms.

'The *bastinado* will knock out some of your peasant insolence.' The sergeant took a few steps backward and smiled again. 'Both of you, down on the ground!'

The *bastinado* was a form of torture that Cardona and his men utilised to keep the villagers in line. They would whip the soles of their feet until they bled. Dinu knew various villauroresi who'd suffered the punishment in the carabinieri barracks, and they'd gone home with their feet so badly injured they'd never walked again.

He wouldn't let the carabinieri do that to him.

Keeping his gaze fixed on the sergeant, Dinu bent his knee as if he were going to lie down. He put one hand on the ground and the other on his belt so that he could draw the pistol from beneath his shirt. He could see Francu standing proudly, refusing the command, while the submachineguns trembled in the hands of the young guards.

Out of the blue, a falcon swooped down with a zipping sound, causing all three carabinieri to yelp and step back. Giving thanks to God, Dinu took advantage of the distraction to edge in the direction of one of the younger police officers – while Francu crept towards the bamboo thicket. With a grunt, Dinu hit the young carabiniere with his forearm and knocked him to the ground.

'Run!' he shouted to Francu.

Francu sped into the bamboo, and Dinu ran for the olive grove. Feeling a quick sense of exultation, he launched his body midair to dive between the two sturdy trees that would shield him and, as he did so, he drew the pistol free from beneath his shirt.

Except, the sergeant had already swung his rifle up and now aimed a lethal shot.

The bullet tore into the flesh at the side of Dinu's abdomen and his body was racked with pain. He fell like a dead bird between the two trees, then tried to get up, but his legs had gone numb and he couldn't make them move.

Pistol in hand, he twisted around and stared at the sergeant, who was shaking his rifle in the air in triumph. Dinu's trousers filled with blood, the liquid warm and sticky. He gritted his teeth and squeezed the trigger of his pistol.

The sergeant's black cap with its white piping flew in the air as he crumpled to the ground. It was an almost impossible shot with a pistol at that range, but Dinu got the impression his own hand had travelled with the bullet and had smashed it like a sharp blade through the sergeant's eye.

Deathly silence descended. Even the cicadas stopped their incessant twittering.

Moaning in agony, Dinu rolled into the bushes. He tried to get up again and this time his legs obeyed him. But only one leg sprang forward, while the other dragged behind. His crotch was warm and sticky, his trousers soaked, his vision cloudy.

Then he fell – not to the ground, but into an endless, red-tinted black void of nothingness.

16

Lucia was waiting for Gero to come for supper. He'd been more than generous in bringing food for the family since she'd agreed he could ask Pa for her hand in marriage last month. Pa's acceptance had thrilled Ma perhaps more than it had delighted Lucia – she still had mixed feelings about the whole idea. But she knew she had to be practical. Times were harder than ever, and Gero represented a lifeline. In more ways than one. He'd saved her from a fate almost worse than death – simply the thought of Giulianu Cardona being intimate with her made her want to retch.

As for her concerns about Dinu, she'd decided to put off worrying about him until the time came for her to go to America with Gero. Maybe her brother would come too; she'd make every attempt to persuade him.

She remembered their carefree childhood in Brooklyn, where they'd lived in a rented apartment in Fourth Avenue, between Sixth and Seventh Streets, next to the local firehouse. Lucia had loved it; she could hear the station's bells ringing when their windows were open, and also see the Williamsburg

Tower from their front stoop. She and Dinu had attended elementary school on Seventh Avenue, a walk of three and a half blocks. Every day, after class, they'd chalk the sidewalk in front of the apartment block to play hopscotch with the neighbourhood kids. But the best game was stoop ball. She liked boys' games, preferred them to girls' games like jumping rope, and didn't care a jot when she became known as a tomboy.

Of course, now they were both adults, life would be different in the USA. All she knew, though, was that it would almost certainly be better than the poverty and chaos they were experiencing in Sicily.

A knock sounded at the door, and Lucia went to open it. She couldn't help her heart fluttering at the sight of Gero. He looked so handsome in his army uniform; his beautiful chocolate-brown eyes, chiselled chin and white-toothed smile made her knees grow weak. Would she grow to love him? One thing was sure, although she'd marry him, she wouldn't let him make love to her until she did. If that ever happened…

'Guess what I've got?' He kissed her on each cheek.

'Oh, dear Lord.' She gasped as he produced a walnut wood-encased radio from behind his back. 'Where did you get that?'

'It was left behind by the previous fascist mayor. I thought you might like it.'

Before Lucia could say a word, her father approached, his face wreathed in smiles.

'*Grazie*, Gero,' he said. 'I presume this is for me?'

'Yes, and the rest of the family, of course.'

Gero winked at Lucia before taking the set over to the sideboard with her father. They plugged it in and tuned to the public service broadcaster. Soon, the sound of a light entertainment programme echoed in the air. The entire family except Dinu – who'd gone off with Francu somewhere – gathered around in awe, and Ma and Annita clapped their hands with clear glee.

'This will make a tremendous difference to our lives,' Lucia whispered to Gero. '*Grazie.*'

They sat at the table to enjoy Ma's signature dish of beef *involtini*. They'd almost finished eating when the broadcast was interrupted by the voice of Prime Minister Badoglio.

'The Italian government, recognising the impossibility of continuing the unequal struggle against an overwhelming enemy force, in order to avoid further and graver disasters for the nation, has sought an armistice from General Eisenhower, commander-in-chief of the Anglo-American Allied forces. The request has been granted. Consequently, all acts of hostility against the Anglo-American force by Italian forces must cease everywhere. But they may react to possible attacks from any other source.'

Ma and Pa leapt to their feet, sending the cutlery flying.

'It's over. The war is over.' Their voices rang with jubilation.

But Gero soon put them right. He shook his head and said, 'Badoglio mentioned your forces may react to possible attacks from any other source. I'm sorry to have to say this, but Hitler won't let up. He'll garrison the mainland and fight to hold on to it.'

Ma sagged back into her chair as Lucia and Annita cleared the dishes, and Gero and Pa went outside for a smoke.

'Was Gero right about the Germans?' Annita said, drying the plate Lucia handed to her.

'Probably.' Lucia gave a shrug. Her *fidanzato* was right about most things.

The radio programme had switched back to light entertainment and, when Gero and Pa came back indoors, Lucia and the family sat down at the table to listen again.

'I suppose I should make tracks,' Gero said after about half an hour.

'I'll see you out.' Lucia scraped back her chair.

She followed him onto the front step so she could wave him off, but he turned and lifted his hand to stroke her cheek. She stood rooted to the spot while he leant in to kiss her gently on the mouth.

'Sorry,' he said. 'I couldn't help myself. Your mouth is so beautiful. You are so beautiful.'

'It was nice.' The words came out before she could think. The press of his warm lips against hers had made her chest tingle.

'Nice?' He met her gaze.

'I mean, wonderful.' She could feel her face burning.

'Shall we do it again?' He took her hand.

'Oh, yes. Please. I'd like that.'

He inclined his head towards hers and kissed her. She'd never been kissed properly by a man before and had no clue what to do. But something stirred within her, and she curled her fingers in the hair at the back of his neck and parted her lips.

'Hey, what are you two doing out there?' Pa's voice came from inside the house. 'Think about your reputation, Lucia. Get indoors this instant.'

'Oops.' She pulled back with a giggle. '*Buona notte*, Gero. I'll see you tomorrow.'

* * *

The next morning, Lucia was leaning over the table, making pasta with the wheat Gero had bought for the family. Ma and Annita had gone to fetch water, so Lucia was on her own. Her arms ached with the effort of rolling out the dough, but she soon got into the rhythm of it. *At least Italy is no longer at war with America,* she thought. Maybe the paperwork for her to marry Gero would come through more quickly. A warm, fuzzy feeling filled her chest as she thought about their kiss last night. She'd been surprised by how much she'd enjoyed it.

Loud banging at the door interrupted her musing, followed by a shout.

'Oi, you in there!' came Giulianu Cardona's voice. *'Aprite la porta!'* He commanded that the door be opened.

Lucia dusted off her hands and hurried to comply. The marshal was standing on the front step, accompanied by two of his carabinieri.

'What do you want?' Lucia asked.

'We've come to take your brother into custody.'

'What? I don't understand—' Her chest grew cold, and she shivered despite the warmth of the day.

'He shot and killed my sergeant, who was trying to detain him for smuggling grain.'

Lucia's legs began to give way, and she held on to the door jamb to stop herself from crumpling to the floor.

'I'm sure it wasn't Dinu.' Her voice trembled. 'He'd never do anything like that—'

'I'm afraid you're wrong,' Cardona sneered. 'He dropped his ID card. There's no doubt it was him.' He pointed a finger at his men. 'Besides, these two are witnesses. Your brother is a murderer and we've come to arrest him.'

'He isn't here,' she said.

'I don't believe you.' The marshal looked her up and down and gave another sneer.

'Feel free to take a look.' She waved her hand around the room.

Cardona trooped into the house with his men. There was nowhere anyone could hide, but they carried out a thorough search, pulling the mattresses off the beds, upending the hay bales, opening cupboards and rifling through their contents.

Lucia stood and watched, her pulse racing.

Eventually, the marshal commanded his men to stop rummaging.

'You must report to me when your brother returns home, Lucia.' Cardona stamped his boot in obvious anger. 'If you don't, I'll charge you with the crime of assisting a felon.'

The blood drained from her face and she felt nauseous.

Cardona edged closer, and she caught a whiff of the garlic on his breath.

'He has an accomplice, by the way. Do you know who that could be?'

Lucia shook her head – her mouth had gone completely dry.

Lucia barely had time to catch her breath. Shortly after Cardona left, Ma and Annita returned with the pails of fresh water. Lucia sat her mother and sister down to tell them what had occurred.

Annita burst into tears, while Ma prayed to the blessed Virgin Mary and all the saints to keep her boy safe.

'What shall we do?' Lucia asked. She could hear the despair in her voice.

'We can only wait until your father gets home.' Ma twisted her apron and gave a heavy sigh.

Suddenly, Francu's voice resounded from outside the front door.

'Open up!' he shouted.

Lucia did as he'd asked and spotted that her cousin was shirtless.

'Where's my twin brother?' She glanced behind Francu. 'Giulianu Cardona came by looking for him. He said he'd shot and killed his sergeant. Please tell me it isn't true.'

'Dinu's wounded.' A pain-filled expression crossed Francu's face. 'That bastard carabiniere shot him first. I stemmed the bleeding with my shirt. I came to tell you before I went to fetch the doctor.'

There was a shocked silence, followed by a strangled cry from Ma.

'My only son,' she wept, pleating her apron. 'I must go to him—'

'Cardona will have people watching us, Ma.' Lucia took charge of the situation. She touched her hand to her mother's arm before turning to Francu. 'He came by looking for Dinu because he'd dropped his ID card, but he doesn't know you were involved. All he knows is there was an accomplice.'

'The two guards at the scene were scared shitless.' Francu curled his lip. 'They wouldn't recognise their mothers if they'd been there. I can rustle up a dozen witnesses who'll swear I was in Villaurora last night and in the early hours of this morning.'

'Where have you left Dinu?' Lucia pushed up her sleeves, a plan forming in her mind.

'In that shepherd's hut between Gero's baglio and the crags overlooking the village.'

'I'll meet you there,' she said. 'Let me give you one of Dinu's shirts before you go.'

'*Grazie.*' Francu placed a hand on his chest.

Ma saw him to the door, then said, 'You won't let me go to

him, Lucia, yet you'll take the risk of leading Cardona to him yourself—'

'I'll dress in boys' clothes. No one will know it's me.'

'Take care, daughter,' Lucia's mother sighed in resignation.

* * *

Lucia changed into the outfit she wore for rabbit hunting, tucked her hair up in a cap, and then headed out of Villaurora as discreetly as she could. But at the village boundary, she came to an abrupt halt.

Giulianu Cardona was marching down the hill with a group of carabinieri. Lucia froze, and her heart almost beat out of her chest. Had he seen her? Although she was in disguise, she had no identity papers for the boy she was pretending to be.

Nonchalantly, she turned off into a side street, where she crouched behind an upturned donkey cart. She peered through the wooden slats and prayed the police officers wouldn't come her way.

Tramping footfalls echoed from the main road, and Lucia's pulse pounded. Sudden relief welled up in her – Cardona and his men had carried on marching down the high street.

Lucia waited until she was as sure as she could be that they weren't coming back again and then, composing herself, she set off once more, walking slowly, so as not to draw attention.

Worry for her brother constricted in her throat. She hoped that Francu would manage to persuade the village physician, Dottor Rizzu, to attend to Dinu – and that they'd succeed in making their way to the shepherd's hut without being seen.

Pa had mentioned some time ago that the doctor was no friend of the carabinieri. He'd had to treat too many people who'd suffered the *bastinado*. Hopefully, he'd see her brother as yet another one of their victims.

With every step she took, she recited a prayer until, finally, she'd distanced herself from Villaurora, had skirted Gero's baglio, and was approaching the place where she trusted she'd find Dinu.

When Lucia entered the shack, she stifled a gasp. The seconds seemed to slow down as she took a step back. Dinu was lying on a pallet of straw, a blood-soaked shirt around his middle. His eyes were open, but there was a glaze over them.

'*Soru*,' he murmured. 'You came—'

'Of course I came, *frati*.'

She went to crouch beside him, took a handkerchief from her pocket and wiped his sweat-covered forehead. He drifted in and out of consciousness, and all Lucia could do was comfort him and pray while she waited for help to come. At long last, Francu arrived with Dottor Rizzu.

'Sorry we took such an age,' Francu said. 'The carabinieri have set up roadblocks. We had to go across country.'

'Thank God you made it,' Lucia said, hugging him.

She stood aside while the doctor examined Dinu. He gave him a shot of morphine, then cleaned and dressed the wound.

'The bullet appears to have gone through the body between the ribs and the hip,' he said. 'It must have missed the liver, otherwise he'd be dead. But he's lost a great deal of blood—'

'Will he live?' Lucia met the doctor's gaze.

'That depends on whether he succumbs to an infection. He should really be in the hospital.' Dottor Rizzu sighed. 'But, under the circumstances—'

'We can't leave him here.' Lucia choked on the words. 'It's too exposed, and who would look after him?'

She racked her brains, trying to come up with a solution.

There was only one answer. She would have to ask Gero to let him stay at the baglio. How to convince her future husband? Dinu had broken the law, a law whose enforcement Gero was supposed to oversee. He would never agree to harbour a criminal.

'I'll make my own way back to the village.' Dottor Rizzu interrupted her thoughts. 'If I'm stopped, I can just say I've been doing my rounds.'

'Thank you for treating Dinu, *dottore*.' Lucia shook his hand. 'My *fidanzato*, Gero Bonanno, will pay your fee.'

'I'd heard you're engaged to him, my dear. A fine match.'

'Yes, well.' She smiled. 'We are now family.'

She would play that card when she asked Gero to let Dinu stay with him, she decided. Family was everything. As a true Sicilian, how could Gero refuse?

After Dottor Rizzu had left, Dinu fell into opiate dreams. Lucia asked Francu to tell her what had happened after her brother had been shot.

'I was in the middle of a bamboo thicket.' Francu's mouth twisted. 'I laid myself down on the ground and waited for the two surviving carabinieri to go after Dinu. I planned to ambush one of them and relieve him of his gun. But they scurried off, leaving their dead sergeant behind.'

'The cowards,' Lucia said, glad of the fact.

'I ran to the olive grove where Dinu had disappeared. I found him with his pistol still clutched in his hand. I took the weapon and thrust it into my belt. When Dinu's eyes opened, I almost wept with relief, and I tried to help him to his feet.' Tears ran down Francu's cheeks. 'There was a gaping hole in his side. I propped him up against a tree, ripped off my shirt and wrapped it over the wound to staunch the blood. Then I carried him here.'

'You did well, Francu.' Lucia gave him a hug. 'I'm going home now to tell my parents everything. Are you all right to stay here with Dinu until my father comes?'

'Absolutely. Someone should be with him at all times.'

'It won't be easy with Cardona watching us. But we'll find a way.'

Lucia set off forthwith. She would never forget her perilous walk back to Villaurora, how she'd had to skirt around the carabinieri roadblocks, then make her way to Pa's *campagna* by cutting across the fields.

'If only he hadn't given up his identity card. I could have asked my fellow farmers to swear they'd seen him working here with me,' Pa said after she'd explained what had happened.

'They would have arrested him, anyway.' She wiped tears from her eyes. 'Now, if he survives, he'll have to live in the mountains, like other fugitives.'

The highlands of Sicily were rampant with men like Dinu, who'd fled the law.

'I hope it won't come to that, daughter.'

She told him about her plan to ask Gero for his help.

'Good idea,' Pa said. 'I'll stop work now, pretend I've been taken ill. Then I'll pack a bag of essentials and some food before going to Dinu.' A tear trickled from his eye. 'My poor boy. How it's come to this, I'll never know.'

* * *

Lucia spent the rest of the day fretting. It was hard to concentrate on her chores, but Ma insisted.

'It will take your mind off things,' she said, handing Lucia a broom.

But even as the words came out of Ma's mouth, she started to weep. Lucia put her arm around her, and Annita did the same, and the three of them wept hot tears of worry for Dinu.

The hours ticked by, with no news.

'Remember the saying, "no news is good news",' Lucia said by way of encouragement. 'If something had happened, we'd have heard about it.'

'I pray you are right,' Ma said.

Lucia and Annita helped her prepare a simple meal. Their hearts weren't in making anything other than maccheroncini with a pesto sauce. Gero would come by as usual to eat with them any time now. Lucia couldn't help her heart fluttering at the thought of seeing him. She touched a finger to her lips, remembering their kiss. Did he know about Dinu? Lucia suspected it was the talk of the village.

She wasn't wrong. The first thing Gero said when she opened the door to him was, 'Your brother has well and truly done it this time—'

'Come with me, Gero,' she said, taking his hand and leading him to where she'd already placed two chairs in the far corner of the room. 'I need to speak with you.'

'As I do with you, sweetheart.'

'You go first,' she said when they'd sat down.

'Colonel Rinelli wants me to work with him at the AMGOT office in Palermo for the next month. While I'm there, I'll get the last of the paperwork sorted for our wedding.'

Lucia's heart shrank with disappointment at his news.

'I'll miss you, Gero.' And she would, it occurred to her.

'I'll miss you too,' he said. 'But I'll be back before you know it, I promise—'

She chewed her lip, her thoughts chasing each other.

'Gero,' she said. 'Dinu was shot by the carabiniere sergeant before he fired back. He has a horrible wound on his side and has lost a lot of blood.' She fixed her fiancé in her gaze. 'You won't tell anyone, will you?'

'Please don't put me in a difficult position, Lucia. The less I know, the better.'

'Oh, okay.' She leant across and brushed a quick kiss to his cheek. 'Would it be all right if me and the family spent time in your baglio while you're away?'

'I'm not going to ask you why. But I can guess, and I'm worried you might be getting into something you'll later regret.'

'Now we're engaged, you've become part of my family, haven't you?' She gave him a look. 'Family sticks together through thick and thin. The code of *omertà* isn't just in Cosa Nostra – it applies to ordinary families as well.'

'Of course.' Gero got to his feet, and helped her to hers. Then he wrapped his arms around her.

She snuggled into his chest and breathed in his clean scent. He tilted up her chin and kissed her on the mouth. She gave herself over to his kiss, threading her fingers into his shirt and clinging to him.

'*Ti vogghiu beni*, Lucia.'

He said that he loved her, but she wouldn't tell him she loved him back, for that would be a lie, wouldn't it?

17

JESSICA, JUNE 2005

By the time Jess made her way down to the village, the church bells had stopped ringing. She parked in front of the grocery store and went inside.

A stack of shopping baskets had been placed by the door, and Jess picked one up before making her way to the fresh fruit and vegetables aisle. The choice was limited, but she felt pleased to have found a punnet of apricots and a packet of mixed salad leaves, which she put into her basket before going to the deli counter.

A young woman served her the one hundred grams of pecorino she requested, and the same weight of cooked ham. Jess thanked her and headed for the baked goods section.

Suddenly, her skin tingled. Her senses widened, and she took a deep breath. Someone was watching her. Slowly, she turned around. But no one was there – just the lingering sensation she was being observed. Was it simply her imagination? Or perhaps it was merely a curious villager checking her out.

She selected a loaf of sliced wholemeal bread, a packet of

breakfast brioches, and picked up a jar of strawberry jam to replace the one the ants had got at. All she needed to get now was some butter, milk and yoghurts, so she went to the chilled dairy products cabinet and slid back the glass door.

Again, her skin prickled, and this time she turned around quickly. A short, stocky man occupied the periphery of her vision. He caught her eye, then drew a finger across his throat before slipping out of sight.

The cutthroat gesture sent a chill of fear through her. She hurried to the till, paid for her purchases and, on reaching her car, put her shopping in the boot and made haste to open the door. Her gaze landed on a note, tucked behind a windscreen wiper, almost certainly a flyer advertising something. She picked it up, and read:

Torna a casa. Il baglio non è suo.

Go back home. The baglio isn't yours.

Her stomach churning, Jess glanced up the street. The man she saw in the grocery shop was mounting a motorbike. He kicked it into action and roared off, making a familiar noise. It was the same bike Jess had heard at the baglio; she was 100 per cent sure of it.

* * *

The next morning, a text arrived from Jess's cousin, Mel.

> You never got back to me after your second visit to the farmhouse. Hope all is well!

All good here. Sorry I've been quiet. I still haven't made my mind up about taking it on. Kind of daunting, if you know what I mean.

Mel didn't know the half of it, but now wasn't the time to go into details. Jess's encounter with Motorbike Man had unsettled her.

Her cousin then asked if she was having fun, and Jess responded that the owner of the winery had been super friendly and that he was going to give her some advice about the baglio.

That's nice. Is he hot?

A typical Mel question.

Very, but also very unavailable.

Aw. Shame. Don't go silent on me again, Jess. I was worried about you.

I won't. And there's nothing to worry about, silly.

If you say so.

Jess signed off with kisses and heart emojis before going to get ready for the pool. A short time later, she was lying on a sun lounger, attempting to read her book. But she couldn't concentrate. Who was that man and why had he warned her away from her inheritance?

The sound of children's voices interrupted her thoughts, and she looked up to see Piero approaching with two kids and Cappero at their heels. He introduced his son Gigi, and daughter Teresina, both of whom politely shook Jess's hand while the dog flopped down in the shade.

'They're under strict instructions not to make too much noise,' Piero said.

'It won't bother me if they do. I like children—'

'That's a relief.' Piero wiped a hand across his forehead. 'These two aren't the quiet types. I've asked them to speak English when we're with you, by the way, as they need the practice.'

'Can we get in the water now, Papi?' Gigi, Piero's mini me, hopped from one foot to the other.

'Off you go! I'll be with you in a minute.'

Gigi ran to the pool and jumped in with a splash, closely followed by his little sister, her blonde curls flattened to her head as she came up for air.

'Have you had a swim yet?' Piero put towels on a sunbed and smiled at Jess.

'I was just about to—'

'Why don't you join us? There's plenty of room—'

Jess was running across the hot decking before she could think twice. She executed what she hoped was a neat dive into the water, then surfaced. Piero had already taken the plunge and was swimming towards his son and daughter. Jess felt a little reticent, so she stayed in the deep end, while Gigi and Teresina took it in turns to clamber onto Piero's shoulders and jump off them. Eventually, they seemed to tire of the activity and challenged each other to races instead.

'*Ciao*,' Piero said, coming up to Jess.

'You're so good with your kids. Really patient.'

'Thanks.' His hazel eyes crinkled with a wistful smile. 'Being a part-time dad isn't easy. When they're with me, I want to give them the world. But I have to be careful not to spoil them.'

'I can imagine. From what I've seen so far, you're doing a good job.'

'Papi, can we swim a relay race?' Gigi called out. 'You and me against Teresina and Jess?'

'I think it would be fairer if it was you and Jess against Teresina and me.' Piero chuckled. 'Are you up for it, Jess?'

'Of course. But I'm not that fast a swimmer—'

'Doesn't matter. Gigi will make up the difference, you'll see.'

'I'm in the swimming team at my school.' Gigi puffed up his chest with pride.

'So am I.' Teresina clearly didn't want to be outdone.

'Right,' Piero said. 'I suggest the four of us go to the shallow end and take it from there.'

Jess and Gigi won the race, but Teresina was a good loser and quickly came up with the idea for another competition.

'Let's play chicken fight,' she suggested.

'What's that?' Jess asked.

'I sit on your shoulders. Gigi sits on Papi's and we try to push each other off. The first one to fall loses the match.'

'Could you face another game, Jess?' Piero asked.

'I'd love to.'

Gigi explained the rules. Neither Jess nor his dad could use their hands. All they were allowed to do was manoeuvre their passengers into the right positions.

For the next ten minutes or so, Jess needed to steel herself. Piero's muscular body clashed with hers frequently as he moved his son around the shallow end of the pool. Each time, he apologised, and each time, her insides fluttered.

Finally, Teresina leapt off Jess's shoulders onto her brother, which caused him to topple into the water.

'Yay, I won,' Teresina squealed.

'You cheated.' Gigi wagged a finger at her. 'You were supposed to stay on Jess.'

'*Pace!*' Peace. Piero held up his hands. 'We should head back to the house for some lunch.'

'Can Jess come too?' Teresina asked.

Jess held her breath while Piero considered the question. He glanced at her and raised an eyebrow.

'It will just be a plate of pasta and some salad.'

'There's nothing I'd like better,' she said.

18

LUCIA, OCTOBER 1943

A month after Dinu had been shot, Lucia was getting ready for her wedding. Although her brother had been extremely ill at first, he'd made a steady recovery, which was why her nuptials were still going ahead.

She would always remember the emotional reunion when Ma went for the first time to visit him, the day after Pa and Francu had carried him to Gero's baglio. With tears in her eyes, she'd watched her mother kiss Dinu, stroke his hair, and weep over his wound. The entire family then took it in turns to stay with him. Dottor Rizzu also visited, but only under cover of darkness for fear of arousing suspicion.

Marshal Cardona must have realised something was up. For all his faults, he clearly wasn't stupid, but he couldn't send his men into the property of an AMGOT civil affairs officer. The carabinieri answered to Gero, not the other way around.

At first, Dinu had been too sick to remember he'd lost his identity card, and thought Cardona had no clue it had been he who'd killed his sergeant. Dinu spoke of going home, and of how long it would be before he could work again. When he'd learnt the truth from Lucia, that Cardona was after him for murder, and their parents' house had already been searched, he'd been shocked. He'd become a *fuorilegge*, an outlaw, and might have to live the rest of his life as an exile.

Lucia's heart wept for her brother, despite everything he'd done. After he'd recovered enough not to need constant attention, he'd gone to stay in a cave high above the village with Francu. From what Pa had said, they lived off the rabbits they hunted and prickly pear fruit. Pa had forbidden Lucia to take the risk and visit them and, for once, she'd obeyed him.

Apparently, Dinu maintained he merited a pardon. The sergeant had shot him for smuggling two sacks of grain – hardly a capital offence – and he was unconcerned that he'd retaliated by killing the carabiniere. Pa said that Dinu was more worried about the effect his being an outlaw would have on *la famiglia*.

Sighing, Lucia wished her brother could be at her marriage to Gero. Dinu would have relished the fact that don Nofriu would be the guest of honour at the banquet, however, so perhaps it was for the best. The festivities after the ceremony would be held in Gero's baglio, and the godfather had offered the services of his personal chef as a wedding gift. She felt a little ashamed that the food had been bought on the black market, when so many of the poor in the village were starving, but Gero had insisted on paying for it.

'You deserve nothing less, *amuri*.' He'd called her 'love'. 'If I hadn't bought it myself, someone else would have done so. It's the way things are, unfortunately.'

'I get what you mean,' she'd said, slightly consoled because any leftovers would be eaten by her family.

Lucia breathed another sigh. So much had happened in the past month since the post-fascist Italian government had signed the armistice. Everyone she knew hoped the Allies would rapidly occupy the entire peninsula. But Nazi Germany was putting up fierce resistance; they'd even liberated Mussolini from imprisonment and had set him up to lead a puppet government in the north. On 9 September, the US Fifth Army under General Mark W. Clark had landed near Salerno, 150 miles up the western coast from the straits between the mainland and Sicily. American troops had run into searing fire from the moment they'd hit the shore. It had been a hard battle but now, at last, the whole of southern Italy was in Allied hands.

Would they break through to Rome soon? Gero had told her that the Germans were only giving ground slowly, and he feared they were preparing defensive lines. Lucia prayed fervently for peace, for a time when the black market would cease to exist and people could go back to living their lives as they'd done before the world went to war.

'You look lovely, daughter,' her mother said, busting up to her and interrupting her musing. 'That outfit suits you so well.'

Her wedding gift from Gero. Not a bridal gown – the conflict had turned such a purchase almost into an impossibility – but a pretty pale blue flannel dress with padded shoulders and a nipped-in high waist. God only knew what he'd paid for it. In Sicily, the wedding dress could never 'sleep with the bride', which meant it couldn't stay in the same house as her. It was kept by one of the family's womenfolk until the wedding day, and Ma's sister – Francu's mother – Giuseppina had looked after it for Lucia.

Annita now approached, wearing one of Lucia's second-hand outfits.

'I wish I had new clothes too,' she said wistfully, smoothing her skirt.

Lucia wanted to promise her she'd buy her a pretty dress as soon as the war ended. But how would she do that? She had no money of her own, and pride would forbid her from asking Gero.

'Come, Annita.' She took her sister's hand. 'I think Pa is waiting for us outside.'

But before Lucia could leave the house, Giuseppina, as the eldest woman of the family, gave her the traditional blessing by scattering a handful of uncooked rice on her head – a symbol of prosperity and fertility for Lucia's own future family.

Lucia couldn't help worrying. Would she and Gero have children one day? The very thought made her squirm with anxiety that she'd never grow to love him enough for their marriage to be consummated. She would keep to her resolve on that.

As she stepped through the front door into the freshness of the October afternoon, her eyes widened. Pa was standing at the head of a borrowed donkey cart, and the beast was all dressed up for the occasion. Bows, ribbons, bells, decorated harnesses, and red and yellow plumes at its brow and pommel. Even more vivid red, yellow and orange decorations covered the entire cart. Helmeted knights and crowned kings in dramatic scenes from the legends of Charlemagne and Roland – those ancient heroes of Sicilian folklore. Not to mention sacred images of the Virgin Mary. Lucia couldn't resist clapping with glee. Pa helped her into the cart, followed by Ma, Annita and Aunt Giuseppina.

'Let's go,' Pa said, stepping forwards, leading rein in his hand. 'We mustn't be late.'

* * *

The wedding mass passed in a flash, and soon Lucia was walking down the aisle with her arm through Gero's. They emerged into bright sunshine, the ringing of the church bells echoing across the square.

'You look so beautiful,' Gero whispered to her.

'And you look very handsome,' she said, gazing at him.

He was wearing his army major's dress uniform. The button closures glinted on his khaki cotton jacket, as did the gold metal relief of the Great Seal of the United States on his drab olive wool peaked cap. Could she ever love this man? She'd grown to like him more than she'd thought she ever would.

'I believe our car has arrived, *tisoru*.' Darling. Gero's face lit up with a wide smile.

One of don Nofriu's *picciotti* had driven his boss's Fiat 1100 onto the square. The man leapt out and opened the door for Lucia.

Gero took her hand to help her into the back seat, got in beside her and took her hand again as the driver started the engine.

'*Ti vogghiu beni*, Lucia.' He loved her.

But she could only grip his fingers in return.

* * *

Sitting next to Gero during dinner, with don Nofriu on her other side, Lucia swept her gaze around the courtyard. Trestle tables had been set up, where her family, including Aunt Giuseppina, her husband Carlo, and their brood of six children – minus Francu – had joined them. Candles, placed in empty wine bottles, flickered in the dusky light.

Lucia's stomach tightened with nerves. How would she make conversation with the godfather? She feared him and had nothing in common with him except Gero. Shifting her weight in her chair, she told don Nofriu about how she'd met her husband when they were both children in Brooklyn. Before too long, Gero began contributing tales of Coney Island, the candy stores and the ice cream parlours.

'I've never been to la Merica,' the godfather said. 'Maybe one day—'

Their antipasto course arrived – *caponata*, the classic Sicilian cold salad dish made with aubergines and fried peppers with black olives, tomato sauce, onion, pine nuts, capers and raisins.

'I see you haven't invited the maresciallo of the carabinieri.' Don Nofriu smiled knowingly.

'Yes, well,' Lucia said. 'I turned down his proposal to marry Gero instead.' There wasn't much that went on in Villaurora the capo didn't know about, she thought.

'An excellent decision.' Don Nofriu chuckled.

'I think so too.' What else could she say?

'And where is your brother?' The godfather's eyes glinted. 'I haven't seen him about the village for a while.'

Was the boss joking with her? She decided to ignore his question and distract him by commenting on the deliciousness of the food.

'Your cook has produced a wonderful meal for us, don Nofriu. Thank you.'

'You're most welcome,' he said, getting slowly to his feet. 'A toast to the bride and groom!' He raised his glass of Nero d'Avola red wine.

Everyone stood and toasted with their glasses. '*Gli spusi!*' To the bride and groom.

Later, after a feast fit for royalty – tagliatelle with seafood sauce, shrimp risotto, roasted sea bass and, for dessert, cassata cake – Lucia's Uncle Carlo picked up his accordion, and Gero led her onto the paved patio to dance a waltz.

Their eyes locked together and it occurred to Lucia she should be happy. This should be the happiest day of her life, but all she could think about was her brother, exiled in a cold cave up in the mountains. The thought festered at the back of her mind, together with her anxiety about sleeping with Gero.

While he was in Palermo, he'd bought a walnut double bed. It had arrived by lorry just last week, not long after Dinu had gone into hiding. Swallowing the lump of concern in her throat, Lucia thought about the tradition of the *cunzata dò lettu*. Her sister and her cousin Tilde – Aunt Giuseppina's eldest daughter, who was fifteen, like Annita – had been tasked with making up the wedding bed. Only unmarried women could do that job, and the sheets had to be pure white, traditionally hand-embroidered and accompanied by silk pillowcases. They weren't new, of course – Ma had kept those from her own wedding to Pa – but they were beautiful. Annita and Tilde would have applied the finishing touch, sugared almonds, another symbol of fertility, scattering them over the bed before locking the room to prevent the bride and groom from seeing it.

'Shall we slip away now, sweetheart?' Gero broke into Lucia's thoughts.

'Yes.' She mustered a smile, her heart unexpectedly pounding.

The wedding party erupted into loud applause as he led her towards their bedroom door. Lucia's face grew hot with embarrassment as he produced a key to unlock it. Inside, she eyed the bed – which had been prepared exactly like she'd expected. She went to the chest of drawers and, with trembling fingers, extracted the white cotton nightdress which Annita had put there for her.

'Turn around, Gero,' Lucia said.

He did as she requested, while she undressed herself and slipped on the nightie. She faced him again, and her heart skittered through a beat. He'd stripped to his underpants, and she couldn't help staring at him – he was so muscular and well-proportioned.

'Are you going to sleep like that?' she asked, blushing.

'I usually sleep naked.' He winked.

'You're kidding, I hope.' She took a step back.

'Sorry, I couldn't resist.' Gero laughed.

He went to open a drawer and retrieved a pair of pyjamas while she removed the sugared almonds and got into bed. White-knuckled, she gripped the sheets, and the mattress dipped as Gero sat on the other side.

'Relax, *amuri*. I won't do anything you don't want me to do.' He smiled and there was tenderness in his expression. 'Can I hold you?'

Lucia nodded, and he took her in his arms. She shivered, although the heat between their bodies was intense.

'You must think I'm being so silly—'

'Not at all, sweetheart.' He kissed her on the forehead, tucked a strand of hair behind her ear and rocked her gently. 'I'll take care of you, *tisoru*. Till the end of my days. I'll never hurt you.'

Gradually, the raucous voices outside on the patio, the accordion music and the laughter faded into silence. At last, Lucia was alone with Gero in the baglio, her new home. She found herself relaxing in his hold.

'Would you like me to sleep on the sofa?' he asked.

Lucia pondered his question. He hadn't pushed himself on

her and had seemed to be keeping his promise to wait for intimacy.

'No. Stay with me, please. I trust you.'

'Phew, that's good to know.' He kissed the tip of her nose and switched off the light.

She nestled into him, and soon his breathing slowed. Sleep was coming for her too, but she couldn't help worrying about Dinu up in the mountains. She missed him so much and prayed he'd receive a pardon soon so that he'd return to the bosom of his family.

19

DINU, DECEMBER 1943

It was Christmas Eve, and Dinu had gone down to the village with Francu. He left his cousin at Francu's front door and made his way to his family home. After stepping over the threshold, he smiled. Lucia was there without that godforsaken husband of hers; she ran into his arms and he gave her a hug.

But there was something different about her, as if a barrier had formed between them. She stiffened in his arms and squirmed herself free.

'What's wrong?' he asked.

'I wish with all my heart you hadn't shot that carabiniere and become an outlaw.'

'It only happened because I was trying to do my best for the family.'

'There was no need. My marrying Gero has taken care of everything.'

Jealousy made Dinu's stomach harden. Gero Bonanno had usurped his position, and the bitter taste of resentment constricted in Dinu's throat. He wouldn't let Gero win, however; one day, he'd show everyone who was boss.

Dinu's heart lightened as his mother rushed up; she hadn't changed towards him and he was thankful for it.

'My only son,' she said between kisses, 'how happy I am to see you.'

'And I you, Ma.' He breathed in a delicious, salty aroma coming from the stove. 'My mouth is watering. What have you been cooking?'

'Pasta with sardines.' A smile lifted the corners of her mouth.

Rubbing his stomach, Dinu said he couldn't wait. It was what he'd eaten every Christmas Eve, since he was a small boy. From the corner of his eye, he discerned Lucia heading out the door and he asked where she was going.

'Gero will be back from Palermo and I want to be at the baglio when he arrives,' she said. 'But I'll see you tomorrow, Dinu. My husband is bringing a ton of food with him and I'll be making you all lunch.'

'Ah, okay.' Dinu smirked to himself – he'd corner Bonanno and urge him to intercede with don Nofriu and get him pardoned. Holding on to that thought, he waved his sister off before swaggering across the room to the supper table.

* * *

The following morning, Dinu was still deep in dreams when he heard his father shouting from the street outside the front door.

'Paola, open up! The carabinieri are here—'

Dinu knew for a fact Pa always left the door open when he went to morning mass. Cardona must have guessed Dinu would come home for Christmas and had intercepted his father. Heart thumping, Dinu leapt out of bed, scrambled into his clothes and, taking one of Pa's hunting rifles, slipped out of the back door.

Should he head back to the mountains or wait to find out what was happening? He decided on the second option and made his way stealthily to the alleyway at the bottom of the road, from where he could see all the way up to his family home. Before too long, Cardona and a posse of police officers had spilled out onto the street and were crossing the road to Francu's.

The hair on Dinu's nape stiffened as he watched the carabinieri march his cousin to a waiting lorry. Gripping his father's rifle, he ran after the vehicle, hoping to catch it before it left the village square. It slowed down to go round the corner, and he took aim, shooting randomly through the windows. He only gave up when the carabinieri returned fire; he was one man against seven and risked getting killed, so he ducked behind a donkey cart then hurried out of the village before Cardona could send his men after him.

Up in the mountains, he made his way to a different cave than the one where he and his cousin had been living, in case Francu was tortured to reveal the location of their hideout. It was a cold, lonely Christmas for Dinu on his own, with nothing to eat except prickly pear fruit. His family would be enjoying the food Bonanno was bringing from Palermo, he remembered, and the thought made jealousy flame through his veins again. Hunger gnawing at his stomach, Dinu slept fitfully, and the next morning, he made his way to the provincial jail.

* * *

Freezing rain fell as Dinu hid behind a truck parked outside the prison gate, watching the people going in and out of the compound. A tall man, who appeared to be a gardener, given the tools he was carrying, had stopped before a sentry, who gave him access to the premises. Hunching into his coat, Dinu waited until the man came back out again, then approached him.

'I wonder if you can help me,' he said.

'Depends on what you mean by help.' The tall man glanced at him.

'Is there a bar nearby here where we can talk?'

'Sure, just up the road.' The man pointed towards a taverna. 'My name is Aspanu. What's yours?'

Dinu introduced himself and, once he'd bought a glass of wine for Aspanu, explained that his cousin had been unjustly imprisoned.

'The country is in chaos. So many men are ending up in jail and having to wait a long time before being brought to trial,' Aspanu said in a morose tone of voice.

'Precisely.' Dinu sighed. 'If I give you one thousand lire, could you take me into the compound with you as a fellow gardener?' It was almost all the money Dinu possessed, but it would be worth it if he could free Francu.

'I won't ask you why you want to get into the premises. A thousand lire would help me pay off a few debts,' Aspanu said. 'The prisoners are let out into the garden to get exercise every afternoon. Meet me outside the gates at two o'clock.'

'Sorry for not trusting you, Aspanu. But I won't pay you the money until you've got me into the compound.'

'I expected as much.' Aspanu laughed. 'Least you can do is buy me some lunch.'

Which is what Dinu did. While eating, the two men chatted about the progress of the war and how long it was taking the Allies to defeat the Germans. Dinu guessed Aspanu was desperate for the cash he would give him, and he thanked God for sending him the right man for the job.

After they'd eaten, Dinu settled the bill and walked back to the prison entrance with Aspanu. He held his breath while Aspanu explained to the sentry that he'd brought his nephew to help him. The sentry looked Dinu up and down, then nodded and let him through.

Dinu again thanked God that he knew a thing or two about gardening, and soon he was pruning trees alongside Aspanu and keeping his eye out for Francu among the prisoners exercising in the yard.

When he spotted his cousin, he put down his pruning shears and made his way across the yard. If anyone asked what he was doing, he'd say he needed the toilet. But no one asked, and he boldly went up to Francu, swept his gaze around to make sure it was safe, and then greeted him.

'*Mizzica!*' Francu smiled. 'What are you doing here, *kuxinu*?'

Dinu explained he wanted to break him out of the jail and asked if there was any way he could do that.

'The window of my cell overlooks a side street. If you come by tonight with a metal file to cut the bars, I can escape.'

'How will I know which window is yours?'

'I'll tie a handkerchief to it.'

'Perfect,' Dinu said. 'See you later, cousin.'

* * *

It had stopped raining by the time darkness had fallen and Dinu, one thousand lire the poorer, but with a metal file he'd persuaded Aspanu to give him, hurried down the narrow street flanking the prison. He spotted the handkerchief tied to a window bar and passed the tool through to Francu.

Pulse racing, Dinu paced the alley while he waited. His cousin was making a hell of a racket filing the iron window bars. What if the guards realised something was up? It wouldn't take them long to put two and two together and come for Dinu.

Finally, his cousin's head appeared at the window. Dinu reached up to help him wriggle out.

'It's not just me,' Francu said. 'I'm bringing some like-minded men with me, and we've also broken into the prison armoury.'

'You're brilliant,' Dinu said, setting him on his feet and slapping him on the back. 'Well done!'

The entire operation progressed without a hitch. It was clear the guards were shirking in their duties as ten men escaped from the prison with Francu. They brought the rifles they'd stolen from the arsenal with them and agreed to form a band with Dinu and Francu up in the mountains.

Hiking back to Villaurora under the light of a full moon, Dinu couldn't help feeling proud of himself for doing what he'd set out to do. God was on his side, he thought. His family didn't need Bonanno when they had him. Lucia should have trusted him and not rushed to marry that American.

20

JESSICA, JULY 2005

Teresina slipped her hand into Jess's as they strolled between the vines. It was the children's last day at the tenuta. Tomorrow they'd return to their mother in Palermo, and it occurred to Jess she would miss them. Gigi and Teresina had included her in their walks with Piero and Cappero every morning since she'd met them three days ago. It had meant getting up early before the heat became too intense, but she didn't mind. She enjoyed spending time with Piero and his kids – it had stopped her from dwelling excessively on Motorbike Man – and her chest deflated at the thought of Teresina and Gigi not being around any more.

'This one has black spots,' Gigi called out as he skipped ahead with Cappero to inspect the rose bushes while the dog snuffled in the soil. 'Come and look, Papi!'

'Well done, son,' Piero said, going up to him. 'I'll come back and check the health of the vines later.'

'Can I come also?' Gigi asked.

'Of course.' Piero ruffled the boy's hair. 'I'm proud you're showing an interest.'

'I'm interested too,' Teresina added.

'I know, sweetie. *Sei bravissima.*' You're very good.

'Are you coming to the pool with us, Jess?' Teresina tugged at her hand. 'We can play chicken fight again.'

The kids never tired of that game, it seemed. Teresina was a determined character, but had learnt not to cheat. She no longer launched herself off Jess's shoulders; instead, Jess was under strict instructions to keep a tight hold of her legs.

Jess agreed to the suggestion and soon she was standing in the shallow end, gripping Teresina tightly as sunlight sparkled on the water.

'I'm shattered,' she said later after five bouts of the competition, two of which Teresina had succeeded in winning – perhaps because Gigi let her.

'I'm dead beat too,' Piero said, his smile flooding Jess with warmth.

They climbed out of the pool and sauntered over to the sunbeds where they'd left their towels. Cappero left his shady spot under a bougainvillea and padded across the decking to lick their hands.

'Gigi and Teresina have boundless energy,' Jess said, gazing at the two children – who'd stayed in the pool.

'They do, indeed.' Piero grinned. 'But at bedtime, they fall asleep as soon as their heads hit the pillow.'

'Nice for you to have some peace and quiet, then.'

'It's the only time I can catch up on some work.'

'I'm not looking forward to going back to the daily grind in Bristol.' Jess pushed the damp hair off her face and stretched out on her sunbed. 'Constant target setting has become a bit of a nightmare.'

'Why don't you chuck it all in and come and work in Sicily? I mean, you have a house already. All you need is a job—'

'I'm a bank manager, Piero.' She gazed across the vineyards towards the distant mountains. 'I'd have to start at the bottom in this country. And I'm sure the Villaurora bank is fully staffed, as it's such a tiny branch.'

'I'm not saying you should manage a bank here. Didn't you mention your qualifications are in accounting and finance? There's a lot of freelance work available in that field. You'd just need to study the Sicilian regulations—'

'I don't know. It would be a tremendous change in my life.'

'Of course. Sorry I mentioned it.'

'No. Don't be sorry.' She eyed his apologetic expression. 'I'll give it some thought. But first, I need to decide about the baglio.'

And solve the mystery of Motorbike Man. Just the thought of him made her skin prickle.

'How about I go there with you the day after tomorrow?' Piero suggested.

'Thanks.' Jess smiled. 'I'd certainly appreciate your advice.'

The following morning, Jess made her way to her car. The winery appeared so forlorn without the children. Even Cappero seemed dejected; he was lying under a pomegranate bush and, not bothering to get up, simply thumped his tail on the ground.

'I know how you feel, boy.' Jess walked over to him and patted him on the head. 'We're missing Gigi and Teresina already, aren't we?'

The dog whined plaintively in response, and Jess wished she could take him to the farmhouse with her – he'd soon alert her if there was an intruder. But she couldn't, of course. His job was to guard the winery, not her baglio. Hopefully, Giovanna or Angelo would be there. Jess resolved to get them to be more forthcoming. After all, she'd said they could continue farming the land that once belonged to Lucia...

Heat shimmered off the road as Jess drove across the dusty valley. Sprinklers sent out jets of water, irrigating the vineyards, and the ubiquitous prickly pears had turned grey under the unrelenting sun. Would she tire of this climate if she were to live here permanently? Not as much as she tired of the constant wind and rain in Bristol, maybe.

She changed gear to head up to Villaurora, and her insides quivered. Motorbike Man had got to her – no doubt about it. That cutthroat gesture, the note warning her off. Who could he be and why had he approached her? If he was, indeed, the person who'd driven his bike up the hill behind the property, what was he doing up there?

Before too long, Jess was parking in front of the low white farmhouse. After spending half an hour taking more photos of the baglio's rooms, she went back outside and made her way around to the back of the building. Her heart gladdened as she spotted a figure, who looked like Giovanna, working in a distant field.

'*Ciao*,' Jess said, going up to her. 'How are you? I'm pleased to see you, cousin.'

'As I am you.' Giovanna leant on her spade. 'What can I do for you?'

'Is there somewhere we can talk?' she asked, determined to get her cousin to address her concerns.

'What do you want to talk about, Jess?'

She explained about the man in the supermarket, the note and the motorbike.

'It's the same bike I heard here last week,' she added. 'I'm sure of it.'

'There's more than one motorbike in Villaurora.' Giovanna's tone came across as curt. 'How can you be so certain?'

'Call it a sixth sense. And also, that the man in the supermarket was riding it. It must have been him who left that note.'

'It's extremely strange, I agree.'

'Have you any idea why he would warn me off my inheritance?'

Giovanna frowned and slanted her body slightly away from Jess.

'I have no clue,' she said, shaking her head vehemently.

'One thing that's been puzzling me.' Jess changed tack. 'How did my grandmother come to own this property? It clearly didn't belong to your family—'

'Don't you know?' Again, the curt tone.

'Remember, I told you there was a rift between her and my mother—'

'Let's go and sit in the shade.' Giovanna's tone had softened, and she led her to a bench beneath one of the olive trees. She passed her a bottle of water, and Jess took a sip. 'In Sicily, we don't talk about certain things. Especially anything to do with Cosa Nostra.' Giovanna met Jess's eye. 'The code of silence – *omertà* – forbids it.'

Jess remembered her conversation with Piero when he told her about the crime boss in Villaurora, and her heart set up an uncomfortable beat. The discussion with Giovanna had become extremely odd. Why on earth had she brought up the Mafia?

'There's one thing I've been meaning to ask you,' Jess said, changing tack again. 'I know Lucia's married surname was

Bonanno. But what was her maiden name? It must have been the same as your grandmother's.'

'Pavano. The family name is Pavano.'

'Is there anyone around still with that name?'

'No one in Villaurora.' Giovanna fidgeted with the water bottle.

Jess stared at her cousin. Was she telling the truth? She'd lied about not hearing the motorbike, and her body language suggested she'd lied again. But why would she fib about her family? It was all too weird for words.

'Thanks for talking to me,' Jess said, realising she wasn't getting very far with her questions. 'I'll let you get on with your work now. But I'm coming back tomorrow with Piero Sacca. He's promised to give me some advice on restoring the baglio.'

'So you're still planning on keeping it?' The curt tone was back again.

'It all depends...' It was Jess's turn to be reticent. Two could play at the same game. She took her leave of her second cousin and returned to the farmhouse.

Inside, she paced the courtyard, imagining her grandmother doing the same. Lucia was in Villaurora at the same time as that *mafioso* Piero had spoken about. She might have known him. And what about Lucia's husband, her own mother's father? Lucia had taken his surname, Bonanno. Could the baglio have been his?

Jess had a light bulb moment. Perhaps she'd been barking up the wrong tree. Maybe she should be looking for members of the Bonanno family. She'd ask Piero for his help. Jess couldn't wait to bring him here tomorrow. She really needed to make up her mind about her inheritance. It was July already, and she only had ten days left in Sicily before she had to go back to Bristol.

From the corner of her eye, she discerned a rickety wooden chair, which had been placed near the entrance door, its seat made of woven straw. She couldn't remember seeing it here on previous visits. The chair appeared old, but it looked sturdy enough.

She sat in the shade and swept her gaze around the courtyard, just like Lucia must have done all those years ago. What had her life been like? How had the war affected her? Had her husband been Sicilian like her? So many questions, so little chance of getting them answered. Jess drew in a deep breath and released a heavy sigh.

21

LUCIA, JANUARY 1944

Anticipation tightened in Lucia's chest as she swept the courtyard. Gero was coming home later today, and she wanted everything to be perfect. It had been three months since their wedding, and so much had happened during that time. Italy had finally declared war on Germany, thereby becoming a co-belligerent with the Allies. From now onwards, military government would be restricted to the combat zone, and a control commission would supervise the Italian administration elsewhere. Gero had been needed in Palermo to assist with the start of the transition process and had relinquished responsibility for local affairs to don Nofriu, the mayor of Villaurora.

Dust stung Lucia's eyes, along with sadness. When he wasn't with her, she missed Gero with an intensity that had surprised her at first. But when he'd suggested that she might like to live in Palermo with him, she'd baulked at the idea. The Allies had bombed the city to bits prior to the Americans' arrival, and she had no friends nor relations there. At least in the village, she had her family. Life was better now, and the freedom that came with her new status as a married woman, with no longer needing to be chaperoned in public, had made her feel better about herself.

Her body tingled as her mind filled with images of her husband. He'd been so patient with her in the bedroom. She loved being kissed by him; she loved it when he held her close; she loved the sensation of his warm lips on hers. Recently, their kisses had become more passionate, and she'd open her mouth so their tongues could dance and light a fire that made her burn for him. Was she ready for physical love? For them to become one? She almost thought she was...

She remembered Christmas. Gero had showered her with gifts of nylon stockings, candies and scented soaps, not to mention providing all the ingredients for her to make a traditional feast for the family. She'd prepared homemade ravioli, stuffed with ricotta cheese, followed by roast pork with potatoes and artichokes. For dessert, she'd made Sicilian almond cookies. But the entire day had been spoiled by Dinu.

When Ma, Pa and Annita arrived for the meal Lucia had made, they told her everything that had happened after Pa had got home from mass. The carabinieri searched the house and discovered nothing. They threatened Lucia's father with summary arrest if Dinu's hiding place wasn't revealed, but Pa had refused. Ma spent the entire lunch weeping, Pa couldn't stop berating Cardona for his actions, and Annita said she'd lost her appetite.

A couple of days later, Gero informed Lucia about her brother's success in springing Francu from the jail, and that Francu hadn't come out alone, but with ten others. Dinu and Francu had now formed a band of thugs up in the mountains – they'd truly become outlaws.

Her belly twisting with worry for her brother, Lucia carried on sweeping until the courtyard was spotless, then went indoors to the kitchen. It was a big step up from her family home down in Villaurora. There was running water, pumped from a well behind the house, a wood-burning stove provided warmth to the interconnecting rooms in the chill of winter, and she'd polished the red-brick floors until her face practically shone in them. There was also a telephone – the height of luxury – but an absolute necessity for Gero to keep in touch with his office when he came to visit.

Lucia wasn't complacent, however. With her father's help, she'd already started digging the soil to prepare for spring sowing. The baglio had once been the home of a family of tenant farmers who'd worked the land on behalf of don Nofriu. When their son had died fighting in Russia for Mussolini and Hitler, they'd lost the will to carry on and had moved to live with relatives in Agrigento.

After checking the *canazzu* she was cooking for the evening meal – a vegetable side dish of potatoes, aubergines, tomatoes and bell peppers she would serve with *involtini* as the main course – Lucia went to wash and then change into clean clothes. Gero had phoned yesterday to say he'd invited don Nofriu and an associate of his for dinner. Lucia's chest squeezed with trepidation and she prayed her culinary skills would be up to the mark.

'My compliments on a fine dinner, Lucia,' don Nofriu said after she'd poured him a glass of homemade *ammazzacaffè* bitter digestive liqueur.

She took her seat next to him on the wooden chair, its seat made of woven straw, and smiled. Everything had gone well, despite her reticence at being sat with Gaetano Sacca, the son of Aurelio Sacca di Melita – the new mayor of Palermo. Gaetano was running the *latifondo* estate on behalf of his father and was a leading member of the Sicilian Separatists – a movement which had existed for about eighty years, since the unification of Italy, apparently, with the aim of splitting the region from its Italian masters.

Gero had explained to her earlier, before their guests had arrived, that in the early days after the Allied landings last July, the American Special Services had done everything they could to foster the organisation. Now, however, the Allies could no longer sponsor the movement; they couldn't incite civil war in the territory of a co-belligerent.

'If that's the case, why are you meeting with Gaetano Sacca, Gero?' Lucia had asked.

'So that I can pretend support, when what I'm really doing is gathering intelligence.'

From what Lucia knew, Rome governments had treated Sicily as a poor colony from the outset, imposing high taxes and draining her of her resources. None of the money that was taken from the island had ever been reinvested in it. She welcomed the idea of Sicilian independence, she'd realised out of the blue.

'You shouldn't spy on a fellow Sicilian, Gero,' she'd said. 'Promise me you won't!'

'We'll talk about it after the dinner, my love,' he'd responded.

Conversation around the table now focused on how a Separatist army would fight for an independent country, either as part of a future United States of Europe, or with permanent independence guaranteed by America and Britain.

'Our worst enemies are communism, monarchism and clericalism.' Gaetano fixed his gaze on Lucia. 'Would you be able to help in the distribution of our leaflets to discourage people from following those politics?'

'I'd love to.' She swallowed hard, truly surprised.

Lucia had been brought up firmly anti-communist; the king of Italy had been born into the aristocratic house of Savoy in Piedmont, which was at the opposite end of the country and as removed from Sicilian affairs as it could be. As for clericalism, she believed that the Church had no business meddling in politics.

'Here, have this.' Don Nofriu took a small ceramic figure from the bag he'd left by his feet. 'It's the emblem of Sicily.'

Lucia stared at the turquoise sculpture. Three human legs had been arranged around the head of a medusa in a shape that reminded her of a swastika. She found it both beautiful and repulsive at the same time.

'Thank you,' she said, taking it from the godfather.

Before the men left, they taught Lucia the movement's secret sign.

'It's like the British V for victory, but with three fingers extended instead of two,' Gaetano said.

'To represent the three joined legs?' Lucia asked.

'*Esattamente.*' Gaetano smiled. 'We'll reconvene here next month, all going according to plan.'

'I'll look forward to it.' Lucia returned his smile.

'I'm proud of you, *tisoru*,' Gero said as he helped Lucia clear the dishes – something neither her father nor her brother had ever done at home. 'You cooked us a delicious meal and held your own with don Nofriu. But be careful of that man. He's only a

Separatist for one reason, and that is because he thinks it will benefit him.'

'Thanks for the warning, Gero,' she said, keeping to herself that she didn't need cautioning. She'd been wary of the godfather for years.

'You can never be too careful with the Friends of the Friends,' Gero said. 'For the last hundred years, like thousands of spiders, they've spun a gigantic web over all of life in Sicily. Don Nofriu now stands in the centre of that web.'

'I'll take care,' she said. 'Cosa Nostra sickens me too much to do otherwise.'

'Brava.' Good girl.

Gero went to his briefcase, which he'd left by their bedroom door. He withdrew a sheaf of documents.

'These are the deeds to the baglio. Before I return to the city, I'd like your signature on them.'

'Of course, but why?' Lucia ran a hand through her hair.

'I want to transfer the property to you.' He handed her the papers and a pen. 'The Palermo office looks as if it will only run on a skeleton staff once the transition to the local authority is complete. I could be sent to the mainland, and I'd like to leave you with some security.'

'You're so good to me, Gero. I don't deserve you.' Sudden tears welled up in her eyes.

'Don't cry, sweetheart.' He brushed her tears away and kissed her on the nose. 'You're worth everything I can do for you, and more.'

'Thank you,' she said, sniffing back a sob.

'Sign and then we'll get ready for bed.' He lifted her wrist, kissed it.

She did as he asked, and he put the documents back in his bag.

'I'll get it all notarised when I'm back in Palermo, *tisoru*. Now, let's go to bed.'

* * *

In their room, they undressed quickly in the cold night air. Lucia placed the three-legged ceramic figure on her bedside table, got into bed, and turned to face Gero. She trailed her fingers down his cheek to his lips.

He kissed her palm and pressed his body against hers. She felt his desire and, for the first time, returned the gesture, pressing herself into him and relishing the look of longing in his eyes. She loved him, she realised. He'd come to mean everything to her.

'I want you to make love to me, Gero,' she said. 'I'm ready now.'

'Are you sure, *amuri*?' He sounded surprised.

'I've never been surer of anything.'

Then his lips were on hers, and she opened her mouth to him before he kissed his way down her body until he arrived at her most intimate part. He pressed kisses there, ran his tongue over her nightdress, creating a hot wetness that sent tingles to her core.

'Oh, Gero,' Lucia sighed.

'You're so beautiful, *bedda*.' He lifted off her nightgown and gazed at her, his dark eyes glowing. 'I love you so much.'

She luxuriated in his gaze. 'I love you too, Gero. *Ti vogghiu beni.*'

'I've waited so long to hear you say that, Lucia,' he said.

He took off his pyjamas and held her in his arms, skin against skin, kissing her passionately. Lucia moaned, losing herself to the pleasure as his mouth explored her breasts. She couldn't think of anything but him. Her one and only love. Her thighs fell open for him, and he covered her with his magnificent body.

She threaded her fingers into his thick dark hair, and he kissed her, his tongue caressing hers with such love it brought a lump to her throat. At the moment he rocked into her, he was so gentle she barely felt any pain. Exquisite sensation filled her body.

Afterwards, Gero stroked her hair and held her tight. He looked deep into her eyes, repeated how much he loved her, and she told him again that she loved him in return. Gero completed her, she realised. A much brighter future beckoned with him by her side.

He fell asleep within minutes. But Lucia lay awake, gazing at the three-legged figurine. In the morning, she would beg Gero not to report on the Separatists to his superiors. He was Sicilian by heritage, and his loyalty should be with Sicily, like hers. Then, closing her eyes, she said her prayers in her head, praying for Dinu's safety like she always did before dropping off.

22

LUCIA, FEBRUARY 1944

It was late in the evening, well past suppertime, and Lucia was waiting for Gero to arrive. Three weeks had gone by since she had seen him and she'd found herself longing for him every minute of every day. Finally, the rumble of a car engine sounded. Her heart racing, she ran to open the heavy wooden entrance door.

'Lucia, *amuri*.' Gero's deep voice made her heart flutter. He put down his bag and enveloped her in his arms. 'I've missed you so much,' he said before lifting her chin up and kissing her.

She breathed in his wonderful, clean scent and told him she loved him. '*Ti vogghiu beni*, Gero.'

They kissed again, and their heads switched sides, tongues dancing, lips sliding. The heat of passion crackled between them as Gero smoothed his hands into the swell of her hips, drawing her closer. Lucia pressed herself against his hardness, yearning for him. He gripped her tighter and their kisses became frantic. But then, without warning, he stopped.

'We need to talk, *tisoru*,' he said with a regretful groan.

'What about?' A niggle of concern tightened in her chest. She could guess what was coming. It had been on the cards for weeks.

He picked up his bag and led her into the kitchen, where she poured them both a glass of wine. She sat next to him and Gero took her hand, planting a kiss on the inside of her wrist.

'Sicily is about to be fully restored to Italian administration,' he said.

'But you'll stay in Palermo to supervise, won't you?' Lucia gave voice to the forlorn hope.

'Charles Rinelli has ordered me to go to Naples with him.' Gero shook his head.

'I don't want you to go,' she said, dread gripping her. 'The *napolitani* are terrible people. The city is full of disease.'

'Don't worry, my love.' Gero appeared to be choosing his words carefully. 'I won't take any risks. I'll be fine.'

'Please, promise you'll be careful.' Hot tears wet her cheeks.

'I'll be careful. I promise,' he said, kissing her tears away.

Lucia lifted his sweater, ran her hands up his strong stomach. She lowered her head and kissed his chest, the muscles hard against the softness of her lips.

'Don't get killed,' she whispered against his warm skin.

Looking up at him, she felt her heart fill with absolute unconditional love. This man. This incredible man. No longer the person she didn't know if she could love, but her adored husband.

'Make love to me, Gero,' she said.

* * *

They made love until the early hours before falling into a deep sleep. In the morning, they made love again before Gero got the tin bathtub out of storage and Lucia heated water on the stove. They took it in turns to climb into the tub, soaping each other and laughing like two little kids.

After they'd dressed, they had breakfast – ersatz coffee and the bread Lucia had baked the day before, warmed up in the oven, then smothered with fig jam. When they'd finished eating, Gero pulled a sheaf of papers from his bag.

'These are the notarised deeds to the baglio, *amuri*. I'll leave them with you when I set off.'

He'd told her last night, as they'd lain in each other's arms after lovemaking, that he'd stay with her for a week before heading to Palermo, where he'd board a ship that would take him to Naples.

'*Grazie*.' Lucia took the documents from him. 'I wish you didn't have to go—'

'I'll be back as soon as I can get some leave, sweetheart,' he promised.

They talked about the war – about how the Germans were fighting doggedly in terrain crossed by rivers and mountains well suited for defence. Italy's cold winter had exhausted the Allies, Gero said. Highly mechanised forces such as the US Fifth and British Eighth Armies found that vehicles were often more of a hindrance than a help. Rain frequently suspended what little mobility they had.

'Have you any idea when they'll capture Rome?' Lucia asked.

'Hopefully soon. Problem is, they've encountered fierce resistance at Monte Cassino.'

'Where's that?' Lucia's knowledge of Italian geography was sketchy at best.

'Halfway between Naples and the capital.'

Lucia's heart sank at the thought of him going so near to the front line. Thankfully, he wasn't a combatant, but an occupied city like Naples undoubtedly would be extremely dangerous for the occupiers…

The chime of the bell by the kitchen door broke into her thoughts.

'Someone has come to visit.' Lucia got to her feet. 'I wonder who it can be—'

Gero went to check while she took their dishes to the sink. He was back within minutes, his face wreathed in smiles.

'Look who's here!' he said, Lucia's father in tow.

'*Bon jornu.*' Pa wished her good morning. 'I have a message for you both from don Nofriu.' He dug into his pocket and extracted a piece of paper.

Gero took it from him and read the words out loud.

Dinu and Francu will come to a meeting at your place tomorrow evening, under cover of darkness. I will be there, along with Gaetano Sacca. There's no need to prepare a meal.

'It appears we've been issued with a command.' Lucia glanced at Gero. 'Hope that's all right with you—'

'More Separatist monkey business, I expect. Not sure you should get involved with that, Lucia.'

'It will give me something to keep me busy while you're away. What harm can it do?'

'I'm concerned that Dinu and Francu have been invited.' Gero wrinkled his brow. 'What on earth could don Nofriu and Gaetano Sacca want with them?'

'We'll find out tomorrow, no doubt,' Lucia said, touching her hand to his arm.

'Perhaps I should also be there?' Her father edged forwards. 'So I can keep an eye on things when you're away, young man.'

'That's an excellent idea,' Gero said.

* * *

The following evening, Lucia waited impatiently for her brother to arrive. It had been a couple of months since she'd seen him – not since Christmas Eve, in fact. She'd asked her father to send a message to him and Francu that they were to arrive early and have supper with her and Gero before the meeting with don Nofriu and Gaetano Sacca.

When Dinu stepped into the courtyard, Francu at his heels, Lucia stood back to look her brother up and down.

'You seem well, *frati*,' she said. 'The mountain air has done you good.'

'It's damn freezing up there at the moment.' Dinu flinched away as she went to kiss him. 'I envy you your cosy baglio.'

'Come inside, everyone,' she said, leading them into her warm kitchen, where Gero was already uncorking a bottle of red wine.

Drinks were poured, and Lucia went to take the *pasta 'ncasciata* she'd made earlier out of the oven – baked maccheroni prepared with meat sauce, hard-boiled eggs, aubergines and caciocavallo cheese. She carried the dish to the table and told everyone to help themselves. They ate hungrily, smacking their lips and complimenting her.

'I haven't had delicious food like this since I left home,' Francu said, rubbing his stomach.

'I'm glad you enjoyed it, cousin. Tell us how Dinu succeeded in springing you from the prison after you were captured at Christmas,' Lucia said.

She kept her gaze on her brother while Francu recounted the tale. There was something in Dinu's expression that unsettled her, a tightness around his mouth, his wide, darting eyes.

'Maybe you shouldn't brag about such things in front of me.' Gero made a tutting sound.

'Lighten up, Major.' Dinu smirked. 'Remember, I'm here to meet don Nofriu and Gaetano Sacca. I'm hoping they'll wangle a pardon for me.'

'I hope they do, son,' Pa said.

They carried on eating and, at the end of the meal, Lucia served *sfinci*, deep-fried pastry balls dipped in sugar with nuggets of raisins inside. She'd only just cleared the dishes when the doorbell chimed and Gero went to answer it. Within minutes, he was back with don Nofriu and Gaetano Sacca.

After the godfather had introduced Gaetano to Pa, Dinu and Francu, Gero placed a bottle of grappa on the table, and Lucia went to get clean glasses, which she handed around.

'We know you have a band of followers up in the mountains, Dinu,' Gaetano Sacca said without preamble. 'We'd like you and Francu to help strengthen our striking force by recruiting more men and collecting arms.'

'For what purpose?' Dinu asked, furrowing his brow.

'To set up a western wing of the Separatist army under your command,' Gaetano responded.

'Also to subdue the communist menace,' don Nofriu chipped in. 'And you'll be licensed to carry out guerrilla warfare against the carabinieri.'

Lucia glanced at Gero and took in his startled expression. She shook her head at him. He wasn't involved in Sicilian affairs any more. The Allies had handed over control to the local authorities, and that meant don Nofriu here in Villaurora.

'What's in it for Francu and me?' Dinu came right out with the question.

'We'll give you money for the purpose, and you'll be formally invested as colonel,' Gaetano said, smiling.

'Hold on a minute,' don Nofriu said. 'Didn't we agree Dinu would raise the funds by kidnapping and ransom?'

'I'm no bandit,' Dinu said scornfully.

'My son is not a murderer either,' Pa said, bristling.

'Indeed,' the capo said. 'But as colonel of the western Separatist army, if you kill anyone, Dinu, it won't be considered murder but an act of war.'

'And my pardon for killing that carabiniere last September?'

'Leave it with me,' don Nofriu said.

* * *

After the party had broken up, and their guests had gone back to where they'd come from, Gero helped Lucia clear the table and then they both went to get ready for bed.

Gero went to fetch a bed warming pan from the kitchen. When he'd filled it with hot ashes from the stove, he came into the bedroom and pushed it under the bedclothes, grasping the handle and moving it up and down to get rid of the cold and damp.

Lucia had already put her nightdress on. She got into bed and waited for Gero to join her. He'd want to talk about the events of the evening, no doubt. She steeled herself to listen to his disapproval of don Nofriu's offer to Dinu, and didn't have to wait long.

'I wish Charles Rinelli had never ordered me to appoint

that mafioso as mayor of Villaurora,' Gero said, wrapping his arms around Lucia and holding her close.

'But didn't you say there was no alternative?' Lucia was sure she'd heard Gero tell her so a while ago.

'I did, Lucia. Unfortunately, the only other person available would have been the fascist who'd held the post before him. But I fear the Allies haven't done Sicily any favours by giving people like don Nofriu positions of power.'

'We've been ravaged by Rome and the *fascisti*,' Lucia said, snuggling into the warmth of Gero's chest. 'At least the men of honour are Sicilians—'

'You've become a true *siciliana*, Lucia.' Gero kissed her on the forehead.

'I think of myself as more Sicilian than American these days,' she said. 'But I'd still like to go back and live in New York.' She kept to herself the hope that Dinu would also move with her, and resolved to ask for Gero's support when the time was right.

'I can't wait to take you there.' He stroked her shoulders. 'I'd like to expand my father's film importing business. Maybe you'd like a job with us?'

'I'd love that.' A bubble of happiness formed in Lucia's chest. 'But I'd also like to start a family with you, if that's what you want too—'

'Oh, wow, Lucia. You've made me the happiest man alive. Maybe we should get started on that wish of yours right away?'

'Are you saying what I think you are saying?' She giggled.

'I am.' He moved his hands down her body, and need sparked between them. He kissed her mouth, her breasts and further down. Soon she was begging him for more, and when he took her, the waves of pleasure built and built until she was climaxing and calling out his name.

Later, they lay in each other's arms, kissing and whispering, '*Ti vogghiu beni*,' until their breathing slowed and they fell asleep.

'I've had an idea,' Gero said after kissing Lucia awake in the morning. He pointed towards the ceramic emblem of Sicily on her bedside table. 'Why don't I get some cement and set this into the wall of the baglio? Every time you look at it while I'm away, you can think of me.'

'You'd do that even though you don't approve of the Separatists, my love?' Delight gripped her.

'If you want to be a part of that movement, then I won't try and stop you.' He grinned. 'It wouldn't do any good anyway. I can see you've got your heart set on it.'

'I'd give it up in an instant for you, Gero,' she said, taking his hand and kissing it.

'There's no need. Even though I despise that man, don Nofriu won't let anything bad happen to you, my darling. He considers you family now.'

'I'm not sure if that's a good thing or not. He's taken Dinu under his wing, it seems. My brother has wanted to be part of the godfather's circle ever since we came to Villaurora.'

'Let's hope his wish doesn't lead to his downfall.' Gero sighed.

'By getting involved with the Separatists, Dinu might well become a respected member of society. Another reason for me to be part of the movement, so I can encourage him.'

'Good idea, now you mention it.' Gero smiled. 'You've always looked out for him and I won't try to persuade you otherwise.'

Lucia took a deep breath as she thought about how cold Dinu had been towards her when he'd arrived last night and had flinched away from her kiss. Sadness blurred her vision and her heart ached. Her beloved twin had changed, no doubt about that; his lawlessness had turned him into a different person.

23

DINU, MARCH 1944

A feeling of being able to conquer the world spread through Dinu as he perched on a boulder, cleaning his pistol outside the largest of the caves where he was living with his band of men. He smiled with satisfaction – he'd recruited several new members and also increased the group's stash of weapons by stealing them from people who were hoarding them for sale.

His satisfaction quickly turned to dissatisfaction, though, when he remembered there was still the thorn in his side of the lack of a pardon. Don Nofriu had yet to deliver on his promise and Dinu had decided the time had come to talk to him.

He, Dinu Pavano, was a force to be reckoned with nowadays. No one dared mess with him, of that he was sure. He pulled in a deep breath, remembering how last month he'd gone down to Villaurora after dark to visit his family – even though he'd discovered that Cardona, realising the need for a better information service, had employed several petty spies in the village.

As Dinu approached his family home, he'd seen a gangly young man who was hanging around in the street outside.

When he'd slammed the door open to leave, he'd found the fellow lurking behind it. The youth said he'd seen him come down from the mountains and had stood guard for him. The young man's story didn't ring true, but Dinu gave him the benefit of the doubt, cuffed him savagely and told him not to do it again. A few days later, though, Dinu caught him at it for the second time. He grabbed the youth by the scruff of the neck and marched him to a dark alleyway, where he told him to say his prayers before shooting him.

Did he feel any remorse for his actions? Sicily was a land where men killed each other for lesser crimes. The young man was a spy, a godforsaken traitor who'd broken the code, and Dinu had made him pay for it. The sharp heat of anger had inflamed his gut, and his pulse had pounded in his ears. He'd planted his legs wide, every muscle in his body tensing as the youth had bled out on the cobblestones. Coldness seeping through him, he'd then turned on his heel and had left the corpse to be finished off by the rats.

Movement caught his eye now, and he spotted Francu approaching up the stony path.

'I'm setting off to see the boss,' Dinu said, getting down from his boulder.

'I'll take care of things while you're gone.' Francu grinned, his pencil-thin moustache curling above his lips.

'Of that I have no doubt, *kuxinu*.'

As he sauntered down the stony track, Dinu thought about Francu. They were equals as far as both of them were concerned. Dinu had been made a colonel in the Separatists' army and Francu a major, but it didn't matter to either that one outranked the other – they shared decision making like they'd always done.

Once he'd arrived in the village, Dinu paid a quick visit to

Ma, Pa and Annita, then headed for the godfather's house. He paused at the iron gate and rang the bell. One of don Nofriu's *picciotti* opened the door to him and took him through to the capo's living room.

The boss was sitting in an armchair, listening to the radio, his habitual cigar in his mouth. Dinu advanced across the marble floor and bowed before him. He kissed his hand, the traditional Sicilian greeting to a man of higher rank. Don Nofriu indicated towards the seat opposite and told Dinu to sit. He did as requested, eyeing the godfather cautiously.

'I expect you've come to ask about your pardon.' Don Nofriu leant forwards to tap ash into an ashtray before fixing Dinu with a calculating look. 'It will take time, but don't worry. As soon as the war is over and we have a Separatist government in Palermo, I'm sure I can come to an understanding with whoever will be the Minister of Justice.'

'I was hoping that it could be achieved sooner,' Dinu said, narrowing his eyes.

'Be patient, young man.' Don Nofriu paused for a long moment, as if considering what to say next. 'In the meantime, I'd like you to join my family officially under my protection. You can't live in the mountains forever—'

'You do me a great honour,' Dinu said, jerking his head back in surprise.

'I only have female children. No son to inherit the business side of things. You've impressed me with your resilience. If you prove yourself while working for me, you could reach the summit of my organisation in due course. One day, you might even become my right-hand man.'

'Thank you, but what about my cousin, Francu Bagghieri?'

'The youth with the slicked-back hair? What of him?'

'We're partners,' Dinu said. 'We do everything together.'

'He'll need to show he's worthy.' Don Nofriu tapped his chin.

'Francu will do that, I'm sure.'

'Which brings me to a matter of great importance.' Don Nofriu sucked on his cigar and puffed out smoke. 'Communist agitators have invited the regional secretary of their party, Giro-lamo Li Causi, to hold a rally in the village next Saturday. The authorities recently released him from prison where he was serving a twenty-one-year sentence for being anti-fascist. The communists sent emissaries to ask my permission, "*Ccù trasi addimanna permessu.*"'

'What did you say?' Dinu glanced at the godfather.

'I accepted their request, but only on the condition they keep silent about the topic of agrarian reform, the division of the big estates.'

'Why are you telling me all this?'

Don Nofriu owned twelve thousand acres of land around Villaurora that he'd want to protect at any cost, Dinu knew, but he had no clue what the boss wanted of him.

'If we let the communists control Italy after the war, what will happen to the Church? What will happen to our strong family foundations?'

'I'm hoping we'll be independent of Rome by then,' Dinu said.

'There's still the danger of a left-wing government. If the leftist parties win the elections, the day might come when there are Russians in the villages of Sicily.'

'Russians? Why Russians?'

'If the communists run this country, we'll become an ally of Russia. They'd make children go to schools that would teach them that the state comes before God and their own mothers and fathers.'

'I don't understand what you want of me, don Nofriu.' Dinu scratched his head.

'I don't trust those bastards.' The godfather shifted his bulky body in his armchair. 'I agreed they could organise their damned rally on one condition. That they don't mention land reform. I intend to hold them to that promise. If they so much as say one word against me, I'll need you and your men to teach them a lesson.'

'What kind of lesson?' Dinu cocked his head to one side.

'Something to scare them. Remind them who's in charge. I'm sure you can think of an appropriate action.'

Dinu hated the communists' preaching against the Church and their scoffing at the Sicilian institution of the family. But he also guessed don Nofriu cared not a fig for such things. He was more concerned about keeping his land and remaining in control. A left-wing government would be serious about reforms, and would almost certainly try to get rid of the Friends of the Friends.

Smirking to himself, Dinu nodded. He, too, wanted power. Hadn't the boss promised he could eventually work his way up in the organisation and become his right-hand man? To Dinu's way of thinking, a job with don Nofriu would be far more profitable than his position in the Separatist army.

'Leave it with me, capo,' he said.

* * *

The following Saturday evening, their faces hidden by balaclavas, Dinu waited with Francu and four of their men in a lorry parked in the middle of the village square, keeping guard as arranged.

Alberto Spina, the schoolteacher, had organised a podium

for the speakers in front of the local branch of the Banco di Sicilia. Don Nofriu sat some twenty metres to the right of it with his *picciotti*.

A truck pulling an enormous wagon rumbled into the piazza. It came to a halt and about forty communists and socialists from Caltanissetta got out.

Dinu touched the pistol at his waist, relieved that the villagers themselves were hanging back. Strangely, not one carabiniere was present.

The crowd burst into applause as Alberto Spina mounted the stage and welcomed Li Causi to Villaurora. The communist spoke on abstract topics concerning work in the fields and being taken advantage of by large landowners. Then he hurled a bolt of lightning into the proceedings, and said, '...like, for example, the exploitation carried out by don Nofriu Vaccaru's fiefdom.'

Dinu gasped. Li Causi had hit the boss's nerve point.

'*Non e' vero!*' The capo yelled it wasn't true. '*E' falso!*'

Dinu jumped out of the lorry and fired his pistol into the air. Francu and the others followed and began shooting, raining down bullets on all and sundry.

Pandemonium ensued. People were screaming, and a small stampede started among the villagers, who'd been hanging around at the edge of the scene.

Dinu took a grenade from his pocket, pulled the pin, and hurled it into the crowd of communists.

Li Causi crumpled to the floor of the podium, clutching his leg. Others fell to the ground, soaked in blood, writhing in pain.

'Let's go,' Dinu commanded. Within minutes, he and his cohort were on the outskirts of Villaurora, then heading back up to the caves.

Once again, Dinu felt no remorse for his actions. He'd steeled himself, carried out what was necessary. He'd done the godfather's bidding and Francu had also proved himself up to the task. From now onwards, they would be don Nofriu's men, and, in time, they too would have positions of power as great, if not greater, than their capo.

24

LUCIA, MARCH 1944

When Pa arrived the next day, Lucia discovered that fourteen people had been injured by bullets or shrapnel from the grenade.

'At least no one died,' he said, stirring black-market sugar into the cup of ersatz coffee Lucia had brewed for him.

'Thank God for that.' Lucia shivered, sadness seeping through her. 'Dinu had no business shooting at innocent people.' Next time she saw him, she'd reprimand him for sure.

'Don Nofriu put him up to it, I fear.' Pa sighed heavily. 'He told me on his way back to the mountains after going to see the capo about his pardon. But we can't say or do anything because of the *omertà* code of silence. I said as much to your mother. We have to act as if nothing has happened.'

'It's a good thing Dinu was in disguise,' Lucia said. 'How will I tell Gero?'

'Chances are he won't have found out.'

Lucia had only received one letter from Gero in the six weeks since he'd left. It had been routed via Algiers and had taken an age to arrive. She hoped he would get some leave soon; she missed him with an ache that cut deep into her heart.

The Separatist army uniforms on the kitchen table captured her attention. Loose tunics, yellow on one side and red on the other, the colours of Sicily. She'd been tasked with sewing the three-legged emblem onto each breast. Annita and Ma had also become seamstresses for the movement, and they'd done a fine job. Would Dinu ever get to wear one of the uniforms? By throwing in his lot with the godfather, could he have jeopardised his position as colonel? But perhaps he would fight for Cosa Nostra and the Separatists at the same time? After all, both organisations were in cahoots...

Pa took his leave of Lucia, and she got on with her spring cleaning. It would be Easter soon, and tradition called for her to thoroughly wash the household linen, scrub the red-brick floors even more vigorously than usual, and polish the walnut furniture with beeswax. Since their wedding, Gero had added to their collection, and had bought a dining-room table with a sideboard, as well as a cabinet in which he'd placed porcelain crockery and glassware.

He truly was the most generous of husbands, and Lucia couldn't love him more.

* * *

The next morning, Lucia woke with the sparrows. She listened to them chirping, stretched lazily, then drew back the blankets. Sudden nausea gripped her, and she barely made it to the chamber pot in time to vomit. Her skin felt cold and clammy. Had she eaten something that had disagreed with her?

The sickness soon passed, and Lucia got on with her day. She was hoping for a letter from Gero, but none arrived.

Evening came, and she'd been on her own in the baglio the entire time.

I can't carry on like this, she thought. *I need to work in the fields as there's no one else to do it.* In Sicily, women didn't labour on the land, but Lucia couldn't care less. The baglio was hers, and she wanted it to be as productive as possible. No one knew how long it would be before the war ended, and she planned to sell her produce at honest prices.

The following morning, she sat at the table, a cup of coffee in front of her. She breathed in the rich aroma and, once more, nausea swelled up from her stomach. Her feet skidded on the wet earth outside as she ran to the privy to be sick.

Back in the kitchen, she took the calendar off the wall and did some rough sums in her head. She hadn't had her monthlies since December. Could she be pregnant?

She touched her hands to her belly and tried to imagine a tiny life growing inside. But the idea seemed too good to be true. Much as she'd love to have a baby with Gero, for them to become a family, her bleeding could be delayed for a different reason. She'd never been regular.

But neither had she been this late before.

After the nausea had subsided, she went outside to work on the land. She resolved to concentrate on the fields nearest the baglio, which were just about manageable, so she spent the rest of the morning hoeing out weeds from the ground where she planned to plant tomatoes and beans.

It was a mild spring day, and the landscape was awash with green. Lucia loved this time of the year when the countryside was carpeted in bright orange, lilac, yellow and crimson wildflowers, and the almond trees had burst into beautiful white and light pink blooms.

She ate a bowl of spaghetti with pesto sauce for her lunch,

then tiredness overwhelmed her and she went to take a nap. On waking, she felt lonely for company and set off for the village to visit her mother and sister.

A chilly wind had sprung up as Lucia made her way along the winding track to Villaurora. She hugged her coat around her and soon she'd arrived at her old front door.

Ma enveloped her in a warm hug, kissing her loudly on both cheeks, and Annita joined in before going to make coffee for them all.

Lucia sat at the rectangular wooden table. She lamented with Ma about Dinu getting involved with Cosa Nostra, but they both agreed there was nothing to be done.

'He'll find his own way in life,' Ma said, sighing.

Lucia lifted her coffee to her lips, but nausea washed through her and she put the cup down.

'You've gone pale,' Ma said, patting her hand.

'The smell makes me feel sick.'

'Is this what I think it is?' Ma's face broke into a smile.

'I'm not sure.' Lucia shook her head. 'I mean, I'm late, but there could be another explanation.'

'Lateness coupled with nausea?' Ma chuckled. 'I don't think so. You're pregnant, my girl. And about time.'

Lucia's cheeks grew hot. She'd never shared with her mother about her reluctance to consummate her marriage until she was certain that she loved Gero.

'I can't believe I'm going to be an aunt.' Annita leant across the table and gave Lucia a hug.

'And I'll be a nonna.' Ma's voice bubbled with delight. 'You've made me so happy, my dear.'

Joyful tears filled Lucia's eyes as she finally allowed herself to accept she was having a baby.

'What's it like giving birth?' she asked her mother. It was a question she'd kept to herself until now.

'You and your brother were pulled from my body on our kitchen table by a midwife, Lucia.'

'Why the kitchen table?' she asked, wide-eyed.

'To prevent the bed from getting soiled.'

'Did it hurt?' Lucia leant forwards.

'You were both big babies, so the midwife had a difficult time as my pelvis was so small. I thought you were going to kill me.'

'Is that why you waited five years before having Annita?' Lucia asked.

'I forgot the pain once you and Dinu were in my arms. We decided to have more children almost immediately. But the good Lord saw fit to make your pa and me wait for Annita.' A shadow crossed Ma's face. 'And afterwards I became barren—'

'I'd thought it was because you just wanted to limit the number of kids you had,' Annita said.

'In New York, that wouldn't have been frowned upon. But here in Sicily, the size of a man's family is a matter of pride. People criticise his virility every year that he does not produce another child. I feel so sorry for your pa.'

'Pa thinks the world of you, anyone can see that.' Lucia wrapped her arms around her mother. 'Don't feel sorry for him.'

Lucia spent the rest of the afternoon and early evening with her mother and sister, then made her way back to the baglio before darkness fell.

The next morning, she suffered from nausea again and was just about to head down to the village to visit the doctor and get her pregnancy confirmed when the sound of a motorcar engine alerted her that someone was coming up the road.

Could it be Gero, about to surprise her? She hastily checked her appearance in the mirror on the wall of their sitting room, then rushed into the courtyard.

The bell was ringing, so it couldn't be Gero. Lucia swung open the big rustic door and took a step back in shock when she saw Gaetano Sacca standing there. She offered her hand in greeting and wished him good morning. It would be impolite to ask why he was visiting, but she expected it had something to do with the Separatists.

'*Buon giorno*, Lucia.' Gaetano Sacca bowed over her hand and kissed the air above it. 'I'm afraid I have bad news. Is there somewhere we can sit?'

Her stomach grew heavy with dread. Something must have happened to Dinu. She led Gaetano into her living room and indicated towards the armchair while she sat herself on the sofa.

'I received a phone call from Palermo this morning, relaying a message from Charles Rinelli.' Gaetano made direct eye contact with Lucia. 'There's no easy way to tell you this, Lucia, but Gero was killed last week in a Luftwaffe bombardment. I'm so sorry, my dear.'

The blood drained from her face and she shook her head in disbelief as coldness gripped her, squeezing her heart in its icy grasp. Her entire body started to shake.

'It can't be true. Not my Gero—' She clung to the words like a lifeline.

'He was among over three hundred people who lost their lives. There wasn't time for an air-raid warning and they were caught out in the open.'

The room swam around Lucia. She closed her eyes and

willed herself not to faint. A sob welled up from deep inside her, and she emitted a cry that sounded like a wounded animal.

'I should have brought a member of your family with me.' Gaetano leapt off the chair and sat next to her. 'Can I take you down to the village?' He held her hand.

'No, thank you, but I think I'd like to be alone,' she said, her voice choking.

'Are you sure? I mean, I could fetch your mother and bring her back here, if you like—'

'If that's not too much trouble—' She took a shaky breath.

'No trouble at all.' Gaetano got to his feet. 'I'll see myself out.'

When the rumble of the car engine had subsided, Lucia headed for the bedroom. There, she buried her face in Gero's pillow and inhaled the vestiges of his scent. How could he be dead? Not Gero. He'd been so full of life, so charming and so generous. Why had fate dealt him such a blow? It wasn't fair. He'd only been in his early twenties. Far too young to die.

She cradled her abdomen. How cruel that Gero had never known she was expecting their baby. She hugged the pillow and wept until she had no tears left.

Later, she wandered around the baglio, thinking about Gero and remembering the happy times they'd spent together. The kitchen spoke of meals shared and laughter. The sitting room of cosy evenings by the fire. The dining room of entertaining visitors. How was it possible that Gero would never set foot in the baglio ever again?

She made her way over to the ceramic figure he'd cemented into the wall by the entrance door and ran her fingers over the cool turquoise ceramic. Gero had put it there for her and every time she looked at it, she'd be reminded of him. A sudden thought occurred to her. Had he suspected what the future held when he'd signed the baglio over to her? Surely not – he was just being pragmatic, wasn't he?

The distant sound of a car engine alerted her to Gaetano returning with her mother. She swallowed rapidly to dispel the thick ache in her throat. A feeling of numbness had come over her. But when Ma stepped into the courtyard and opened her arms, it was as if a dam had burst. Lucia ran to her and sobbed her heartbreak into Ma's comforting chest.

'I'll leave you to it, then,' Gaetano said, shuffling his feet.

Ma thanked him, then put her arm around Lucia and led her back indoors. She sat her down at the kitchen table and took her hand.

'You must be strong for your baby, daughter,' she said. 'Thank God the baglio is in your name.'

'I would like you, Pa and Annita to move in here. Also Dinu when he's been pardoned.' The idea had just come to Lucia. 'It's what Gero would have wanted, I'm sure.'

25

JESSICA, JULY 2005

Late in the afternoon, the day after Piero took his children back to Palermo, Jess found herself showing him the strange ceramic figurine inserted into the wall at the baglio.

'It's the trinacria symbol of Sicily,' he said.

'I feel a little stupid for not knowing that.' A flush of embarrassment warmed her cheeks.

'How could you possibly know? I don't suppose you've ever seen a Sicilian flag—'

'I didn't realise there was one.'

'It's red and yellow, bisected diagonally,' Piero said. 'Sicily adopted its first official flag in the nineties, but there was a coat of arms at the centre. The current flag, implemented five years ago, has a trinacria. Today's flag was originally used by the Sicilian Separatists.'

'How amazing,' Jess said, intrigued. 'But why the trinacria?'

'The three legs in the symbol represent the three extremities of the island. The head of the woman in the middle is the ancient Sicilian goddess of fertility, Hybla. As you know, Sicilia is an extremely fertile island.'

'I wonder why my grandmother placed it here.' Jess smoothed her fingers over the cool ceramic.

'There was a powerful Separatist movement in this area back in 1944.'

'Could Lucia have been involved?' Jess tilted her head towards Piero.

'Even my father was involved.'

'Gosh! He must have been very young then.'

'He's eighty-three now, but doesn't look it. People tend to live well into their nineties in Sicily.'

'The famous Mediterranean diet?'

'I expect so. But it could well be merely a matter of having the right genes.'

'Probably.' Jess smiled. 'Thanks for telling me all about the trinacria and the Separatists. There's so much I still have to learn about Sicily.'

'It's early days, Jess. Why don't you show me the rest of the baglio?'

'Come with me,' she said.

Later, after she'd given him a tour of the rooms and shared her ideas about adding an extra floor on one side of the building, Jess suggested they went for a walk.

Piero agreed and turned to head through the entrance door at the same time as she did, bumping into her, dislodging her sunglasses, and almost knocking her to the ground.

'I'm so sorry,' he said, gently taking hold of her shoulders.

'It's okay. No harm done.'

Their eyes locked, and Jess's heartbeat echoed in her ears. She took a step backwards, and Piero did likewise.

'You go first,' he said, waving his hand.

Jess pulled her sunglasses down on her nose and went outside.

You're such an idiot, she told herself.

But she couldn't help the fluttery feeling in her chest. Pressing her lips together, she led Piero around to the back of the house, where they came across Angelo watering the vegetables with a long irrigation hose.

'The water is pumped from a well,' Angelo explained as the two men eyed each other up. 'So it doesn't cost us anything. Giovanna and I have been paying for the electricity—'

'How about the property taxes?' Piero asked.

'They're taken care of by the lawyer in Palermo.'

Jess should have asked those questions herself, she realised. She was feeling more than a little out of her depth, and said as much to Piero as they headed back to his car.

'It's not surprising.' He opened the door for her. 'You're new to this country, and it's a complicated place even for us Sicilians.'

It was on the tip of her tongue to say she should let Angelo and Giovanna inherit instead, but an image of Motorbike Man came into her mind. She wouldn't allow him to defeat her. Instead, she told Piero about him.

'No wonder you're feeling daunted.' Piero took the road past Villaurora. 'What a horrible experience.'

'I won't let him put me off. I mean, what can he do?'

'Hmmm. I hate to remind you, but this is Sicily, not England—'

'You're thinking of Cosa Nostra?' Jess felt her blood freeze.

'Precisely.' Piero shifted gear and the engine purred. 'Perhaps it would be best if you didn't go to the baglio on your own for the time being?'

'You're joking, aren't you?' She laughed.

'No, Jess, I'm not.'

'Should I tell the police about what happened?'

It was Piero's turn to laugh.

'The local carabinieri won't interfere with the Friends of the Friends. Only the anti-Mafia police in Palermo would do that.'

'You're frightening me, Piero.'

'I didn't intend to. Let's hope your Motorbike Man is simply a trail bike rider, not wanting you to spoil his fun.'

'Sounds like a logical explanation,' Jess said. 'I mean, why would the Mafia want to scare me off my inheritance?'

'Why, indeed?' Piero glanced at her and raised an eyebrow.

'I wish I knew more about my grandmother's life here,' Jess said. 'Her surname was Bonanno. I'm thinking of asking around the village if anyone knows a family with that name.'

'Why don't you leave it with me? I could ask my father if he knew your grandparents. He supported the Separatists for a short while back in the day. The trinacria on the wall might signify they were also Separatists.'

'Did the Mafia back the organisation?'

'I believe so. It was within their interests to wrest control from Rome.'

'Why did your dad support the Separatists, Piero?'

'He was ardently anti-communist, as were they. In the 1940s, the communists were stirring up the farm workers to revolt against the big landowners. My father saw Separatism as a way of carrying on with the life into which he'd been born. He was wrong, of course. Times were changing and agrarian reform finally took place after the war. Our latifondo was reduced by one half.'

'That must have taken some getting used to.' Jess caught her lip between her teeth. 'Do the Separatists still exist?'

'They do indeed and, just last year, the movement reconstituted itself. They're aiming for complete independence from Italy.'

'Would you like that too?'

'I don't think it would be good for Sicily,' Piero said. 'We have our own regional government, our own flag. Being independent from Italy might make us more vulnerable.'

Jess nodded, and they lapsed into silence while they listened to Piero's eclectic choice of music. When they arrived back at the tenuta, Jess thanked Piero for going to the farmhouse with her.

'I like the baglio a lot,' she said, 'despite all the mystery surrounding it.'

'I agree it has masses of potential. Let me make a couple of phone calls.' He smiled. 'Would you like to have a light meal with me at my place later? We can talk more about it while we eat.'

'Thank you. That would be lovely,' she said.

* * *

After a quick shower, Jess put on a sleeveless white cotton dress, pinned her hair up in a bun, and made her way back to the main building. She found Piero sitting with Cappero under the Judas tree, his phone on the table in front of him.

'There you are,' he said, getting to his feet. 'Supper is waiting for us upstairs.'

She followed him and the dog inside and up a spiral staircase to the first floor.

'Your apartment is lovely,' she said, eyeing a comfortable-looking dark brown leather sofa in front of a fireplace. The floor had been tiled in terracotta, and a bookcase filled with paperbacks held pride of place on the wall opposite the hearth.

'Thanks. I'm very lucky to live here.' Piero smiled. 'Come through to the kitchen. It's time to eat.'

They passed under an archway into the next room, where he pulled out a chair at a round marble-topped table. She lowered herself onto it while Cappero flopped down on the floor. Through the open window, the sky had pinked with a magnificent sunset. Her ears rang with the song of the cicadas, serenading the dusk of the day in the courtyard below.

'A glass of wine?' Piero offered.

'*Grazie,*' Jess said.

He opened the fridge, removed a bottle of *Melita Brut*, the sparkling white wine she'd tasted the week before, and poured them both a glass.

'*Salute!*' he said. 'Good health!'

'*Salute!*' She clinked her glass with his.

'We have a selection of cold dishes. I hope you don't mind, but the weather is too hot for cooking—'

'You cook?' *Is there no end to his talents?*

'I enjoy the creativity of it, when I have time. How about you?'

'I'm a terrible cook,' she admitted. 'Thank God for ready meals.'

'I have to confess that I didn't make what we're about to eat.' He chuckled. 'So you could say this is a ready meal. The dishes were prepared by Maria, the winery's cook.'

'Looks delicious,' Jess said as Piero placed a couscous salad, caponata, and cold cuts on the table.

'I've phoned my builder, and he's available to join us at your baglio tomorrow evening,' Piero said, pouring Jess more wine.

'Thank you, but are you sure you can spare the time?'

'Absolutely. We're not due to harvest the grapes for another couple of weeks. My evenings are my own for the time being.'

'I don't know what I'd do without you,' she said.

'Just glad I can help.' He took a sip of his wine. 'I've also talked to my father. He said he'd like to meet you.'

'Did he know my grandparents?' She held her breath.

'He did indeed,' Piero said. 'I asked him to tell me about them, but he said he'd prefer to speak to you in person.'

'Oh, my God!' She almost fell off her chair. 'I can't believe it—'

'It's a small world, for sure.'

'I'm flabbergasted. This is beyond my wildest dreams.'

'Papà asked me to bring you to the villa in Mondello. My mother will organise lunch for us.'

'I don't want to put your parents to any trouble.'

'My father wouldn't have invited you if it was a problem.'

'Then I happily accept his kind invitation. When are we expected?'

'I told him you're only in Sicily for another week, so he suggested Sunday, the day after tomorrow, if that's all right with you.'

'My stay here has gone by so quickly. I wish I had more time.'

'If you decide to take on the baglio, you'll be back before you know it.'

'Yes, well. It all depends.'

They carried on eating and drinking, talking about different options for renovating the property, and how to get planning permission for a pool.

'I can't manage another mouthful,' Jess said eventually. 'The food was truly delicious, thank you.'

'Cappero and I will walk you back to your accommodation, if you like.' Piero put down his fork.

Outside, the night air was a warm caress to Jess's bare arms. Gravel crunched under her feet and, before too long, they'd arrived at her front door. As she slipped her key into the lock, the dog scurried off and she turned to thank Piero, catching him gazing at her.

Before she could utter a word, he tilted her chin up, his hazel eyes questioning. She nodded, and he touched his mouth to hers. Her heart pounding, she raised herself onto the tips of her toes, kissing him back, looping her arms around his neck as he pulled her against him. She wanted him so badly it hurt, but she had to be sensible, so she pushed against Piero's chest.

'We can't,' she said.

She'd been in danger of letting things go further. Piero was still in love with his ex-wife. If Jess had sex with him, she would open her heart to him, which would only lead to pain. Her breakup with Scott had given her enough heartache to last a lifetime.

Was it disappointment she could see in Piero's expression? Tears of regret welled in her eyes. She turned away before he could see them.

'*Buona notte*, Piero,' she said as she went inside.

Jess half expected him to follow her, and was only slightly relieved when he didn't. Upstairs, she got ready for bed before slipping under the cool sheets. She'd done the right thing, she told herself.

To distract herself from thinking about Piero, she focused on the events of that afternoon. The revelations about her grandparents and the Separatists. The fact that Piero's father had known them. She couldn't wait to meet him and find out more.

26

LUCIA, OCTOBER 1947

Lucia's heart filled with love as she sat by her daughter Carula's bed, while the child took an afternoon nap. It had been the little girl's birthday yesterday – she'd just turned three – and she'd been so over excited from celebrating that she'd barely slept the night before.

A smile warmed Lucia's lips. There was more excitement to come. Gero's parents were arriving at the baglio for a visit, and then they would take her and Carula back to America with them. They'd disembarked in Palermo from a steamship last week and had been staying in a hotel. Tomorrow morning, they'd pay for a taxi to bring them all the way to Villaurora.

Lucia felt her anticipation tinge with sadness and not a little worry. It would be a wrench leaving her family, but it was what Gero would have wanted. And she did as well – of course she wanted a better life for herself and her daughter. There were far more opportunities for them both in New York. And she needed to get away from Villaurora, where don Nofriu ruled the roost and Giulianu Cardona had been sniffing around again, hinting that he'd like to become Lucia's second husband. But, and it was a big 'but', she would be leaving Dinu without her steadying influence. He'd refused point blank to go to New York with her, saying he was doing well enough in Sicily and saw a brilliant future on the island. That this future would be with Cosa Nostra caused Lucia's chest to constrict with concern.

She thought about how life had changed since the war. The Separatists had agitated so much that, last year, Sicily had been granted autonomous region status, with its own Statute, under the new Italian constitution, as well as its own parliament and elected president. Lucia hadn't been part of the movement since Gero's death. But he'd have been so overjoyed to know that, in the elections, women had been given the right to vote for the first time. It was something that he'd maintained should have happened years ago.

Next on the agenda would be agrarian reform to abolish the large feudal agricultural estates and divide them into smaller farms like hers. Lucia was grateful Pa was now farming her land for her – she had plenty to cope with, looking after her child and managing her widowhood.

She missed Gero terribly, and it had been a godsend having her father, Ma and Annita live with her. Pa still went to work on his *campagna*, and the produce from both properties kept them well fed, with more than enough left over to take to market. Added to the rent they were paid from their old house, Lucia and her family lived far more comfortably these days.

She would never forget the first letter she'd received from Alberto and Filomena Bonanno soon after the war had ended. Their words described their heartbreak at Gero's death and they said he'd written to inform them of his marriage not long before he was killed. Military personnel could write home, of course. Lucia had to wait until normal lines of communication were restored until she could tell them about Carula's birth – not that she'd gone into the gory details, the interminable labour, the intense pain. It had all been worth it when she'd held her baby in her arms. That moment had been bitter-sweet, and she'd cried hot tears of grief that Gero hadn't been with her – they'd mingled with her tears of happiness at the birth of her child.

Parcels from the Bonannos began arriving then. There were things Lucia had no idea existed: biscuits that tasted of mint, tinned spaghetti, tinned herring and tinned orange juice; and clothes for her and Carula, packets of chewing gum hidden up the sleeves. There were even pens, pencils and safety pins. Filomena Bonanno had thought of everything. She wrote all the time, sending long letters with dollars folded in their thin leaves, always repeating the same words: the good Lord, the Sacred Heart, the Holy Virgin, her promise to the Madonna, her daughters, her husband's film importing business, the wonderful people of New York.

Dinu had laughed out loud when Lucia had offered him some of the money she'd received, saying he was making more than enough working for don Nofriu. Lucia asked him about his job with the godfather at that point, and her twin explained he was being trained as an accountant. If only his boss wasn't the village godfather, then she'd be pleased he was doing so well and not so concerned about leaving him.

She reached into her pocket and retrieved the letter she'd received from Filomena last year, and reread it for the umpteenth time.

Dear Lucia,

    I want to come over and bring you and Carula back with me to America. I think about it every moment. First of all my husband, Alberto, was ill. Now, thank God, he's better. But my eldest daughter, Lina, is expecting a baby in the first days of the New Year. If it's Our Lady's will that everything goes well, I'll be in Italy before the end of 1947…

A yawn came from Carula's cot, alerting Lucia that her child was awake. She went to lift her out and place her on her hip.

'Mamma. I'm thirsty,' Carula said.

'Let's get you a glass of water, sweetie.'

'*Grazie.*' The little girl dimpled a smile.

Lucia's breathing slowed as she thought about Gero. Carula had his dark hair and chocolate-brown eyes, as well as his trusting nature. She was as bright as a button and would do well in America, Lucia was certain.

As for herself, she was looking forward to getting a job as soon as Carula started school. Alberto and Filomena had already said she could work for them in their film importing business. They had an empty apartment, among the many they owned and rented out, where Lucia and their granddaughter would live. In the meantime, they'd sorted out the necessary paperwork with the immigration authorities. Lucia was a war bride, had been born in the States, and had the right to a US passport on which Carula could travel. Last month, Lucia had gone to the American consulate in Palermo – a hot, dusty bus ride there and back – to pick up the document. Apparently, Charles Rinelli had been most helpful in expediting the bureaucratic red tape.

* * *

The next day, after spending the morning dusting and cleaning and helping Ma prepare a welcome lunch for the Bonannos, Lucia was waiting with Carula in the courtyard, her chest tingling with nerves.

Lucia had tied and retied the bow in Carula's hair so many times it had frayed. The child fidgeted, begging to be allowed to go play with the puppies their dog had recently produced.

'You'll get dirty if you do that, *tisoru*,' Lucia said. 'You don't want your American nonno and nonna to think badly of you, do you?'

'Why do I have an American nonno and nonna? I've already got a nonno and nonna here.'

'They are your daddy's parents. Remember I told you? Italian nonno and nonna are my parents.'

'My daddy in heaven?' Carula's sweet little face clouded with a frown. 'I wish he didn't have to be there—'

'Me too, *amuri*. But you'll meet him one day when you go to heaven, I'm sure.'

'When will that be?' The question was wistful.

'Not for a long time, I hope.'

The rumble of a car engine coming up the hill made Lucia get to her feet. She lifted Carula onto her hip and, with her heart in her mouth, went to the entrance door.

The Bonannos had aged since she'd last seen them, of course, but they were instantly recognisable as her parents' friends from the Bronx. Lucia greeted them and introduced Carula, who burrowed her face shyly into her chest.

Ma, Pa, and Annita erupted onto the scene, and there was much kissing of cheeks between the women and back slapping between the men. Pa helped Alberto retrieve the Bonannos' suitcases from the trunk of the taxi, the driver was paid, and everyone trooped inside to get out of the midday sun.

Alberto and Filomena went to the newly installed bathroom to freshen up, then came into the kitchen carrying gifts – a battery-operated radio for Pa, an electric razor for Dinu (when he decided to grace the company with his presence) and clothes galore for Lucia, Carula, Annita and Ma.

Talk during lunch was filled with reminiscences of when Lucia and her family lived in Brooklyn and tales of Alberto and Filomena's childhood in Villaurora. The Bonannos asked about Dinu, and Pa told them he was busy working for don Nofriu. Lucia only prayed she'd get the chance to say goodbye to her brother before she left for America. She'd try to persuade him again to leave with her; she wouldn't give up trying and would keep on at him by letter once she arrived there. There was always hope...

'Ugh, what a lot of flies there are!' Filomena said, waving them away with the back of her hand.

Five days had passed since the Bonannos had arrived, and Filomena had been repeating the complaint non-stop ever since. They'd brought DDT powder with them, but the flies were never ending; you only had to open the window and they entered in droves. It was obvious Gero's parents were suffering – they hardly touched their food on account of the flies settling on plates, glasses, meat and bread.

Filomena cursed Sicily, saying she'd expected it might have been different, newer and cleaner; instead, it was worse than ever.

There were two sides to Filomena's disappointment, it occurred to Lucia. She and her family weren't the starvelings Filomena had imagined them. It made Sicily not having improved as much as she'd hoped even harder to bear. She'd obviously been expecting to find Ma and Pa in dire straits, to be fitted out with her clothes and nourished by her tins of vita-minised food. But, nowadays, there was no shortage of bread, olive oil, milk, meat or eggs. If Lucia and her family had been as destitute as Filomena had thought they'd be, perhaps she'd have borne the primitive state of her birthplace better.

When Filomena ranted, for the umpteenth time, about all the illnesses that came from flies, Lucia's mother, a little crossly, said, 'You and I grew up with flies, there were more than there are now, and, thanks be to God, we're in good health.'

Filomena didn't mention flies any more, but Lucia could see she was counting the days remaining that she and Alberto had to spend in the country. Long days of flies and dust. Nights so humid that if you left the windows open the sheets stuck together, and if you closed them it was like an oven...

Carula kept the pot of resentment from boiling over, though. She took to her American grandparents like a duck to water, sitting on their laps for cuddles and telling them stories about the puppies.

'Can I have a puppy in New York?' she asked Alberto.

'Of course, sweetie. If your mamma agrees.'

How could Lucia refuse? A dog would be good company for Carula, help her settle into her new life.

'I think it's a great idea,' Lucia said.

* * *

On Lucia's last full day in the baglio, Dinu finally came to visit. She took him outside so they could sit and talk under the shade of an olive tree – where Pa had built a bench.

'There's something I need to say to you, *frati*.' She took a quick breath. 'I'm worried don Nofriu is leading you astray.'

Dinu laughed, took her hand and gripped her fingers.

'You haven't changed since we were kids in New York, *soru*. You always thought of yourself as my guardian angel, made it your business to keep me on the straight and narrow. Remember when you used to stop me from shoplifting and getting involved in playground fights? All it took was one piercing look from you and I'd crumple.'

'Those days are long gone, I fear,' she said. 'You've thrown your lot in with a terrible man. I just hope he doesn't turn you into someone whom I'd wish wasn't my brother—'

'Hey, *soru*. I would never do anything to hurt you or Carula. You have my word on that. Hand on heart.' Dinu placed his fingers on his breast. 'We're twins and will always have a deep bond. Under no circumstances would we break the code and betray each other.'

She nodded. What else could she do? Of course she'd never be disloyal to Dinu – he was her twin brother, after all.

'Promise me you'll take care of Ma, Pa and Annita,' she said. 'I'm going to miss them so much. And you, too, of course.'

'But you'll come back and visit, won't you?'

'Of course. I couldn't bear it if I never saw my family again.'

'Good.' He pulled her to her feet. 'Let's go get some breakfast. I'm starving.'

Indoors, Carula ran into Dinu's arms and he swung her high above his head, unleashing a peal of giggles from her.

Dinu sat at the table like a *signorino*, a little lord, and Ma and Filomena fussed around him, serving him coffee and homemade cakes.

Even Alberto Bonanno deferred to him, letting him speak

without interruption. It was clear he thought Dinu was doing well for himself by working for don Nofriu.

Lucia sighed to herself. Pa had once told her, after she'd expressed her worry for Dinu, that most ambitious young men like her brother sought to be part of the dominant culture of the Friends' world. Pa maintained Dinu knew if he could worm his way into the Cosa Nostra orbit, he would never lack for anything. Once her twin had made enough money, he would go legitimate, Pa said. Lucia hoped against hope that it would be so.

Dinu left soon afterwards, and Lucia spent the rest of the day packing. A feeling of unreality took hold of her as she placed a dress in her suitcase. Was she really leaving for America? It had been her dream since she was twelve years old. Now, at twenty-four, she was going back at last. She couldn't wait to take Carula to Coney Island, couldn't wait to go to the movies and watch Disney cartoons with her, couldn't wait for her to attend school and get a wonderful education. She could see a bright outlook for her daughter and would make every sacrifice possible for that to happen. If only she didn't have such a bad feeling about leaving her brother behind...

She slept fitfully that night, her mind abuzz. Then morning came, and it was time to go. Gero's parents had booked the same taxi that had brought them to Villaurora. They would have breakfast in Palermo before embarking on the liner that would take them to New York.

'Time to leave, *zuccareddu*' – little sugar – Lucia said, lifting Carula onto her hip. 'Let's go say goodbye to Nonno and Nonna.'

'Italian Nonno and Nonna?' Carula clarified. 'And Aunt Annita?'

'Of course.' Lucia's voice trembled as her throat clogged with sudden tears.

Her family were waiting for her out in the courtyard, a forlorn little group.

'I've loaded your luggage into the taxi's trunk,' Pa said. 'Filomena and Alberto have climbed in already.'

Lucia went into his arms, and he enfolded her and Carula in his warm embrace. Then Ma and Annita joined in and they all hugged and wept and made promises they would see each other again as soon as possible.

'We'll look after your baglio,' Pa said. 'But it will always be yours. Come back and visit, Lucia. It's what Gero would want.'

Her father was right. The baglio was hers, and then it would be Carula's and, God willing, it would belong to Carula's children. When Gero had signed it over to Lucia, he'd done it to protect his legacy through her. It must be kept in the family – Gero's and her family. The thought consoled her, lessening the sorrow of saying goodbye.

'*Arrivederci*,' she said to her parents and sister. Until we meet again. She took a deep breath to calm her nerves.

27

JESSICA, JULY 2005

A comfortable warmth radiated through Jess as she smoothed her fingers over the ceramic trinacria. Piero was accompanying Domenico, the builder, to his car. The three of them had spent the past hour inspecting every nook and cranny of the baglio, and Jess was feeling more than encouraged by Domenico's positive remarks.

She'd been expecting a touch of coldness from Piero after she'd pushed him away last night, but he'd been the perfect gentleman and had driven her to Villaurora earlier with the same friendliness as usual. It must have meant nothing to him, but Jess was still mortified by what had occurred.

They'd met Domenico beforehand in front of the farmhouse and, when Jess opened the rustic door, the builder had exclaimed with delight. Domenico only spoke Italian, and Jess was grateful for Piero's translations of technical terms. The property was structurally sound, there was a septic tank for domestic sanitary wastewater, which undoubtedly needed updating, and the electrics and plumbing were also old. Domenico had suggested investing in solar panels and the installation of a rainwater collection system, which would be vital if Jess installed a swimming pool.

When she'd asked him about adding an extra floor on one side of the building, Domenico said he thought it wouldn't present any problems. He said that, once she'd made up her mind about accepting her inheritance, he'd come back and do a full survey and a comprehensive estimate for the renovation work.

'That went well,' Piero said when he came back into the courtyard. 'Domenico is an excellent builder, and trustworthy. His quote will be competitive, but you could get a second opinion—'

'No need.' Jess smiled. 'I'll go with your recommendation. And I've decided I'll make an appointment with that lawyer in Palermo to get the deeds transferred to my name.'

'That's excellent news. I know you won't regret it.' Piero jangled his car keys in his pocket. 'Let's go back to the tenuta. Maria has made rice salad and other cold dishes, perfect for a hot summer's night. Would you like to join me?'

'You're too kind to me, Piero.' Jess felt her cheeks heat up and thought about mentioning her overreaction to his kiss yesterday, but decided against it. Best forgotten.

They headed for Piero's car, and he opened the door for her. She settled herself into the comfortable leather seat and enjoyed listening to the sultry tones of Mina coming from a CD while he drove them towards the winery.

She was wearing shorts and, at one point, she caught him glancing at her tanned thighs, a glance that made her insides tingle. *Get a hold of yourself, Jess.*

The car park was busy on account of new guests arriving, meaning that Jess would no longer be on her own by the pool, but she'd already resolved to see more of Sicily and go on some day trips for the rest of her holiday.

Upstairs in Piero's apartment, he offered her a glass of the *Nozze d'Oro* white wine she'd tried at the wine and food tasting, which she gladly accepted.

'Where's Cappero?' She glanced around for the dog.

'Stefania has him. When the place is swarming with guests, we can't give him free rein so he stays with her as not everyone likes dogs.'

Piero fetched the food from the fridge and placed it on the table – not only rice salad but also a cold pasta dish and an array of cheeses and cold cuts.

'*Buon appetito!*' He clinked his glass with hers.

'*Altretanto!*' Jess said. You too.

She helped herself to a portion of rice salad, prepared with sun-dried tomatoes and fresh mozzarella.

'So delicious,' she said after chewing a mouthful.

'Try this!' Piero handed her the pasta salad, and she took a small helping.

The corkscrew-shaped fusilli were topped with bell peppers, tangy cherry tomatoes, and tuna. When Piero passed her the cold cuts and cheese dishes, she declined.

'The salads are perfect, thanks,' she said, trying not to gaze into his hazel-coloured eyes.

While they ate, they talked about the proposed renovations to the baglio and the costs involved.

'I'm happy to help with the work,' Piero said. 'Painting wooden window shutters can be extremely therapeutic.'

That I'd like to see, Jess thought, an image forming in her mind of his toned body flexing as he wielded the paintbrush.

'You'd do that?'

'Of course. We'd have fun getting dirty together.'

Jess felt her chest flutter and knocked back a gulp of her wine. Was he doing this on purpose? Choosing his words? Flustered, she imagined them having hot, sweaty fun, splashing each other with paint, then showering together and...

'Let me top you up.' Piero broke into her thoughts.

'Thanks.' Jess fanned her face with her hand. Time to change the subject.

'I'm looking forward to meeting your parents tomorrow,' she said.

'It's terrible that your grandfather, Gero Bonanno, was killed in an air raid in Naples.' Piero looked her in the eye. 'That must have been such a shock for your grandmother.'

'Excuse me?' Had she heard him correctly? Jess put down her fork.

'Oh.' Piero put his glass down. 'You didn't know?'

'No,' she said, picking up her own glass and taking a substantial sip. She tried to blink away the tears that prickled her eyes. 'Sorry, it's just – poor Nonna. And poor Gero. It's the first time I've heard his name.'

'You're trembling,' Piero said, coming around to her side of the table. He helped her to her feet and enveloped her in a hug. 'I'm so sorry. I thought you knew—'

'Do you remember I told you about the rift between my gran and my mum?' Jess sighed. 'All I knew was that Nonna moved to New York after the war. I had no idea she was widowed beforehand—'

'Come, sit on the sofa and I'll fetch you a brandy. I'm sorry for giving you such a shock.'

'Thanks,' Jess said, doing as he suggested.

'Brandy cures all ails, I think,' Piero said as he poured amber liquid into two glasses.

The liquor tasted fruity and somewhat sweet, but it warmed the coldness that had taken hold of Jess.

'Feeling better?' Piero asked.

'Much better, *grazie*. I feel so silly not knowing about my family history. For years, it's as if a part of me has been missing.' She took a breath. 'I'm hoping your dad will fill in some gaps tomorrow. But I'm also a little scared I'll find out something awful—'

'I understand where you're coming from, but try not to worry. Whatever happened, it happened a long time ago and won't hurt you now.'

'I hope not.' A smile quivered on her lips. 'Well, I suppose I should head back to my accommodation—'

'Before you go, I'd like to apologise for my behaviour last night.'

'I should be apologising to you.' Jess felt her cheeks flame. 'I totally overreacted. I mean, what's a kiss between friends?'

'Is that what we are, Jess? Friends?'

'What more can we be? You're still in love with your ex-wife and I'm going home to Bristol soon.'

'Ah, my slip-up in Licata. I knew that would come back to haunt me. I meant to say that I still love Eleonora, not that I'm still in love with her.'

'What's the difference?' Jess glanced at him.

'Being in love is romantic. Loving someone can be platonic. Eleonora is the mother of my children. I could never not love her. But I'm not in love with her, if you know what I mean—' He took Jess's hand. 'I realise we've only known each other a short while, but we get on so well. Have such a lot in common. What are the chances I'd meet someone who loves *Star Trek* as much as me?' He smiled into her eyes. 'I'm developing feelings for you, Jess. Dare I hope you feel something for me too?'

'Oh, Piero. How can I not be attracted to you? You're the kindest man I've ever met.' She squeezed his fingers. 'And charming, good-looking, intelligent and such a good father. But we live in different countries—'

'Ah, yes, thanks for the compliments. I should have told you how attractive I find you as well. Your beauty, sense of humour, willingness to try new experiences, I could go on and on. You're absolutely perfect. As for us living in separate places, I can't help hoping that will only be temporary. Once your baglio has been restored, would you consider moving to Sicily to work as a freelance accountant, like I suggested?'

'Hmmm. How about we take things one step at a time?' Jess gave a sigh. 'I don't want to rush into anything.'

'Fair enough.' Piero took her brandy glass and set it down with his on the coffee table. He opened his arms and she went into them, snuggled against him.

'Now I must head back to my accommodation,' she said.

'Is that what you really want?'

'Yes. No. Maybe.' Indecision tightened in her chest.

She closed her eyes, and he touched his mouth to hers, his tongue seeking entrance. And she couldn't help herself, she gave in to him. Before she knew it, she was lying back on the sofa and he was covering her with his body. Her heartbeat echoed in her ears as he pressed his fingers along the tops of her shoulders and traced them down to the curve of her hips.

'Mmm, that feels nice,' she said.

Piero caught her eye, and she nodded. She wanted him so badly every nerve in her body was on fire, and she couldn't stop herself from reaching for his shirt buttons as his lips found hers. Whimpering with pleasure, she arched her back.

'You're so beautiful,' he said, tearing his mouth from hers.

'So are you.' She held his face close.

Piero kissed her again and she burnt with need as he tugged her shorts down. It felt so right, so natural, to wrap her legs around him. So natural as he eased himself into her, his eyes fixed on hers.

They rocked to the same rhythm, and she lost all sense of time and space. She forgot about Scott and his treatment of her, and her worries about what she might discover about her grandmother, even about the stresses of her job at the bank. All she knew, all she cared about, was this amazing man and his ability to make her feel so wonderful.

Afterwards, they lay in each other's arms, kissing and cuddling.

'Spend the night with me, please, Jess,' Piero said.

And, so help her God, she said yes.

It was only after they'd moved to the bedroom, and made love for a second time and she was drifting off to sleep, that she thought about Lucia again.

How sad that Gero was killed. Carula must have been born in Sicily. Jess had always thought it had been in New York. What had prompted Lucia to move to America? Jess burrowed into Piero's chest, relishing the closeness – she'd find out from his father tomorrow, no doubt.

28

LUCIA, APRIL 1969

Lucia pulled in a deep breath as she sat in the front pew of St Peter's, New York's oldest Roman Catholic church. Today was Carula's wedding day, and Lucia couldn't have been prouder.

She gave a sigh of pure happiness. Finally, Carula had settled down. She'd gone through boyfriends like a dose of salts while at Cornell University. After majoring in Biological Sciences, she'd begged to be allowed to undertake postgraduate research at Oxford University in England. Lucia had agreed, hoping it would broaden her horizons even more than they'd been broadened already. It was there she'd fallen in love with Iain Turner, a fellow researcher. Lucia had been over the moon when they'd both found jobs in the veterinary pharmaceuticals industry in New Jersey. They would rent their own apartment and start work as soon as they'd returned from their honeymoon.

Lucia gazed at Iain, who was standing by the altar with his best man, a fellow Brit. She'd first met Iain nine months ago, when her daughter had brought him home for the summer vacation. It had been clear that Carula and Iain were deeply in love – they listened to each other, accepted each other's differences, and respected each other. The attraction between them was palpable, and Lucia could see that they'd formed a deep connection. She had every confidence their bond would be long lasting.

Lucia turned her attention to Filomena, dressed in lavender and sitting on her right. Alberto would walk Carula down the aisle. It was hard to believe almost twenty-two years had gone by since Lucia and Carula had travelled to America with them. Lucia closed her eyes, remembering her first sight of the Statue of Liberty after being away for so long. It hadn't taken her any time at all to slip back into her American ways – regular visits to the movie theatres, eating out at diners, lazy summer days at Coney Island. And Carula had adapted quicky; she'd soon begun speaking English, making friends at kindergarten, and watching TV like it was going out of style.

But Lucia missed her family. She thought about them constantly and wrote long letters every week, describing her life in the States and begging them to come and visit. She, herself, couldn't spare the time. Her job with her in-laws was all-consuming as she'd taken over the organisation of film festivals in conjunction with Italian consulates throughout the USA. Besides, she'd decided it would be too unsettling for Carula to travel with her back to Sicily.

Thankfully, she made enough money to afford airline tickets for Ma, Pa and Annita to come over every other year or so. When Annita married a local villaurorese, she no longer visited as often, given that she was too busy with her husband – a post office employee – and, eventually, her son and daughter. It was she who would welcome Carula and Iain to the village, where they would be accommodated in the baglio for some of their honeymoon. Ma and Pa would stay on in New York to give them some privacy. They still lived on the property and Lucia's father had carried on working on the land, despite his advancing years.

Lucia nudged her mother, sitting on her left with Pa next to her.

'I'm so glad you are here, Ma,' she said. 'And that you'll be staying with me while Carula and Iain are away.'

'Just wish your brother could have torn himself away from his businesses,' Ma muttered.

Lucia sighed – she hadn't seen her brother since she'd left Sicily. As time had passed, her reluctance to return to Villaurora had increased, and she'd used the excuse of being too busy. There were simply too many memories at the baglio, and that was that.

Oh, Gero, how I miss you still.

There would never be anyone else for her, she'd realised not long after she'd come back to America. Men asked her out on dates, but she always declined. No one could match up to Gero – he'd been unique, a one-off, and she didn't want to even think about being with any other man.

As for her brother, it had become clear they were no longer as close as they were when young. She and Dinu wrote to each other from time to time, but whereas she recounted everything about her life in New York, his letters were brief. The partnership between him and Francu was stronger than ever, apparently. The two of them had left Villaurora after don Nofriu had passed away fifteen years ago as they'd always wanted to make it big in Palermo, and Dinu wrote that they were now in the world of finance. Ma and Pa saw little of him, they said. When Lucia had asked them if her twin was still involved with Cosa Nostra, they'd related he'd told them his enterprises were totally legitimate.

'Carula and Iain will get in touch with Dinu, I'm sure,' Lucia whispered to her mother. 'Maybe that will encourage him to visit you more often—'

He could at least have made the effort to attend his niece's wedding, she thought. She wouldn't let sadness about Dinu spoil her day, though. Her daughter was getting married, and she was determined not to let thoughts of her twin brother ruin her happiness.

The organist launched into 'The Arrival of the Queen of Sheba' and Carula and Alberto started their procession down the aisle. The congregation stood and turned to gaze at the bride. Wearing a high-waisted, empire-silhouetted long white silk dress, with a short train and an antique lace veil which covered her face, Carula looked absolutely stunning and Lucia's eyes welled with emotion.

* * *

Later, after myriad toasts and enough food to feed an army in the Dolce Vita restaurant in Coney Island, Lucia smiled as Iain guided Carula onto the floor for their first dance.

Lucia couldn't help being reminded of her own wedding, how she and Gero had danced under the stars in the courtyard of the baglio while Uncle Carlo had played his accordion. If she closed her eyes, she could still feel Gero's strong arms, whirling her around, hear his deep voice, and feel his gentle kisses. Such wonderful memories...

Carula and Iain had kept things simple, only inviting close friends and relations. Iain's parents had flown over from the UK. Blond and fair-skinned like their son, they contrasted with the swarthy Sicilians in the party.

Before too long, it was time for Carula and Iain to leave for their honeymoon, and Lucia pulled her daughter in for a hug.

'Have a great time in Sicily, sweetie,' Lucia said. 'And say *ciao* to that brother of mine, if you track him down.'

'Will do.' Carula hugged her tight. 'I'll ask Aunt Annita to get hold of him when we're there.'

29

CARULA, MAY 1969

'Villaurora sure is quaint,' Carula said to Iain as they strolled hand in hand across the village square towards the Bar Centrale. They'd arrived in Sicily a week ago and had spent the first three days in Palermo before picking up a rented car and heading to Cefalù for the night. After a morning visiting the charming seaside town, they'd driven inland to Enna, and then on to the baglio.

'It's not how I expected,' Iain said. 'I thought there'd be a lot more people about.'

Carula shivered despite the warmth of the day. She felt eyes on her, but when she looked around, there was no one to be seen.

In the café, she ordered cappuccinos for herself and Iain. Her mamma had brought her up speaking Sicilian and she felt entirely at home in the language. Just like she felt at home in the baglio. Her grandparents were looking after it beautifully for Lucia, who'd told her it would be hers one day. Not for ages, Carula hoped. Mamma was only in her mid-forties and Carula prayed she would live a long, long life.

She gazed at her husband, her heart brimming with love. How lucky she was to have met him – he grounded her and had become her rock. Although Mamma had patently done all a single parent could do for her child, Carula had always felt there'd been a huge hole in her life. She hung on every word her mother told her about Gero. At the baglio, she'd caressed the trincaria, feeling a tangible connection with her father, and she could sense a vestige of his presence in the farmhouse, the place where her parents had been so happy. It was a shame Lucia hadn't returned since she'd moved to America. She always maintained the memories were too painful, but surely enough time had passed...

'This coffee tastes great,' Iain said, breaking into her thoughts. 'Can I get you another cup?'

'Thanks, I'd love that.' Carula smiled.

She glanced at the counter while Iain went to order their coffees. A man dressed in a carabiniere uniform had come into the bar and was leaning against it, drinking an espresso. The thin grey hair at the sides of his head had been combed over his baldness. He lifted the cup to his fleshy red lips, and met Carula's eye.

Not wanting to be caught staring, she quickly glanced away. But the man came up to their table when Iain returned.

'Excuse me,' he said. 'I couldn't help noticing your similarity to someone I used to know. My name is Giulianu Cardona. You aren't, by any chance, Carula Bonanno, Lucia Pavano's daughter?'

Surprised, Carula confirmed that she was before introducing Iain and saying her married name was now Turner.

'We're on our honeymoon, staying at my mother's baglio,' she added.

'I'm an old friend of Lucia's,' the carabiniere said. 'I knew your father, Gero, very well.'

'How amazing!' Carula widened her eyes. 'My grandparents are in New York still, but my Aunt Annita is here and I'll be meeting my Uncle Dinu tomorrow in a restaurant in Castronovo. We're heading there after we've visited the temples in Agrigento.'

She translated the conversation into English for Iain before turning to Cardona.

'It's strange my mother never mentioned you—'

'When you see her next, please give her my regards.' The carabiniere smirked. 'I've never forgotten her, you see.'

Carula didn't know how to respond to Cardona's words and was glad when she didn't need to as the policeman gave her a bow and then marched out of the café.

The next day, excitement making her chest feel light, Carula was walking across the main square of Castronovo, high in the mountains to the north of Agrigento, hand in hand with Iain. She was finally about to meet her Uncle Dinu, her mother's twin. Mamma had told her so much about him, how they used to hunt rabbits together, how close they were until the chaos of World War II and Carula's decision to move to America drove them apart.

When Carula pressed her mother for details, she'd said that Sicily had gone through massive turmoil during and after the Allied occupation, and the less said about that the better. Mamma had also lamented her brother's lack of letter-writing skills – she knew very little about his life these days, and hoped Carula would find out more from him.

Carula's heart pounded. The man picking at the dish of olives in front of him on the outside terrace table of the restaurant couldn't be anyone but her uncle. When she'd asked her Aunt Annita how she would recognise him, Aunt had said he was the image of Lucia in male form. And she was right.

Dinu scraped back his chair and came forward to greet her and Iain. They spoke to him in English and he replied in the language of his childhood.

'I remember you as a little girl,' he said, kissing Carula on both cheeks before leading her and Iain back to the table. 'Let me introduce you to my cousin, Francu.'

Everyone shook hands and a waiter appeared to take their food order.

'What do you recommend, Uncle?' Carula asked.

'This is our first time here.' Dinu shrugged. 'But you can't go far wrong with *pasta alla norma* followed by grilled sea bass.'

Carula explained the dishes to Iain.

'Sounds good,' he said, glancing at her. 'Shall we have the same?'

'Great idea, honey.'

Movement caught her eye, and she pointed in the direction of the far side of the square. 'Look, there's Giulianu Cardona.' She smiled. 'He introduced himself to us at the bar in Villaurora, and we told him we were planning on meeting up with you.'

Carula's smile vanished as she caught her uncle's expression. His nostrils flared and his eyes had turned cold and flinty.

'You betrayed me, Carula.' He spat the words. 'How could you?'

'What?' She stared at him blankly.

Before Dinu could clarify, all hell broke loose. Cardona was racing towards them, followed by a posse of carabinieri.

Carula gasped as Dinu drew a pistol from under his jacket. Cold sweat spread down her body and she held her breath.

Bullets caught Cardona on the side of his face and neck, spinning him around. His body crumpled to the ground, his eyes unseeing.

Carula had never seen anyone killed before and nausea swelled her stomach. She started screaming.

'Duck!' Iain shouted, pulling her under the table.

Guns roared. Bullets flew.

'Run!' Dinu yelled at Francu.

Carula's heart nearly stopped while she watched them as they set off across the piazza, ricocheting bullets raining down while the carabinieri pursued them, both sides firing.

A bullet caught Dinu's arm. He grasped hold of it and he swore with pain.

Carula's eyes widened. Her uncle and Francu had reached a car, parked on the other side of the square. Francu bundled Dinu into the passenger seat and got behind the wheel. Bullets crashed into their rear window, smashing it to smithereens.

And then Carula felt herself falling, down into blackness as the world spun around her. The last thing she heard before she fainted was Iain muttering that Dinu and Francu had got away.

30

LUCIA, MAY 1969

Lucia was waiting in arrivals at John F. Kennedy International airport, worry churning her stomach. Carula had phoned from Palermo yesterday, her voice trembling, to say she and Iain were cutting short their honeymoon and returning to New York. When Lucia had asked the reason, her daughter said she'd tell her everything once she'd arrived, and had promptly hung up.

After what seemed like hours, Carula and Iain finally came through the gate. Lucia ran towards them, but she stopped dead when she saw her daughter. Carula's face was pale and Iain had his arm around her.

'Oh, my God, what's happened?' Lucia asked, every nerve in her body quaking.

'Your brother, that's what happened,' Iain said. 'But now is not the place. Carula is in shock. Let's get her home. Then I'll tell you everything.'

They went to the parking lot and, before too long, Lucia was driving them in stony silence to Lower Manhattan.

Occupying the entire top floor of a building overlooking the

MacDougal-Sullivan Gardens near Washington Square Park, her apartment was her refuge and she couldn't wait to get back there. Ma and Pa would be waiting impatiently to find out about their granddaughter and her husband's time in Sicily. Something had gone badly wrong and now Lucia knew it had to do with Dinu, apprehension was eating at her insides.

After she'd parked in the basement, Lucia took Carula and Iain up to her three-bedroom apartment, where the newlyweds went straight to Carula's room and closed the door.

'What's going on?' Ma asked, rushing up to Lucia as she stepped into the living room.

'Dinu.' Lucia only needed to say the word for Ma's face to fall.

'Is anything wrong?' Pa asked from where he was sitting in an armchair.

'Iain said he'd tell us everything once he's got Carula settled. She's in shock, apparently.'

* * *

'How could you have suggested Carula contact her uncle? The man is an outlaw, wanted by the police.' Iain came right out with the statement a short time later after he'd come into the room where Lucia was waiting with her parents.

'I had no idea. We all thought he'd gone legitimate, didn't we?' Lucia glanced at Ma and Pa.

Her parents looked at each other and nodded.

'We haven't seen much of him since he left Villaurora to seek his fortune in the capital,' Pa said. 'Whenever he phoned, he'd say he was too busy. We haven't heard anything bad, which is why we thought it would be fine for you to get in touch—'

'The police told me they'd been looking for Dinu and Francu for years, but they'd been keeping a low profile while spending their time wreaking devastation by setting the big Palermo crime families against each other, probably with a view to taking over one day. It's suspected that the Mafia war between rival clans, sparked by a quarrel over a lost heroin shipment, had been instigated by your brother and Francu, Lucia.'

Her head spun with shock, and her stomach rolled.

Iain went on to recount that the carabinieri's informers had revealed that Dinu and Francu's underground existence had become one of their most feared traits: none of the Cosa Nostra clans knew who they were or what they looked like. Nobody ever saw them, they only saw the bodies in the aftermath of their passing. Their mystique had grown – no one knew for sure whether they were just hit men or held more important roles. The fact that they'd evaded the authorities successfully while notching up several murders had fuelled the mythology surrounding them.

'It was only Carula's innocent remark to Cardona that led to a breakthrough,' Iain added.

'Can you tell us what happened?' Lucia met his eye.

'We were at the bar in Villaurora, having a coffee, when a guy, who introduced himself as Giulianu Cardona, approached. He said he was an old friend of yours, Lucia. The guy appeared genuine, he told us he used to visit you, so we got chatting and Carula let slip we were meeting Dinu the next day in a restaurant in Castronovo.'

Lucia's blood turned to ice, and she shivered.

Damn you, Giulianu Cardona.

'He and Dinu go back a long way. My brother had a run-in with him at the end of the war,' she said. 'They were hard times, and Dinu had got involved in smuggling and other illegal activities.'

'Bloody hell,' Iain said. 'You could have told me.'

'It was a long time ago.' Lucia sighed. 'Dinu left Villaurora fifteen years ago. We truly believed he'd turned over a new leaf.'

'Obviously not. Cardona turned up in Castronovo with a team of carabinieri. As soon as he saw him, Dinu accused Carula of betrayal.' Iain grimaced. 'Then, cool as a cucumber, Dinu shot Cardona dead.'

Lucia's heart sank.

'No wonder Carula's in shock. You too, Iain. I'm so sorry this has happened.'

'Us too,' Ma added, and Pa echoed her.

'Too late to apologise now.' Iain sighed. 'Carula had to witness a scene she'd only ever watched in the movies. Her uncle and his cousin pursued by law enforcement officers shooting at them. We hid under the table until the carabinieri returned.'

'Did they catch Dinu and Francu?' Lucia asked.

'No. They got away.'

Lucia didn't know whether to be relieved or not. She loved her brother, but hated him right now.

'It was then that the police told us Dinu and Francu were fugitives from the law and gave us the same information I've given to you.' Iain blew out a long, slow breath. 'Carula and I caught the next flight back to New York. She didn't stop crying for hours and can't keep any food down.'

'My poor baby.' Lucia's voice strangled on a sob.

* * *

For the following two days, Carula barely left her room, barely even spoke. Lucia carried her meals to her on a tray and Iain stayed close.

On the third day, Alberto Bonanno came to visit.

Lucia took one look at him and dread filled her.

'Carula and Iain need to leave the country,' Alberto said after Lucia had taken him through to the living room. 'Charles Rinelli has been in touch. Although he has now retired, he heard through his contacts that people will come for them.'

Lucia couldn't believe what she was hearing.

'People? What people?'

'Friends of friends. You know who I mean—'

Lucia gasped and her mother burst into tears. This was concrete confirmation Dinu was involved with the Mafia, if anything was. But how could her brother even think of putting out a contract on his own niece? His twin sister's daughter? She was truly shocked that Dinu had turned so spiteful and vengeful. He'd become evil. No other word would describe him.

'Where can Carula and Iain go?' Pa asked.

'Back to England. They should be safe there,' Alberto said.

Pa rubbed a hand through his thinning hair.

'But isn't Cosa Nostra active in England?'

Alberto shook his head.

'Rinelli told me that the Mafia wanted to move to London when casinos were legalised, but the local criminal gangs were so established that it would have been difficult to arrive from overseas and hire suitable local enforcers, and since any armed and known foreign gangsters would not get further than being turned away at the airport, they thought it not worth the trouble. Besides, England never had the number of Italian immigrants that we received here in the US.'

'Oh, God,' Lucia sobbed. 'How am I going to tell my daughter and son-in-law that they can't stay in America?'

'That's not the worst of it, my dear,' Alberto said. 'Charles Rinelli stressed that Carula and Iain must have no contact with you. Just in case—'

'No, that can't be right.' Lucia stared at him, saw that he was serious. She hardened her heart. 'I will never, ever forgive my brother for this.'

* * *

Ma and Pa went back to Sicily two days later, two days during which Lucia spent her time organising Carula and Iain's departure. When Carula was told she'd need to leave the country, she wept and begged Lucia to go with her. But Lucia couldn't take the risk. She was well known in immigrant circles; it would be better if she stayed in the US and spread the word that her daughter had gone to Australia instead.

'I'll write to you, my darling,' Lucia said on her daughter's last evening as they said goodnight at her bedroom door. 'And, when everything settles down, I'll come and visit.'

Carula's eyes welled up.

'Iain and I have decided it would be best if you didn't write. Neither do we want you to visit.' She took in a shuddering breath. 'We'd like to try for a baby soon and we don't need the stress. I'm sorry, Mamma. But this is your fault. You knew what your brother is like, yet you still asked me to get in touch with him.'

Carula was right, Lucia realised. It was all her fault. She'd done the unforgivable. Put her daughter in deadly danger. For the rest of her life, she would have to live with that.

'I'm so sorry,' Lucia said. 'I will keep you both in my heart and pray for you every day.'

'Good night, Mamma.' Carula's voice choked with tears. 'Iain and I will see ourselves out in the morning. Don't worry about us.'

'Good night, *tisoru*.'

Lucia stepped forward to draw her daughter into her arms. But Carula was already closing the door in her face.

With tears streaming down her cheeks, Lucia went to her room. She sobbed into her pillow, thinking about Gero and how he would have handled the situation. One thing was for sure, he would never have sent Carula to Dinu. How could Lucia have been so stupid? Her only excuse, if there was one, was that she was so proud of her daughter she needed her brother to be proud of her as well.

An image of the baglio came into her mind. She'd wanted to pass it down to Carula and any children she might have one day. It was their heritage. But Lucia would only do that when Dinu was no more. She would never put Carula and her future offspring at risk ever again.

31

JESSICA, JULY 2005

Butterflies danced in Jess's stomach as Piero brought his Alfa to a stop in front of the wrought-iron gates at his parents' villa on a hillside overlooking the Mondello beach resort near Palermo.

'Everything will be all right,' he said, reaching across the space between them and squeezing her hand.

Jess swallowed hard. Gaetano Sacca di Melita had known her grandmother. She still couldn't get over the fact.

Piero jumped out of the car and spoke into the entry phone. Soon after, the electronic gates swung open, and he parked in front of the three-storey house. Piero's parents came out to greet them, and he introduced his father and mother.

'I'm honoured to meet you, Baron and Baroness Sacca,' Jess said.

Piero's father air kissed her hand and his mother aimed kisses at her cheeks.

'Please, call us Gaetano and Valeria,' the baroness said, smiling.

They trooped into the air-conditioned villa, and Jess's eyes widened. The living room was gorgeous – airy, with terracotta floors and traditionally furnished with plush sofas.

'Come, see the view,' Piero said, taking her hand and leading her through enormous glass patio doors to an external terrace.

'Wow! It's so beautiful.' She gazed down at the fine white sands, electric-blue sea, and Liberty-style villas of the town.

'Not as beautiful as you, Jess.' Piero touched his lips to hers. Just a small kiss, but so warm, so... 'I think we should head indoors,' he said with regret in his tone.

'Probably for the best. It is rather hot out here.' Jess fanned her face with her hand.

'And getting hotter by the second.' Piero grinned.

Jess giggled as he took her hand, and they hurried back to the coolness inside.

'Let's have a glass of wine before we eat,' Gaetano Sacca said, uncorking a bottle of *Melita Brut* while Jess sat next to Valeria on the sofa. Piero brought their glasses, and they raised them in a toast to good health before taking a sip.

'You're the image of Lucia.' Gaetano smiled. 'I almost thought you were her when I first saw you, Jess.'

'I wish I'd known her.' She glanced at him. 'What was she like?'

'I only met her a few times, but I was struck by her loyalty to Gero. It was me who took her the news of his death and I could see that she truly loved him.'

'Was he a good man?'

'He was. One of the best. Did you know he was a major with the American army, that he worked in intelligence?'

'I had no idea.' Jess shook her head.

'His commander was working undercover at the tenuta before the Allied landings, then ran the AMGOT office in

Palermo before being shipped to Naples. Gero was based in Villaurora as his parents came from the village. They'd emigrated to the US shortly before he was born. In fact, he met your grandmother in New York when they were kids.'

'My grandmother lived in America as a child?' Jess heard the incredulity in her tone. 'I feel such an idiot for not knowing this—'

'It's not your fault,' Piero said. 'And you're not the first person to have been kept in the dark about their family background.'

'Did the baglio belong to my grandfather?' Jess asked.

'He signed the property over to Lucia before he was transferred to Naples.' Gaetano Sacca nodded. 'It was a good move.'

'She left it to me, and I'm about to make an appointment to visit a lawyer in Palermo to go through all the paperwork and get the deeds transferred to my name.'

'Inheritance law is far less complicated in Italy than in many countries. That shouldn't be a problem,' Gaetano said.

Valeria rose to her feet and said, 'I wish we could have lunch out on the terrace, but the weather is too hot for that so I've prepared a selection of salads and we'll eat in the dining room.'

They went through to a room with a picture window and views of the shore. At the table, they enjoyed pasta with home-made pesto, a salad with herrings, oranges and olives, seafood couscous, and delicious *Sarde alla Beccafico* – butterflied sardines stuffed with breadcrumbs, nuts, raisins, and herbs, rolled up and baked with fresh bay leaves and lemons until golden brown. They really were delicious, and Jess complimented Valeria.

'I'm falling in love with Sicilian food,' Jess said, catching Piero winking at her, making her cheeks burn.

'Did you ever meet other members of my nonna's family, Gaetano?' Jess asked.

'Oh, yes. I met her father and her brother.'

'What were they like?'

'Her pa was a farmer. One of those salt-of-the-earth characters one can't help but admire. As for her brother—'

'Shall we go through to the other room for coffee?' Valeria said. 'You can tell Jess about him there.'

'Good idea.' Piero got up to clear the dishes, and Jess went to help him.

In the kitchen, Jess and Piero loaded the dishwasher, while Valeria brewed espressos. Back in the living room, Piero poured the coffee into small white porcelain cups, and Jess sat next to him on the sofa before lifting the cup to her lips.

'Piero told me about the Cosa Nostra boss who lived in the village,' Jess said. 'I did wonder if my grandmother had ever met him.'

'I know she did, but it was her brother who came completely under his influence.'

Gaetano went on to tell Jess about her great-uncle's grain-smuggling operation, his killing of the carabiniere, how he and his cousin Francu became outlaws, and eventually how they were recruited by don Nofriu.

'Oh, my God. How awful.' Shock wheeled through Jess and she put down her cup with a shaky hand.

'Perhaps Jess has heard enough about her family for one day.' Piero glanced at her. 'I was going to suggest a gelato in Mondello before we head back to the tenuta.'

'*Grazie*, Piero,' she said.

* * *

After Jess had taken her leave of Piero's parents, thanking them for lunch and for telling her about her family, Piero drove her down the winding road to the seaside town. He found a park opposite the beachside promenade, and they strolled hand in hand, the breeze from the ocean making the walk bearable in the heat.

'I can't believe it was only a week and a half ago that we were walking by the sea in Licata,' she said. 'So much has happened since then.'

'You've borne the news you received today so bravely, Jess.'

'I'm not sure bravely is the right word. It seems surreal, to be honest. I think it will take time to sink in.'

'I expect so. But you mustn't worry. You can look forward to turning a new page in your life, right?'

'I hope so. When I go back to Bristol, I'll need to finalise my divorce. Then I'll have a long think about the future—'

'I won't pressure you,' he said. 'Please know that I'm here for you if you need me.'

Could he be any nicer?

'*Grazie.*' She brushed a kiss to his cheek. 'Let's go find a *gelateria*. I could murder a chocolate gelato.'

Piero laughed and, before too long, they were sitting on a bench licking the dripping ice cream from their cones.

Jess thought about that morning, when she'd woken up in Piero's bed. They'd made love before having breakfast. He was a considerate, skilful lover and he'd made her come so hard she'd almost seen stars. Was this just a holiday fling, or was there more to it? And if there was, what could the future hold for them?

She gazed into Piero's eyes, but there was something flitting at the back of her mind, like a moth beating its wings against an electric light. What had caused the rift between her mother and her grandmother? Jess sighed. How would she ever find out?

'What's wrong?' Piero nudged her.

'Nothing,' she said. 'I'm just a little tired, that's all.'

'No wonder. It's been an emotional day.'

'Thank you for giving up your Sunday for me, Piero.'

'No need to thank me. Your family history has got me hooked. Just like you've got me hooked.'

'I've got you hooked?' She grinned. 'Whatever do you mean?'

'I'm becoming addicted to you, Jess.'

He leant in and kissed her on the lips, and she opened her mouth for him. He tasted of chocolate ice cream and the salt of the sea.

A group of boys skateboarded past, wolf whistling, causing Jess and Piero to break apart and laugh.

'Let's head back to the tenuta for some privacy,' Piero said.

Soon they were in Piero's car, listening to music as he drove out of Mondello. Jess let her thoughts wander. It must have been a tremendous culture shock for her nonna to move back to America with a young child.

However did she cope?

32

LUCIA, SEPTEMBER 2004

Dust motes flickered in the sunlight coming through her living room window as Lucia made her way slowly to her desk. She sat down and rested her weary bones, then gave a heavy sigh; she needed to write an important letter, but couldn't face it yet.

Tears prickled her eyes. She'd been diagnosed with stage 4 ovarian cancer, which had spread to her liver, and she only had months left to live. The devastating news had come soon after she'd found out about Carula and Iain's tragic accident. Although contact with them had been impossible since Dinu had shown his true colours, Lucia had employed a private detective not long after Jessica was born, and the investigator had kept her up to date ever since.

How she still regretted her actions of thirty-five years ago. Not a day went by when she didn't wish she could turn back the clock and warn her daughter off contacting Dinu. Lucia's heart ached. Had she been blind to his faults since they were children, or had he simply deceived her about his real nature? He'd always been hot-headed and it had been up to her to keep him under control. By moving to America, she'd deprived him of her steadying influence, and the dark side of him had obviously taken over completely.

Following her cancer diagnosis, Lucia had got in touch with the same firm of lawyers Gero had used to get the deeds of the baglio transferred to her. She frowned. Before leaving the property to Jessica, she'd had to be sure that Dinu wouldn't pose a threat.

From long telephone conversations with the notaio, Lucia had learnt that, after her twin brother and Francu had left Villaurora, they'd spent their time forming allegiances, moving constantly around western Sicily, where they were sheltered by Friends – trusted mafiosi who knew that none of the locals, not the old men sitting in their circle of chairs in the square, not the heavily pregnant young mothers struggling with shopping and children, or even the local priest, would ever say a word about strangers in town.

The lawyer had discovered they'd often returned to Cinisi, a small municipality on a promontory, a prosperous and peaceful place between the mountains and the sea, which was under the watchful eye of a Mafia boss who'd taken in many fugitives over the years. Nothing escaped the notice of his gossips and spies. And it was in Cinisi that Dinu had met Vera Bruno, the woman who had become his wife.

Lucia had been surprised to learn that he'd taken Vera to live on the outskirts of Bagheria in a luxury villa. The town was once the playground of the rich, a spot where the wealthy of Palermo built grand summer residences. When Dinu took his bride there, Bagheria was still the playground of the rich – just not the old aristocracy but the new moneyed criminal class.

It was in an abandoned ironworks in Bagheria that Dinu and Francu had started their reign of terror. Lucia had felt sick to the stomach when the notaio informed her that her brother and cousin would give people, whom they no longer considered trustworthy, appointments in the building, and once inside the door, said people would never leave.

How could Dinu have turned so evil? Lucia had asked herself this question so often over the years and she asked it of herself again now. She'd been shocked beyond measure when she'd learnt that, after he and Francu had eliminated their rival bosses, they'd taken over the running of Cosa Nostra.

Francu, maddened with power, moved his entire family away from Villaurora and then began to wage war on the state. His strategy of violence backfired, and he was arrested. He'd died in a maximum-security prison some time ago. When Lucia asked the lawyer if he knew what had happened to Dinu, he'd responded that her brother hadn't been seen in public for over thirty years, and it was widely believed that he was dead.

In order to be sure of the fact, Lucia had asked the notaio to employ a private detective on her behalf, but given Dinu's Mafia connections, no one would take on the job. Had her brother really died? The fact that he'd given every impression of having vanished off the face of the earth led her to believe that he had, indeed, passed away. And wouldn't she sense him if he was still alive? They'd always been so much in tune with each other...

There was a glass of water on her desk next to a packet of painkillers. Lucia placed two pills on her tongue and took a sip to wash them down. Tomorrow, she'd be moving into a hospice, so she needed to write that important letter now.

* * *

The next day, Lucia walked around her apartment for the last time. In her American will, she'd given instructions for it to go to her great-niece, Karen, who'd become like a granddaughter to her. In fact, she'd asked Karen to drive her to the hospice. The girl reminded her so much of Gero – she had the same chocolate-brown eyes, as well as his generous nature.

Was Jessica like him too? The English detective had relayed information about the breakup of Jessica's marriage and had sent a photo of her taken from a distance. But it was impossible to know anything about her personality. Lucia only prayed she'd find happiness and hoped she would agree to inherit the baglio, and that it would help her heal from her wounds.

The sound of a key opening her front door alerted Lucia to Karen's arrival. She swept her gaze around her home, then, with sadness in her heart, went to greet her great-niece.

33

JESSICA, JULY 2005

Breathing deeply to calm her nerves, Jess stood on the pavement outside the modern office block in the centre of Palermo. She'd driven here a short time ago and was lucky to have found a parking space at the side of the busy street. The traffic and crazy driving in this city had made her feel as if she'd taken her life into her own hands and she'd broken out into a cold sweat while dodging cars, scooters and motorbikes coming at her from every direction. But she was here now and her heart filled with gladness that she was about to meet her grandmother's lawyer.

She pressed the button on the entry phone, gave her name, and was buzzed inside. A receptionist greeted her on the first floor and took her through to Notaio Gentile.

'*Buon giorno.*' He shook her hand. 'A pleasure to meet you, Mrs Brown.'

'Your English is excellent,' she said to the middle-aged man with curly grey hair.

'*Grazie.*' He smiled. 'Please, take a seat.'

She sat opposite him at the wide glass and metal desk.

'Your grandmother contacted us last year,' the lawyer said. 'I'm glad you've decided to accept your inheritance.'

'Can I ask you about the funds Lucia left me to maintain the property?' Jess asked. 'It needs renovation, and I was wondering if the cash would cover it.'

'Once the baglio is in your name, you'll have access to one hundred thousand euros held by us in an account set up specifically for the purpose. All you have to do is send us invoices for expenses and we'll settle them on your behalf.'

'Oh, my goodness, that's a lot of money.' Jess couldn't help her mouth falling open.

'Indeed. It should pay for any work you'd like to have done on the place.' He grinned. 'Unless you envisage turning it into a palace, of course.'

Jess laughed at the lawyer's attempt at a joke.

He asked for her documents, and she handed over her passport and the fiscal code she'd obtained in Caltanissetta yesterday.

While he went off to get her papers photocopied, Jess gazed out of the window. Time was going by far too quickly for her liking. Was it only three days ago she'd had lunch with Piero and his parents?

She lost herself in thought. The day after, she'd gone sightseeing on her own and had driven to the ruins of an enormous, elaborate Roman villa at Piazza Armerina, where she'd viewed a fabulous collection of stunning mosaics, beautifully preserved by the landslides that had covered them for centuries. When she'd returned to the winery, she'd had supper with Piero and they'd talked for hours about their lives and dreams for the future, and then they'd spent the night together – their lovemaking creating a deepening bond between them.

Yesterday, after she'd queued in a government office to obtain her *codice fiscale*, she'd done some shopping in Caltanissetta, buying deli foods and a box of artisan chocolates for Mel. While strolling through the town, she'd been delighted to find a trinacria wall hanging in a ceramics store. She'd bought it and would take it back to Bristol, where she'd place it in her kitchen.

Last night, Piero had seemed tired – he'd been busy preparing for the harvest and the upcoming wine exhibition in Agrigento. So she'd offered to make supper for him in her kitchenette. Her culinary skills could just about stretch to omelettes and she'd bought ready-made salads in Caltanissetta. They'd sat out on the portico, sipping the wine he'd brought, talking quietly and listening to the night crickets crooning their songs. Again, they'd slept together and, again, their lovemaking had brought them ever closer.

A sigh escaped her now as she thought about her imminent departure – she only had three days left before her flight home. From what Mel had texted her, the weather had turned chilly and wet. She wasn't looking forward to returning to work, neither did she relish finding a flatmate. It might be best to put the apartment on the market and get somewhere smaller once her divorce was finalised...

The sound of the notaio coming through the door made her swivel round. He gave her a copy of the deeds to the baglio, the *atto notarile*, and went through the legalities with her.

After Jess had signed, he handed her a receipt for payment of his invoice – which had come out of her grandmother's legacy – and a thick envelope with her name written on it.

'What's this?' she asked, intrigued.

'A letter from your grandmother. She wrote it to you last year. We had strict instructions only to give it to you once you'd accepted your inheritance.'

'Oh my God.' Jess clasped the envelope to her chest. '*Grazie.*'

* * *

Jess took her leave of the notaio and headed for the first café she could find. It was a simple place, tucked between a motorcycle parts store and a video game shop, but at least it was air-conditioned. She found a table in the corner, ordered a cappuccino and, when her coffee had arrived, prised open the envelope, extracted flimsy sheets of paper, and started to read.

New York, September 10th, 2004

My dearest granddaughter,

It feels strange knowing that you will be reading this when I am gone. I have been diagnosed with stage 4 cancer, and found out soon after I heard about your parents' tragic accident. Although contact between us has been impossible, I employed a private detective not long after you were born, who has kept me up to date over the years. I'm so proud of your accomplishments, darling Jessica, and wish I could have met you. Now that you have accepted my legacy to you, I think it's important that you know about your Sicilian family's history. As I'm the only person left who can recount it to you, please bear with an old woman's rambling while I tell you everything...

Jess read on. She was fully immersed in Lucia's story from the start, transported first to pre-war Brooklyn and afterwards to wartime Sicily. Lucia came across as a wonderful woman, brave, determined, with a loving heart.

Tears spilled from Jess's eyes as she learnt about how Lucia had met Gero when they were children. Dinu had seemed harmless enough at first, but the more her grandmother described his Mafia ambitions, the more Jess disliked him.

She sobbed openly while reading Lucia's poignant words describing how she learnt about Gero's death, and how Carula's birth was her only consolation. Her description of the rift between them, caused by Dinu, made Jess's heart weep.

Her grandmother went on to write about how she coped after her only daughter had cut her off. Lucia immersed herself in her work, had made sure she saw as much as she could of Gero's family, who were good to her, including her in all their celebrations. She formed close attachments to her nieces and nephews, and subsequently their children.

After Filomena and Alberto had passed away, Gero's sisters showed no interest in running the business, so Lucia took over, not only importing movies, but videos and, later, DVDs. When the time came for her to retire, she sold the company. The proceeds were divided between her and the Bonannos, but there was more than enough for Lucia to live comfortably.

As for Lucia's own family, her parents' physical condition had declined rapidly after the Dinu debacle, and they'd died when they were both in their early seventies. Annita also suffered from ill-health and had passed away a couple of years ago. In the meantime, her son had moved into the baglio with his wife. They took good care of it until it become too much for them and they left Villaurora to live with their daughter in Licata. Thankfully, Giovanna and Angelo were able to look after the place and work on the land. Lucia expressed the hope that Jess would allow them to continue to do so.

It was my fault for sending your mother and father to meet my brother. I was so proud of Carula and wanted him to be proud of her, too. When I discovered he'd put out a contract on her, I couldn't believe how evil he'd become. My priority was to keep Carula, Iain, and then you safe. I would have loved to have been in touch directly – I'm sure there were ways we could have managed it – but your mother had hardened her heart. I think what happened in Castronovo made her suffer from post-traumatic stress, which was never addressed. The more time passed, the more difficult it became for her to reconcile with me.

As for Dinu, I'm certain he is dead. No one has seen or heard of him for years. So, I feel confident leaving the baglio to you, Jessica, my only grandchild. I never remarried; I couldn't love anyone as much as I loved your grandfather. I hope you will love the place as much as Gero and I did. We were so happy in the short time we had there and my dearest wish is for you to be just as happy as we were.

Your loving grandmother,
Lucia

* * *

'What an incredible story,' Piero said, handing Lucia's letter back to Jess. They'd just had supper in his apartment and were relaxing together on the sofa. She'd been debating whether to show Piero the letter, then had decided not to hold anything back. Their relationship was becoming ever closer, after all.

'What I don't understand,' she said, 'is how Dinu could have been so malicious as to want to kill his own niece.'

'You recall me telling you about *omertà*? She'd clearly broken the code of silence.'

'But she didn't do it intentionally, I'm sure. How could she even have known about *omertà*?'

'Dinu acted in his own interests, it seems. He needed to come across as a powerful man and get his revenge. Otherwise, his enemies would have taken advantage of what they would have perceived to be weakness.'

'But the child of his sister? His twin sister?' It beggared belief.

'That was how it was in those days, I'm afraid.'

'I hope things have improved for the better, Piero.'

'We no longer hear of so many murders, so I suppose you could say that.' He put his arm around her and held her close. 'The rift between your mother and grandmother is such a sad story. My heart truly goes out to you, sweetheart.'

She snuggled into him and soon they were kissing, and then they were heading for Piero's bedroom to make love.

Afterwards, she pressed kisses to his chest.

'I'm going to miss you so much when I go back to Bristol,' she said, the realisation bringing a lump to her throat.

'Then don't leave.'

'I have to.' She sighed. 'My job. My divorce. My flat. I have a life there—'

'You could make a new one here, darling. If you let yourself.'

Dare she do that? It would be such a big step.

'I'll think about it, I promise.' She couldn't help feeling tempted.

She kissed him and wished him goodnight. Before too long, his breathing deepened and he'd fallen asleep.

But, tired though she was, she couldn't drop off. Her thoughts were filled with Dinu and his threats to her mother. If he weren't dead, she would definitely give him a piece of her mind.

34

JESSICA, JULY 2005

The next morning, on waking, Jess remembered Piero was about to set off for a meeting in Agrigento. He'd invited her to go with him, but she hadn't fancied waiting around while he was working. She put the coffee percolator on the stove while he took a shower, and they had breakfast together before he left.

'Are you sure you don't want to come with me?' he asked as she kissed him goodbye.

'I'm sure, Piero.'

She kept to herself the fact that she intended to go up to the baglio; she was eager to walk around and take everything in, knowing the property was finally hers. He would repeat his warning that she shouldn't be there on her own. But she'd only seen the man on the motorbike once in all the times she'd visited; Piero was probably being over-protective, and she'd be perfectly safe.

An hour later, she parked in front of the rustic door and made her way through to the courtyard. Her chest buzzing with excitement, she wandered through the rooms and imagined how she would decorate them. She would make them as cosy and inviting as the winery's interior. Casual with a touch of sophistication. Could this ever be a permanent home for her, though? It would certainly be a wonderful place for holidays, if there was a pool.

The need to take another look at the area where said pool might be built prompted her to head outside. She strolled around to the back of the farmhouse, where there was a patch of flat land that would be ideal. Giovanna and Angelo were growing tomatoes there, but surely they wouldn't mind relinquishing it, given that Jess had decided they could carry on farming the rest of the property. She strode across the plot – it came to about 10 metres long by 5 metres wide, a good size.

A fresh, cooling breeze had sprung up, chasing fluffy white clouds across the sky. It was the perfect day for a walk. Why not resume her hike up the track towards the shepherd's hut that had been interrupted by the need to go shopping the day after she'd visited Licata with Piero? She remembered it hadn't been half as dangerous as Giovanna had made it out to be.

Jess swept her gaze around to see if her cousins were about, but they weren't at the baglio. With no one to warn her off, Jess made her way up the track. She loved the view from the hillside, loved gazing down at the baglio and the village below. The strip of ragged peaks forming a rocky ridge behind the village towered above as she brushed past the prickly pears and agave plants. She kept her eye out for the long, black snakes that often slithered among the stones, and relished the sight of the big, bright butterflies. Even in the dry heat of summer, the countryside was beautiful. What would it be like in autumn, winter and spring? She couldn't wait to find out.

Her legs ached with the effort of walking as she approached the ramshackle-looking shack she'd spotted before. All the windows were still boarded up and the door was firmly shut. She rattled it, but it was locked.

Something made the skin at the back of Jess's neck prickle. Her heart hammered with sudden fear. Someone was watching her, she was sure of it. And that someone was inside the hut, puffing out noisy breaths.

Without warning, the roar of a motorbike came from lower down the track.

Jess whirled around. She needed to get out of there, but it was too late. Motorbike Man brought the bike to a halt, and it made a tik tik sound as he switched the engine off.

'What the hell are you doing here?' he yelled in Sicilian. 'Didn't I warn you?'

'I don't know what you're on about,' Jess replied in English, her heart pounding and her mouth dry.

She shouldn't have walked up here; she should have done what Piero had suggested and not come to the baglio alone. Pulse racing, she prepared to run, but before she could take one step, Motorbike Man had grabbed her, put his arm around her shoulder and pointed a pistol into her neck.

'Don't hurt me,' she begged as he hustled her through the door.

Jess stared at the old man who'd appeared in front of her, and he stared back at her with piercing grey-blue eyes.

'Who are you?' she asked, eyeing the reading glasses on a string around his neck. He was dressed in baggy grey trousers and a plaid blue shirt.

'I could ask you the same question,' he said in English with a strong New York accent. 'But I know the answer already. You're Lucia's granddaughter, and I'm your great-uncle Dinu.'

'Bloody hell,' she said, shock wheeling through her. 'I thought you were dead.'

'Obviously I'm not.' He turned to Motorbike Man. 'Tie her up, Bastianu. We'll figure out what to do with her later.'

Jess shook with fear as she was manhandled into a rickety old chair, her hands behind her back.

'Sit,' Motorbike Man barked.

'Let me go, please, I beg you. I've done nothing.'

'It's not what you've done.' Jess's great-uncle's tone was threatening. 'It's what you might do.'

With his enigmatic smile, Dinu looked like a simple, harmless old man. But he wasn't, of course. Jess knew about some of the things he'd done, and they made her blood run cold. He fetched rope from a cupboard at the back of the room and gave it to Motorbike Man.

'Who's this person?' Jess asked as the man's garlicky breath assailed her nostrils.

'He's my eldest son, your cousin Bastianu.'

'I can't say I'm pleased to meet you, Bastianu,' she said, her voice trembling as he tied her to the chair.

'Have you decided what we'll we do with her?' Bastianu asked his father.

'Not sure yet, son. In the meantime, let's get on with my packing.'

Jess inhaled a slow breath. She had to keep her composure; she mustn't let fear take her over. To convince her great-uncle to release her, she needed to get into the right mindset. Nausea threatened to overcome her, but she swallowed down the bile that had made its way from her stomach to her throat.

'Please let me go and I'll keep quiet,' she said calmly. 'It appears you're leaving soon. I don't know where you're going, so I wouldn't be able to give information about your whereabouts.'

'You're just like Lucia.' Dinu's lips twisted. 'She was a bossy girl who became a bossy woman. I was glad when she left Sicily and could no longer tell me what to do.'

'You deprived her of her daughter,' Jess couldn't help saying. *This despicable man needs to be told a thing or two.* 'You turned my mother against her. I grew up not knowing anything about my Sicilian family—'

'And now you know too much,' Dinu said. 'Gag her, Bastianu. I can't stand the sound of her voice.'

Jess struggled while her cousin tied a dishcloth around her mouth.

'Sit still or I'll punch you in the face,' he growled.

His words brought home to Jess the danger of her situation. *These men are vile mafiosi who will stop at nothing.*

She watched them busy themselves packing clothes, books, myriad papers and other paraphernalia into cardboard boxes. How foolish she was to have come up here. She really should have listened to Piero. Would her great-uncle kill her? Her skin turned clammy and her pounding heartbeat made her chest hurt.

Dinu and his son had started talking to each other in rapid-fire Sicilian, which she couldn't understand. Her great-uncle must have been on the run for decades. But surely he couldn't have been living in this hut all that time.

No one knew she was here. She wouldn't be missed until that evening, when Piero got back. It might be too late by then.

Oh, God, what can I do?

Bastianu had tied her hands behind her back and had pushed the chair up against the rough stone wall. Stealthily, she rubbed the rope against a sharp piece of brick she could feel jutting into her.

The cord must have been quite old, and soon it began to slacken. Tears of relief welled up in Jess's eyes. Dinu and his son were too busy to notice. But they might see what she'd done at any moment.

It's now or never.

She squirmed from the slackened rope, pulled the gag from her face, jumped to her feet and ran for the door.

At the same time, a shot rang out and blew the lock to the door open. A man in a police uniform rushed in, followed by two others with their guns raised.

Jess stepped backwards with a cry.

For a moment, Dinu looked like a trapped animal, then he composed himself to face his captors.

'You don't know what you're doing,' he said in a low voice.

Was he trying to tell the police agent they'd got the wrong man?

But the officer reached under Dinu's shirt and revealed him to be wearing three silver crosses on a chain.

'You are Dinu Pavano,' the police agent said. 'After thirty-six years on the run the Boss of Bosses has finally been caught.'

Dinu fixed his visitors with a scornful expression, an inscrutable half-smile, offering his hand and his congratulations.

'Did you have any help to find me, I mean from informers?' he asked.

Jess's breath hitched. How could he be so composed?

'No one helped us. We simply intercepted your messages to the outside world, then followed the motorbike,' the police officer said. He pointed to Bastianu and Jess. 'Who are they?'

Dinu remained silent.

'I'm his son,' Bastianu said, puffing himself up to his full height.

'And I'm his great-niece,' Jess added. 'But today is the first time I've met him.'

'Arrest everyone,' the police commander ordered his men. 'Put Pavano in my car and the two others in the van.'

'But... but... I'm innocent,' Jess stuttered. 'This is a mistake.'

'We are taking you in for questioning, *signora*. You can make one phone call from the *questura* in Palermo.' The police HQ.

* * *

Jess called Piero's cell phone as soon as the police gave her permission to do so. To say he seemed shocked would be an understatement. But he told her not to worry, that he'd do everything he could to ensure she was set free.

The police commander questioned her next, making her feel vulnerable and sick to the stomach. She gasped with disbelief when he told her that her great-uncle had been running the Sicilian Mafia while on the run. But then she remembered how he'd put out a contract on his own niece, the daughter of his supposedly beloved twin sister. Dinu was evil, there could be no doubt about it.

A sergeant took Jess to a lonely cell, gave her a tray of food and water to drink, then left her to spend the rest of the day waiting. She sat on a bunk bed, her thoughts whirling. Nonna Lucia had been so certain that Dinu was dead. Except she'd done the same thing to Jess that she'd done to her own daughter, and had sent her to him.

History had well and truly repeated itself.

Finally, the sergeant returned and unlocked the cell door.

'You've been released without charge,' he said. 'Come with me.'

In a room at the back of the *questura*, Piero opened his arms, and she ran into them, shaking so much that her teeth chattered.

'My dearest Jess,' he said. 'I'm so sorry this has happened to you.'

'You and me both.' She sighed.

And the realisation dawned on her she couldn't make this country her home. It was too raw, too complicated, too different from everything she'd ever known.

The sooner she was on a flight home to Bristol, the better.

35

JESSICA, JULY 2005

Piero drove Jess back to the winery and, at first, she kept her concerns to herself – she was emotionally and physically drained. He appeared to pick up on her mood; he didn't question her, simply inserted a CD of soothing classical music.

But it did little to dispel the turmoil within her. Eventually, she couldn't keep silent any more. She had to talk, had to put her thoughts into words.

'How could a fugitive like my great-uncle have been running Cosa Nostra while in hiding?' she asked.

'It's simple, really. He could count on the members of the organisation to protect him. They're not just a bunch of violent thugs, you know. They're also doctors, engineers, politicians. If you can convince people you can kill them at any time and anywhere, even their children, people will do what you want.'

'That's awful.' Jess thought for a moment. 'Do you know who owns the hut where Dinu was living?'

'I believe it once belonged to don Nofriu. It was part of his *latifondo* estate. After the war, the land was divided, but it seems no one laid claim to the hut.'

'It was in an appalling state.' Jess shuddered with disgust. 'The stove in the kitchenette was filthy with baked-on food. He must have been squatting there for months.'

'Was there a bathroom?' Piero asked.

'I think so. Bastianu disappeared into a side room and I heard a toilet being flushed.'

'Someone must have fixed the place up. I mean, a lowly shepherd's hut wouldn't have had plumbing or electricity.'

'What I don't understand is why Giovanna and Angelo denied all knowledge of seeing or hearing the motorbike.'

'Simple answer,' Piero huffed. 'They would have known better than to break the code of silence.'

Jess nodded, recalling her conversation with Giovanna a week ago, when Giovanna had told her that Sicilians didn't talk about anything to do with Cosa Nostra. That conversation should have rung alarm bells, Jess realised now.

'I know you've gone through a horrible experience being held by the police, but at least your great-uncle won't suspect you of informing on him.' Piero glanced at her.

'Oh, God. I hadn't thought of that. Surely he can't carry on terrorising people from prison—'

'Many a mafioso has run his operations from jail, Jess.'

An icy shiver ran through her as she remembered Bastianu making the cutthroat gesture in the grocery store.

'I thought I was brave, but I've never been so scared in my life as I was when Dinu got his son to tie me up. He was a bit incompetent, giving Bastianu an old, fraying rope, which is why I could get free. I'm kicking myself now. If the police had found me being held prisoner, they wouldn't have arrested me—'

'You were extremely courageous, Jess, trying to escape like that. Most people would have frozen.' Piero reached across and took her hand, squeezing her fingers before clearing his throat.

'There's something I need to tell you, sweetheart. This morning, when I stopped for petrol on the way to Agrigento, I phoned my father. I was suspicious about what your grandmother wrote in her letter concerning Dinu having gone missing. He would have known this area like the back of his hand, and the fact that someone was making their way up to the shepherd's hut on a motorbike, and Giovanna and Angelo had denied hearing it, made me wonder if the anti-Mafia police should be informed.'

'Oh my God.' Jess's heart thudded. 'What did your father say?'

'He told me to leave it with him, that he'd call a friend at the *questura*.' Piero exhaled a breath. 'Later, after you'd called to say you'd been arrested, I called Papà back. He told me his friend had informed him that the anti-Mafia squad was already on the case. They'd found notes, known as *pizzini*, that your great-uncle sent to a group of his collaborators who'd been arrested last year. Apparently, Dinu frowned upon the use of telephones – far too easy to be tapped – and issued orders and communications, even to his family, in writing. He used a version of the code used by Julius Caesar in wartime – shifting each letter of the alphabet forwards three places, then replacing letters with numbers according to their position in the alphabet.'

'It's like something out of a crime movie,' Jess said, shaking her head.

'Their enquiries had taken them to Villaurora, and they'd learnt about a stranger in the village who would periodically ride up to the shepherd's hut on a mountain motorbike. They had started keeping the place under observation and also following the trail of the *pizzini*.'

'It was such a coincidence they found Dinu, after years of hiding, on the same day I met him for the first time,' Jess said.

Not once had Piero berated her for going up to the baglio alone, nor had he said she should have accepted his invitation to accompany him to Agrigento. And she was grateful to him for it.

'Have you heard the expression, "Coincidence is God's way of remaining anonymous", Jess?'

'You think it was divine intervention that sent me up there?' Jess heaved a sigh. 'I could have been killed.'

'I'm extremely glad the police arrived in time.' Piero took her hand and kept it in his while he drove.

'You can be sure I won't be going anywhere on my own for the next few days. I never thought I'd be saying this, but I can't wait to go home to Bristol. At least there I won't be in any danger.'

'Don't tell me this has put you off Sicily, *tesoro*,' Piero said.

'Hmmm. Can we talk about it another time? I need to think things through.'

'I'm here for you, Jess. No pressure.'

'Thank you for coming to collect me.' She changed the subject. 'I hope I didn't disrupt your day too much.'

'Hell, no. My meeting was already over when you called. I came as fast as I could after I'd rung my dad to tell him what had happened. It was thanks to Papà vouching for you with his friend at the *questura* that you were released so quickly.'

* * *

Back at the tenuta, Jess declined Piero's invitation to have supper with him. She thanked him, but pleaded tiredness.

'It's been a long day,' she said, kissing him. 'And you must be exhausted, too. I'll see you in the morning, okay?'

'I'll hold you to that promise.' He tilted her chin upward and kissed her on the lips. 'Have a good night's sleep and, hopefully, you'll feel a lot better tomorrow.'

'I left my rental car at the baglio, with my handbag in it, I've just remembered,' she said with a gasp.

'I'll drive you up there after breakfast to collect it.'

Jess thanked him again and, feeling a little numb, went to her accommodation, where she poured herself a glass of wine, then switched on the television.

Dinu's capture was the first item on the evening news. She gulped as a jostling group of law enforcement officers, in balaclavas and bulletproof vests, bundled him from an unmarked police car into the *questura*. A crowd had gathered, and people surged forwards shouting, '*Bastardo! Assassino!*' while he was ushered through the gateway and escorted inside.

The *Telegiornale* went on to mention that the state prosecutors had left their offices in the courthouse forthwith, and had roared straight round to the police HQ to meet their prisoner and make sure everything was in order before transferring him to a maximum-security unit on the mainland. Bastianu would remain in Sicily to face trail on the island.

A sour taste filled Jess's mouth as she listened to a potted history of her great-uncle's crimes, all of which were too horrible to contemplate. How could she be related to this monster? She felt totally mortified. Her entire life, she'd wanted to find out about her Sicilian family. Now, she wished she'd never embarked on the quest. Better to live in blissful ignorance than carry the burden of shame.

But when Piero arrived the next morning, Jess's heart gave its habitual flutter. If she hadn't travelled to Sicily, she would never have met him. He'd become extremely important to her, and she'd developed powerful feelings for him. The thought of leaving him in two days' time made her chest ache.

'*Buon giorno*, Jess,' he said, stepping across the floor in her kitchenette. 'How are you this morning?'

She told him about what she'd seen on the news last night, how ashamed she felt to be related to Dinu Pavano.

'Please try not to feel like that.' Piero wrapped his arms around her and kissed her on the forehead. 'Easier said than done, I know, but you are you, and he is who he is. You are polar opposites.'

Jess pressed her cheek to his chest and inhaled his comforting scent.

'Would you like a coffee?' she asked.

'I've just had one, but you go ahead.'

'I'm good.' She forced a smile. 'Let's go get my car.'

* * *

Piero took the road past Villaurora, and Jess eyed the hill behind the baglio, the memory of what had happened there making her stomach churn.

How would she ever be able to look at that view without being reminded of her villainous great-uncle? She said as much to Piero.

'Give it time, my darling. I hope you'll feel differently before too long.'

They pulled up in front of the farmhouse and she went inside for one last look, sighing as she stepped into the court-yard, its loveliness still filling her with awe. She walked up to the trinacria and touched her fingers to the cool ceramic. Closing her eyes, she imagined Lucia and Gero living here. Her grandmother wrote that they'd been so happy and she wanted Jess to find happiness in the baglio like they'd done.

But how could she do that after what had happened with Dinu?

'Shall we go back to the tenuta, Jess?' Piero approached and took her hand. 'You look tired.'

'I didn't sleep well last night,' she said. 'I couldn't stop thinking about yesterday.'

'With good reason, *tesoro*. Stay with me today, please. I want to look after you.'

She looked down at her hand in his, and a feeling of deep affection spread through her.

They went outside just as Angelo and Giovanna arrived in their Fiat Panda. Jess's chest tightened at the sight of them. The events of yesterday were still fresh in her mind, and they were the last people she wanted to see.

Giovanna leapt out of the car and rushed up to her.

'Did you hear the news?'

'I was there,' Jess said through gritted teeth.

'What do you mean?'

'I was in the hut when Dinu was arrested. You might have warned me—'

'I'm so sorry,' Giovanna said, clearly at a loss for words.

'What happened?' Angelo asked.

'Some other time, Angelo.' Piero held up a hand. 'Jess is heading back to the tenuta now. She's exhausted.'

* * *

On Jess's last evening in Sicily, she was sitting in Piero's courtyard, dining by candlelight under the stars, having enjoyed a replica of the wine and food tasting she'd experienced soon after she'd arrived here. Except, this time, she was alone with Piero, and Stefania had tweaked the menu to offer a different dessert.

'So delicious,' Jess said, savouring the taste of the *biancomangiare*, a delicate pudding made from almond milk and gelatine, sprinkled with candied fruit.

Piero poured her a glass of *passito* sweet wine, and she took a sip before lowering her hand to give Cappero a stroke.

'I'm going to miss him,' she said as the dog snuffled by her feet. 'And you too, of course.' She swallowed the sadness in her throat.

'My brother and his wife phoned today. They said you promised to visit them in Monreale. So you'll have to come back and do that.'

Jess smiled sorrowfully. Yesterday, she'd told Piero that she'd decided to put everything on hold, including renovating the baglio, until she felt up to it.

If she ever did.

'No sweat,' Piero added. 'But you're not getting rid of me easily. I'm coming to visit you in Bristol as soon as I can.'

'That would be wonderful,' she said, her spirits lifting. 'I'd really love you to come and stay.'

'Good.' A smile lit his hazel eyes, and he glanced at his wristwatch. 'It's time for bed now, sweetheart. You have an early start in the morning, don't forget.'

Jess's vision blurred and her heart felt heavy as Piero held out his hand and she placed hers in it.

Up in his apartment, he kissed his way down her face to her neck, making her tingle all over. They undressed and tumbled onto the bed, kissing slowly, passionately, hungrily.

Piero slid into her, and their bodies rocked together. Soon he was pushing her beyond pleasure into such ecstasy that she was no longer herself, but a part of him. The force of his release tipped her over the edge, and she climaxed, calling out his name.

He kissed her gently, beautifully, then gazed deep into her eyes.

'I'm falling in love with you, Jess.'

'Oh, God, Piero. What are we going to do? I think I'm falling in love with you as well.'

'I was worried you didn't feel the same.' He kissed her on the nose. 'We can give each other the gift of time. I know it's a cliché, but time heals most wounds—'

'I hope you're right.' She drew him into her arms.

Piero rolled onto his back and lifted her on top of him.

Jess took a moment, savouring this amazing man, sliding her hands up his toned chest. She did love him. Loved how intelligent and considerate he was. Loved how he was always there for her. If only they didn't live in separate countries. She sighed.

'Something wrong?' he asked, stroking her arms.

'No, nothing wrong.'

He gave her a questioning look and seemed about to say something, but she placed a finger on his lips.

'Shush,' she said. 'Let's not spoil our last night together with depressing talk.'

36

JESSICA, OCTOBER 2005

Jess dropped her front door keys onto the coffee table with a yawn, kicked off her court shoes, and flopped down on her sofa. She felt like a hamster on a wheel, repeating the same actions every day: target setting, dealing with computer melt-downs, the endless paperwork, the 'same old, same old'. But at least she felt safe.

Three months had gone by since she'd left Sicily. Every day, she looked at her digital pictures. The beautiful tenuta, the gorgeous vineyards, the temples in Agrigento, the marina at Licata, the Roman villa in Piazza Armerina. Her favourite photos were of Piero, of course. Also his kids and Cappero. She missed them with an ache that throbbed deep in her soul.

She'd put all her images of the baglio and surrounding countryside in a separate folder on her laptop. They called to her; they were a part of her heritage, after all. But she couldn't face looking at them yet. She hadn't even taken the ceramic trinacria she'd bought in Caltanissetta out of its box.

A feather of excitement tickled in her chest. Piero was arriving tomorrow for a long weekend and she'd arranged to have Monday off work, so she could be with him. How she longed to see him. They emailed each other practically every other day, interspersed with long phone calls. She loved hearing from him, loved learning about his life, loved hearing his voice. The wine exhibition in Agrigento had been a great success, he'd said, and the grape harvest, the *vendemmia*, was one of the best. She, in turn, had unburdened herself when the decree nisi for her divorce had come through.

Jess glanced at her bare finger, devoid of her wedding ring. It felt strange at first, but now the indentation had almost disappeared and she could look at her hand without thinking of her failed marriage.

Piero had helped her put things into perspective. The flat was fully hers – part of the divorce settlement – but she'd decided to put it on the market and get somewhere smaller and closer to work. Having paid off the mortgage after her parents had died and their house was sold, she could afford to stay on here with a flatmate to share the bills, but her heart wasn't in it.

Late the next morning, she could barely contain her excitement as she waited in arrivals at Bristol airport. She scanned the faces of the people coming through the gate, and finally, there was Piero.

Her heart bloomed with love for him. He looked so hand-some, dressed in beige trousers and a dark brown leather jacket. His hazel eyes lit up, and he broke into the biggest smile when she ran towards him. He put down his bag and swept her into his arms.

'*Tesoro*, I'm so happy to see you.'

They kissed, and she wanted the kiss to go on forever.

People jostled past them, but she barely noticed. It was as if she and Piero were the only two people in the world. They came up for air, and Jess couldn't stop smiling.

'Come,' she said, taking his arm. 'Let's get out of here.'

Before too long, she was driving them towards the city centre, taking a shortcut through a picturesque village on the outskirts of Bristol, where rows of slate-roofed cottages had been built with pale local stone.

'I can't believe you're here at last,' she said. 'I feel as if I'm dreaming.'

'I want to make the most of every second I spend with you, *amore*.' Piero heaved a sigh. 'Time will go by so quickly.'

'I hope you don't mind, but tomorrow at lunchtime we're going on a double date with my cousin, Mel, and her boyfriend, Jake. I've told Mel so much about you, and she wants to meet you.'

'That'll be wonderful, darling. As long as the rest of the weekend, I have you to myself.'

'You will, I promise,' she said, warm tingles running through her. She couldn't wait for them to make love.

'How are Gigi and Teresina?' she asked.

'They wanted to come with me, of course.' Piero laughed. 'But they are well.'

'Maybe next time?'

'No way. I'm not sharing you with them when I don't get to see you often enough.'

They carried on chatting about what had been going on at the winery. The food and wine tasting menu had proved popular with guests and many had made return bookings.

'I'm glad we've closed now for the season,' Piero said. 'I relish the peace and quiet.'

'It must be lovely at this time of the year.'

'Come and visit.' A smile curved his lips. 'Come for Christmas! The entire family gets together at the tenuta. You'd be so very welcome.'

There was nothing she'd like more than Christmas with Piero. It hadn't been the same with her Bristol cousins since her parents' tragic death. But could she face travelling to Sicily so soon after her ordeal?

Piero was looking at her expectantly, and she didn't want to spoil things.

'Can we talk about it later?'

'Of course, *amore mio*. No pressure.'

* * *

Time went by in a flash. When they weren't making love, which they spent blissful hours doing, Jess showed Piero around Bristol. After going on a scenic waterbus journey through the harbour to enjoy wonderful views of the city, they visited the Clifton Suspension bridge and gazed down at the Avon Gorge. A climb to the top of Cabot Tower at the summit of Brandon Hill came next, and Jess informed Piero that it had been constructed in memory of John Cabot, who'd set sail in his ship, the *Matthew*, from Bristol in 1497 – and had landed in what was later to become Canada, thus becoming the first European since the Vikings to visit North America.

They met Mel and Jake for lunch in a gastropub, where Piero was introduced to the British tradition of a Sunday roast. He seemed to enjoy the beef and Yorkshire pudding, declaring it to be delicious.

When Jess retired to the ladies' room with her cousin, Mel flicked a lock of blonde hair from her eyes and said, 'Oh, my God, why didn't you tell me how good-looking and charming Piero is?' She painted her lips with a fresh coat of cherry-pink lipstick. 'He's a keeper. Perfect for you, my love.'

'Problem is, we live in separate countries.' Jess sighed as she soaped her fingers.

Mel was the only person she'd talked to about her great-uncle. After giving her a blow-by-blow account of his arrest, Jess had said she never wanted to hear him mentioned again.

'I understand totally,' Mel said now. 'And I know you want to forget about what happened. But, if you don't mind my saying, it's the wrong approach. You need to face your demons, Jess, or you'll be miserable the rest of your life.'

'I suppose so. I just can't do it yet.' Jess sighed again while she dried her hands.

'Don't wait too long. *Carpe diem*. Seize the day. You aren't the first person to be related to someone you'd rather not be. And organised crime doesn't just exist in Sicily. Haven't you heard of the Clerkenwell Crime Syndicate in London?'

Jess shook her head.

'It's one of the most powerful crime organisations in the UK, heavily involved in drug trafficking, extortion, security fraud, blackmail, and murder—'

Jess glanced at her cousin. Mel had always been a know-it-all. She was the same age as her but had taken on the role of guiding her since her parents had died. Went with the territory of being a college teacher, Jess thought.

'Did you look up organised crime in Britain specially?' she asked.

'So what if I did? You need someone like me to tell you what's what. Remember the adage, "a life lived in fear is a life half lived"? Piero strikes me as the kind of man who won't wait around forever. You need to get a grip, sweetheart.'

Mel had her best interests at heart, but even so, her words were a little harsh.

'Let's go back and join the men,' Jess said. 'Then, if you don't mind, Piero and I will head off. We've only got tomorrow left before he goes back to Sicily. I don't want to waste a minute with him.'

'Sorry if I spoke out of turn, sweetie.' Mel pulled her in for a hug. 'I love you lots, you know. I just want you to be happy.'

'It's okay. I get it.' Jess pecked her cousin on the cheek.

* * *

On Monday, Jess took Piero to a vast shopping mall on the outskirts of Bristol, where he bought gifts to take back to Sicily – the latest video games for Gigi and Teresina and traditional English teas for his mother and sister-in-law.

Jess couldn't resist throwing in a rubber dog toy for Cappero, made to look like a pizza slice.

After they'd returned to the city centre for lunch in a Michelin-starred restaurant, where they enjoyed the five-course tasting menu and excellent wine, they went back to Jess's flat to spend the rest of Piero's last day alone.

'I knew this holiday would go by quickly, and it has,' Piero said as they undressed, then stretched out on Jess's bed.

'I'll miss you so much, my darling.' She gazed into his eyes.

'Not as much as I'll miss you.'

Tears prickled, but she wouldn't let them fall.

'I'd love to come to Sicily for Christmas, by the way.' She took in a quick breath. 'Mel talked some sense into me yesterday. She said I should seize the day.'

'Your cousin is right. I must thank her sometime,' Piero said, wrapping his arms around Jess.

She parted her lips, and he kissed her, his tongue playing chase with her tongue, their separate breaths becoming one. She felt his hardness and pressed herself against him. Sparks danced through her, and she reached down to touch him.

'Make love to me,' she said, hooking her knee over him to pull him closer.

And he did. Ardently. Magnificently.

Later, they snuggled together, holding each other as if they never wanted to let go.

'I love you, Jess. With all my heart.'

Her own heart thudded as he cupped her face and kissed her, and she kissed him back, her pulse racing.

'I love you too, Piero,' she said.

37

JESSICA, DECEMBER 2005

Jess's sprits filled with contentment as she sat eating dinner with Piero's family on Christmas Eve. She'd arrived in Sicily three days ago, having succeeded in getting two weeks off work. Piero met her at Palermo airport – it was a late-afternoon flight – and they'd gone straight to his brother's place for the night. It had been wonderful to see Fabrizio and Cristina again, to enjoy a meal with them and meet Damiano, their five-year-old son.

Before they'd set off for the winery, Piero had taken her to visit the stunning Monreale cathedral. Afterwards, they'd gone to have lunch in a restaurant with glorious views of Palermo, the domes of the many churches and the deep blue sea beyond.

'Next time you visit, I'll show you around the city,' Piero said. 'But now we must make tracks for the tenuta. We'll have tomorrow to ourselves and then the whole family will descend on us.'

'How long will everyone be staying?'

'Until New Year's Eve, *amore*.'

She, herself, would leave on 3 January. She'd make the most of the short time she had here, she resolved.

Sitting at the long table now, decorated with a red cloth and candles, where she'd enjoyed the wine and food tasting six months ago, Jess was feeling rather full. Piero's mother, Valeria, had been in the kitchen all day, preparing 'the feast of the seven fishes', *la vigilia*, with Stefania and Cristina's help. It was traditional Christmas Eve fare, apparently. They'd begun with pickled herrings, then moved on to crab and clam arancini, scallops in browned butter, linguine with shrimp, grilled swordfish, calamari and, finally, cod.

'I won't be hungry for at least a week,' Jess whispered to Piero.

He chuckled and poured her another glass of wine.

'This is merely the start of the feasting. We'll be eating and drinking practically non-stop until the new year.'

The day before Gigi and Teresina were due to leave with the rest of the family, while having breakfast with Jess and Piero, they begged to be taken up to Villaurora where, in recent times, the villagers had been enacting a living nativity scene.

'We go there every year,' Gigi said. 'It's fun.'

'I'm not sure Jess will enjoy that.' Piero chucked him under the chin. 'But I'll take you.'

'Aw, Jess, please come with us,' Teresina begged, tugging at her hand.

How could she refuse? The past several days, she'd avoided gazing up at the fever-chart crags that towered above the baglio. It was about time she took a first step towards facing her demons, and a visit to the Villaurora living nativity might be just the ticket.

'I'd be happy to tag along,' she said.

'Yay!' the children chorused.

'Are you sure?' Piero glanced at her.

'Sure as I'll ever be.'

And so, an hour later, she found herself strolling through the streets of the village, hand in hand with Gigi on one side and Teresina on the other, while Piero brought up the rear.

The narrow roads provided the perfect setting and atmosphere to reproduce the ancient town of Bethlehem at the time of Jesus's birth. Villauroresi, dressed in biblical costumes, were going around offering food and wine to adult visitors, candies to the children, accompanied by musicians playing Christmas music on their Sicilian bagpipes.

Jess spotted Giovanna and Angelo up ahead, and her heart sank. But she couldn't avoid greeting them, and it wasn't as bad as she'd thought it would be. Their boys were with them, and Jess introduced Binnu and Turiddu to Piero before they all went for a coffee in the Bar Centrale.

'It's good to see you, Jess,' Giovanna said. 'Are you here for long?'

'Only until the third of January, unfortunately.' Jess caught Piero's eye. 'But I hope to come back soon.'

* * *

The next morning, Piero's father stepped into the kitchen, his face wearing a serious expression. 'Can I have a word with you, son?' he said. 'In private.'

Piero went with him and, worried, Jess busied herself with the children's breakfast. She made them hot chocolate, into which they dunked brioches and left-over panettone.

When Piero came back, Jess asked if anything was wrong.

'I'll tell you later,' he said. 'When we're alone.'

Jess's mouth turned dry. Something bad had happened, judging by the look in Piero's eyes.

She helped Gigi and Teresina gather up their belongings and take them down to their grandparents' car. Gaetano and Valeria would drop them off at their mother's in Palermo before heading home to Mondello.

'Thank you for such amazing Christmas food,' Jess said to Valeria after the children were settled. 'I enjoyed every mouthful.'

'You're very welcome, my dear.'

Valeria hugged her, and Gaetano did likewise. Within minutes, it was Fabrizio and Cristina's turn to say goodbye. Damiano had to be persuaded to stop running around with Cappero and get into their car.

'He's a handful,' Cristina whispered to Jess as she kissed her on both cheeks.

Jess kept silent on the topic. The child appeared to be a more than a little hyperactive, to say the least. She'd only seen him sitting still while eating.

'Christmas with you all has been wonderful,' Jess said. 'Have a safe journey home!'

Piero came up and took her hand after his brother had driven off in a cloud of dust.

'Let's go have a coffee,' he said.

Up in the kitchen, he placed the percolator on the stove while Jess loaded the breakfast plates into the dishwasher. She tried not to let her nerves show – she'd guessed she was about to get some bad news, and could only pray that no one was seriously ill.

Piero poured them both a mug, pulled out a chair, and beckoned her to sit with him.

'Oh, Piero,' she said when he gazed at her. 'Is it... is it your dad?'

'No, *amore*, my father is fine. It's about Dinu.' Piero placed a hand on hers.

'Dinu?' Her heart was suddenly racing as she imagined him breaking out of jail and coming for her...

'I'm sorry to have to tell you this.' Piero squeezed her fingers. 'Your great-uncle is dead.'

'Dead?' she gasped.

'Papà received a phone call this morning. The facts aren't totally clear yet. From what he could tell me, it appears Dinu has been murdered.'

'I thought he was in a maximum-security prison—' Jess's blood froze.

'He was taken to hospital for some tests. It seems to have happened there.'

'But... but... why was he killed?'

'To have survived as long as he did, he must have had powerful protectors who colluded with Cosa Nostra. Perhaps someone was afraid he knew too much. He was a prolific note taker. Every request he granted, every recommendation for an employee or a political candidate, every guarantee he made, is logged somewhere. When he went on trial, he might have ended up dragging others down with him.'

Jess struggled to find the right words. She should have been devastated by her great-uncle's loss, but she wasn't. The man who caused the rift between her mother and her grandmother, the man whose actions meant Jess never got to know her Sicilian family, the man who'd scared the living daylights out of her, was finally no more.

'I'm relieved he's gone,' she said. 'I hope you don't think I'm being cold-hearted.'

'You're not being cold-hearted at all, *tesoro*. If I were you, I'd be dancing around the room.'

She laughed ruefully, and Piero laughed with her.

'I'm still baffled by how everyone thought he was dead, when he was running Cosa Nostra in secret,' she said.

'My father told me the authorities now suspect he was pretending to be a pensioner and living in Palermo for years. It was only when the anti-Mafia police found the notes he'd sent to his collaborators that they realised he was still alive.'

'And, of course, the Friends of the Friends protected him,' Jess said.

'What would you like to do today, the last day of 2005, my love?' Piero asked after they'd talked a little more about Dinu and had finished their coffees.

'How about we go up to the baglio?' She didn't need to think twice. 'It's about time, isn't it?'

'Have you brought the key with you?'

'Yes. Just in case.'

'Let's go, *amore mio*.'

* * *

Rain sheeted across the valley while Piero drove Jess towards Villaurora. She kept her eyes fixed on the distant hills, swathed in clouds, and soon they'd arrived at the farmhouse.

The rain had stopped and sunshine glistened in the puddles as she pulled the key from her coat pocket and unlocked the rustic wooden door. It swung open, and she stepped into the courtyard. A melancholic lump caught in her throat, and she gave a heavy sigh.

'What's wrong, *amore*?' Piero asked.

'I'm feeling sad about the tragedies that happened to my grandmother. She loved the baglio so much.'

'Well, we owe it to her to make this a happy place.'

'I agree.' Jess nodded. 'Will there be time to get in touch with Domenico, your builder, before I go back to Bristol?'

A smile spread across Piero's handsome face.

'I'll phone him as soon as we return to the tenuta.'

Which is what he did.

* * *

There were enough Christmas leftovers to feed an army, so Piero and Jess didn't need to cook. They had lunch on returning to the winery, spent a lazy afternoon in bed making love, and then they took Cappero for a walk.

Shortly before midnight, Piero uncorked a bottle of *Melita Brut* and said, 'I hope you don't mind this being such a quiet New Year's Eve, my love.'

'It's absolutely perfect.' She clinked glasses with him. 'Happy New Year, my darling.'

'Talking about happiness. Would you be happy living in Sicily full time?' Piero took a deep breath. 'I mean, Bristol is such a vibrant city. You would probably miss it a lot if you moved here—'

'That would depend on under what circumstances I'd be living here.' Jess glanced at him.

'I love you, *amore*.' He took her hand. 'You'd make me the happiest man alive if you agreed to marry me.'

Her heart sang, and joy flooded through her. She put down her glass and went into his arms.

'Are you sure? I can't have children, remember.'

He lifted her chin and kissed her.

'We could adopt a brother and a sister for Gigi and Teresina, if you like.'

'Oh, yes, please.'

Happy tears trickled down her cheeks, but then she remembered the baglio and her grandmother's hope that she would find happiness there.

'I'd like to keep the farm,' she said. 'It's my heritage.'

'Of course. We'll renovate it and use it for friends and family to stay in and, sometimes, a bolthole for ourselves.'

'It appears you've got this all figured out.' She smiled. 'Have you also found me a job for when I resign from the bank?'

'Well, now that you mention it, I might be needing a new bookkeeper in the not-too-distant future. The one I have currently has just given notice that she's expecting a baby and won't be returning to work after her maternity leave.'

'That might not be enough time for me to get the proper qualifications to work in Sicily.' Jess couldn't help a wry chuckle.

'I've thought of that, too. I'll hire a temporary accountant until you're ready.'

Jess laughed, laughed with pure delight. It was as if a heavy weight had been lifted from her shoulders. This was where she was supposed to be – with Piero. She could look forward to a much brighter future with him than without him, and she told him so.

'Does that mean you agree to be my wife?' He gazed into her eyes.

'I more than agree to be your wife, Piero. I love you and want to spend the rest of my days with you.'

He pulled her into his arms and kissed the top of her head.

'I want that, too, *amore*,' he said.

* * *

MORE FROM SIOBHAN DAIKO

Another sweeping historical novel from Siobhan Daiko, *Daughter of War*, is available to order now here:
www.mybook.to/DaughterofWarBackAd

AUTHOR'S NOTE

I was inspired to write *The Girl from Sicily* after a conversation with my brother-in-law, an historian, who told me about the rumoured assistance given to the Allies by the Sicilian Mafia during World War II.

Research led me to the character on whom I based don Nofriu, don Calogero Vizzini, the godfather of Villalba – which inspired my fictional village of Villaurora in the province of Caltanissetta. Vizzini was appointed mayor of Villalba by the American Colonel Charles Poletti, on whom I based my fictional character of Charles Rinelli. Lucky Luciano actually existed, and is a person in the public domain.

Dinu is inspired by several Cosa Nostra personalities – Salvatore Giulianu in his youth and Bernardo Provenzano in later life. I based Francu somewhat on the Mafia boss Salvatore Riina. Dinu's arrest takes place in the exact same matter as Provenzano's, but the latter wasn't murdered on a visit to the hospital.

In April 2024, I went on a research trip to Sicily with my husband, Victor. We drove from Palermo to Agrigento, enjoying an amazing wine tasting experience in a tenuta en route. Piero's winery is an amalgam of several on the island.

After visiting the glorious Greek temples, Victor and I travelled to Licata, where the Americans came ashore in 1943, and from there to a baglio which had been converted into a farmhouse holiday establishment, where we spent the night. The picturesque building was to become my inspiration for Lucia's baglio.

To say I was bowled over by Sicily would be an understatement. It's a beautiful island with breathtaking scenery. The people I met were incredibly hospitable, the food fabulous, the culture and history fascinating.

As for the Mafia – it continues to operate throughout Sicily, apparently, entwined with the legitimate economy, but it isn't as violent as it was in the past. When I asked the locals I met about Cosa Nostra, I was told, 'The Mafia is all about local politics and tourists are totally safe.'

The following books provided me with inspiration and information for this book:

Rodney Campbell, *The Luciano Project*
Ezio Costanzo, *The Mafia and the Allies*
Clare Longrigg, *Boss of Bosses*
G. Maxwell, *God Protect Me from My Friends*
Tim Newark, *Mafia Allies*
Gaia Servadio, *Mafioso*

ACKNOWLEDGEMENTS

I continue to be hugely grateful for all the support I receive from the entire team at Boldwood Books.

Last May, I travelled to London from Italy – where I live – to attend two fabulous parties. The first was the occasion of the Romantic Novelists Association annual awards. My indie book, *The Flame Tree* – republished by Boldwood as *Daughter of Hong Kong* – had been shortlisted in the Historical Romantic Fiction category. I met my lovely editor, Emily Yau, for the first time in person – as well as other 'Boldies' attending the ceremony. Previous contact had been only by email, phone and Zoom calls.

The next night I went partying again, to Fulham Palace, for Boldwood's yearly event. It was lovely to be welcomed by their CEO, Amanda Ridout, and to meet other members of the team as well as fellow authors. It truly is a supportive, friendly community and I'm thrilled to be part of it.

The Girl from Sicily has been challenging to write as it's different from all the books I've written in the past. I'd like to thank Emily Yau for her editorial comments and suggestions, which have made this a better book, I'm sure.

Thank you, Joy Wood and Nico Maeckelberghe, for beta reading.

Special thanks to JH, for his input.

Also, I'd like to thank the bloggers who've been such staunch supporters of my work. I'm truly grateful.

Last, but not least, I'd like to thank my husband, Victor, for his love and encouragement as I wrote this book, and for helping me on our research trip. I couldn't have done it without him.

ABOUT THE AUTHOR

Siobhan Daiko writes powerful and sweeping historical fiction set in Italy and in the Far East during the second World War, with strong women at its heart. She now lives near Venice, having been a teacher in Wales for many years.

Sign up to Siobhan Daiko's mailing list for news, competitions and updates on future books.

Visit Siobhan's website: www.siobhandaiko.org

Follow Siobhan on social media here:

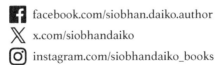

facebook.com/siobhan.daiko.author

x.com/siobhandaiko

instagram.com/siobhandaiko_books

ALSO BY SIOBHAN DAIKO

The Girl from Venice

The Girl from Portofino

The Girl from Bologna

The Tuscan Orphan

Daughters of Tuscany

Daughter of War

Daughter of Hong Kong

The Girl from Sicily

Letters from
the past

Discover page-turning
historical novels from
your favourite authors
and be transported
back in time

*Join our book club
Facebook group*

https://bit.ly/SixpenceGroup

*Sign up to our
newsletter*

https://bit.ly/LettersFrom
PastNews

Boldwood

Boldwood Books is an award-winning fiction publishing company seeking out the best stories from around the world.

Find out more at www.boldwoodbooks.com

Join our reader community for brilliant books, competitions and offers!

Follow us

@BoldwoodBooks

@TheBoldBookClub

Sign up to our weekly deals newsletter

https://bit.ly/BoldwoodBNewsletter